3/22

TEN

Books should be returned or renewed by the last date above. Renew by phone **03000 41 31 31** or online *www.kent.gov.uk/libs*

D1438472

C1

First published in 2017 by Boghopper Books with Print2Demand
Copyright © Chris O'Donoghue 2017

A catalogue record of this book is available from
The British Library
ISBN 978-1-910693-98-8

Typesetting in Minion Pro by Edward Sturgeon
Cover Illustration © Paul Harwood

Printed in Great Britain by Print2Demand

Dedication

Blood on the Tide is dedicated to my late uncle who was a lovely man who I wish I had known better.

Also to my late friend John Weeks, who manfully battled MS for many years and never lost his sense of humour.

My thanks go to my wife and soulmate, Greer, for her continuing support and expertise in editing my manuscript and to Paul Harwood for the great job he has done in designing the cover of the book

Wednesday

Marline spike - *a tool used in marine rope work. Shaped in the form of a polished metal cone, tapered to a rounded or flattened point, it aids in such tasks as untying knots.*

THE TYRES of a small Bedford lorry crunched across the shingle, the sidelights barely cutting through the dark; the engine, at low revs, making little noise. The vehicle coasted to a standstill, the engine was cut and the passenger door opened. Two shadowy figures crept quietly out and went to the back of the truck, one tall and broad, the other, short and slight, limping as he walked. Still maintaining silence, they carefully dropped the tailgate and started to manoeuvre a bulky object, wrapped in rough cloth, out on to the ground. With a low grunt from one of the figures, they lifted the dead weight, carried it to the edge of the quay and rolled it over the side. There was a gentle splash as it hit the water, the high tide near the top of the quay muffling the sound. The figures retraced their steps, climbed back into the Bedford, the engine was started and it drove off.

The cloth-wrapped bundle bobbed, just level with the surface of the water, and slowly began to drift out to sea. The low moon lit a glittering path across the rippled surface, the pale pattern breaking and remaking as the motion of the tide gently rocked the waves.

The three men were quiet as the lorry retraced its route, travelling away from Compass Point. Then the driver spoke, raising his voice above the noise of the engine: 'Won't the body be found?'

The small man in the middle seat replied: 'That's the idea. I've calculated the tide and it will bring it back up the estuary sometime tomorrow.' His voice high, almost shrill, carried the trace of an accent - barely noticeable. 'Anyway,' he went on, 'you have nothing to worry about. No one knows you have any connection with this, so you can have a clear conscience. Meanwhile, please take us back to the brickworks so we can get some sleep.' The large man on the other side of him grunted his agreement. 'Then you can go back to the barracks before you're missed.'

Captain Salt, RN retired, stood on the quayside at Compass Point, dressed smartly in double-breasted blue blazer, with brass buttons gleaming, and grey slacks with knife-edge creases. Sporting a peaked cap above bushy eyebrows and a neat iron-grey beard, he puffed on his pipe and surveyed the damp mud and sand left by the outgoing tide, shimmering in the weak morning sun. Boats lay at rakish angles, mooring ropes festooned with weed, leading from bow or stern to buoy or bank. Below, ferryman Jack Spratt's pale blue boat was tied up at the bottom of the uneven passenger steps. He knew where Jack would be now and that he wouldn't appear until there was enough water to row across the river.

Drawing his eyes back from the misty horizon and looking closer to the quay wall he could see Mitch's two men, Stan and Wally, busy digging in the shingle which was gradually silting up the estuary, making ready to lay new moorings. Farther over was a line of fishing boats but Mitch hoped to attract some of the yachtsmen who were starting to see this stretch of coast as a suitable cruising ground. As the owner of the land that Mitch's boatyard stood on, Captain Salt was keen to promote more leisure activities at Compass Point. It was true that trippers were starting to come down, usually on the train, occasionally by car, but with the war several years behind them and rationing gradually fading, he felt tourism was just about to start in earnest.

He reached into his pocket and pulled out a slender leather pouch. Deftly flicking the flap open he pulled out a plug of Players Navy Cut tobacco and pushed it into his pipe, tamping it down with a thumb. He replaced the pouch, clamped the pipe between his lips and took out a box of matches. Opening the box he took a match out, struck it on the side, applied it to the bowl of the pipe and sucked greedily. Soon the tobacco was glowing and gouts of smoke came from the corner of his mouth. With a contented sigh, he turned and made his way back through the yard. He picked a path between upturned boats and piles of timber then crossed the railway line and walked along the track to the Shipwrights Arms. Pushing the door open he nodded a greeting to Jack, who, as expected, was propped against the bar, and took his place on the stool reserved for him.

'Mornin', Skip,' Jack growled, his blue eyes bright spots in his weathered face, ruddy under a battered flat cap. His dark blue jersey was ragged round the cuffs and elbows and his grubby, baggy grey flannels were tucked into rubber boots, the tops turned over. Despite the fact that Alf, the landlord, had opened the bar only a few minutes earlier, Jack was already halfway down his first pint. No wonder the ferry often ran late, or not all. Salt made a mental note to do something about it, if the hoped for tourists started coming but, for now, he was content to leave things as they were.

'Morning, Jack, you're looking cheerful. Have you come into some money?'

Jack looked startled. 'Why!' he exclaimed. 'What 'ave you 'eard?'

'Oh, nothing.' Salt was surprised at the reaction. 'Just an observation.' He grinned and raised his bushy eyebrows then faced the bar as Alf put a steaming mug of tea before him. He turned to pour a tot of rum from a bottle on the shelf into a short glass, then placed it on the worn but well-polished bar. Salt nodded his thanks, poured it into his mug, raised it to his lips and took a deep draught. He looked quizzically at the ferryman. '*Have* you come into some money?'

Spratt shifted uneasily from one foot to the other, shrugged and muttered. 'No,' he replied, belligerently. 'Wouldn't tell you if I 'ad.' He turned away and buried his nose in his beer. Salt winked at Alf and raised his mug again.

The Shipwrights Arms was a modest building, with stone walls, tiny recessed windows and a pantiled roof. It sat right at the end of the quay, next to the station, hunkered down against the weather. It had withstood any number of gales and powerful storms and had survived, battered but unbowed. Inside was a small, low-ceilinged room, the once white paintwork now the colour of nicotine, stained dark from years of coal fires and the smoke of a lifetime of tobacco pipes. The woodwork was an even deeper colour, with a tar-like quality. Indeed, tar may well have been used as a ready substitute for paint. The room served as the solitary bar and a door marked **PRIVATE** led to Alf's compact accommodation. The landlord was far from being the archetypal mine host. Rangy and thin, he barely spoke more than a sentence at a time, always wore a suit and tie and had bookshelves crammed with classics in his living room. He stood, impassive, in front of a brace of barrels of ale sitting on a rack behind the wooden counter. There was a foxed mirror on the wall above a shelf, reflecting a line of brown bottles. Below the barrels, shelves held clean, upturned glasses; pints and halves. The floor was bare floorboards, with a dusting of sawdust and sand and apart from a couple of stools, the only other seating was comprised of three chairs that had seen better days, arranged around a battered tin-topped table, next to the unlit fire.

The morning sun slanted through the small windows, dust motes dancing in the rays. An old clock ticked on the wall, and apart from the occasional squeak as Alf polished glasses, all was tranquil. But, suddenly, the peace was shattered as the door flew open and Stan burst in, closely followed by Wally, both breathing heavily after the exertion of running.

'Skip! Skip!' Stan panted, 'You've got to come! Come and see what we've uncovered!'

'And come quick!' Wally added, 'It might go off any minute!'

Unflustered, Salt turned towards the men. 'Now calm down. What have you found and why's it going to go off?'

'It's a b-b-b-bomb!' Stan gabbled.

'A *what*?!'

'A bomb! It must have been there since the war,' Wally said. 'We was digging to lay the new moorings and hit something hard.'

'Yeah, and I was scrapin' it with me shovel when we realised what it was,' Stan added. His eyes were wide and he was shaking, and not just from the effort of running.

Salt's naval service on the Atlantic conveys ensured he was quick to assess the situation and make swift decisions.

'Right then you two,' he said. 'Let's find Mitch and we'll take a shuftee.' He drained his mug and followed them out through the door, leaving Alf to his polishing and Jack to his pint. Those two weren't going to get worked up about some ancient piece of ordnance.

Salt had to walk fast to keep up with the others as they retraced their steps across the railway level-crossing and into the yard. Cries of 'Mitch! Mitch!' brought the men's boss out from the boatshed, asking what all the racket was about. He quickly picked up on their urgency and the four of them made their way to the edge of the quay. They peered down at a blackened and rusty metal object that had been revealed by the digging. A couple of hastily discarded spades and an overturned wheelbarrow lay close by. It was clear from the bulbous shape and fins that it was indeed a bomb, probably dropped by a returning German plane, and would have lain there for upwards of ten years.

Salt immediately took charge.

'Right men, stay well away.'

'We aint got no intention of goin' anywhere near it again,' Stan said.

'Mitch, phone the police at Collinghurst and get them to send a bomb disposal crew,' Salt said. 'You two,' he barked, pointing at the ashen faces of Stan and Wally, 'put up a barrier, this side of the level crossing, and don't let anyone come past until the army arrives. The next train from Collinghurst is due soon and I don't want people wandering down here. Got it?' They nodded, and rushed off to collect timber and trestles.

Despite his outwardly calm appearance, Salt was disturbed. If this was a live bomb, and it did go off, it could affect his plans for developing tourism at Compass Point very badly. He hoped the military would get a move on...

$\sim$O$\sim$

'Right, Sir.' Salt was pleased to note that the Army captain had the correct amount of deference. 'If you'd like to keep all personnel well back, we'll make our way to the UXB. How long before the tide turns?'

Salt removed a large fob watch from his breast pocket and consulted the dial. 'Hmm. I'd say you've got about an hour and a half before the water starts lapping round your ankles.'

Captain Valiant turned to the soldier who'd driven the truck: 'Come on Rankin, we'd better get a move on.'

The lorry they had arrived in was painted olive green with distinctive red mudguards. Removing canvas rucksacks from the back, they made their way to the edge of the quayside and clambered down the rusty iron ladder. Salt watched as they walked across the damp sand to the spot where, not long before, Wally and Stan had hurriedly abandoned their digging.

The two soldiers peered at the bomb. 'Could be a tricky one, Sir,' Sapper Rankin said, 'especially as those blokes might have disturbed it.'

'Oh, I don't know,' Valiant replied. 'We've had worse.' The captain had the build of a sprinter, his well-cut uniform fitting neatly on his light but muscular frame. 'Looks like an SC fifty, so only a baby.'

He knelt down and, opening the rucksack, removed a stethoscope. He pushed back his cap, clipped on the earpieces and placed the diaphragm on the metal casing. Rankin, coarsely dressed in ill-fitting khaki, stood by with an extinguisher, ready to douse the fuse if necessary. After a few moments, Valiant sat back on his heels and smiled. 'Silent as a grave. I think this one is going to be okay. Let's see if we can get the cover off.'

Working skilfully, he scraped away carefully at the accumulated mud and grime revealing a raised metal plate. The screws were so corroded there was no chance of undoing them. 'Rankin, chisel and toffee hammer, if you please.' The sapper reached into his pack and passed his superior a slim cold chisel and lightweight hammer. Tapping gently, the captain drifted the remains of the screw heads off the plate, then, using the chisel as a lever, prised it away from the metal casing.

He and Rankin had been a team for several months, usually working alone, only with a larger group when necessary. Despite their differing backgrounds they worked well together, rarely needing more than the minimum of words to communicate what required doing. This was somewhat surprising as Rankin was not popular with the other men at the barracks. It was suggested that he wasn't trustworthy and not completely honest. However, Valiant was prepared to make allowances as he was a good right hand man although he had found it necessary to defend him on more than one occasion.

The timing device was exposed, in surprisingly good condition, considering the length of time it had been buried. Probably, both men agreed, silt and mud covering it had preserved it from the ravages of seawater. Valiant took the proffered wire-cutters that Rankin had anticipated he would need. With a muttered thanks, he reached into the exposed cavity, snipped twice then exhaled noisily.

'Phew, that's it then.' Leaning back he looked out towards the horizon. He could see a thin line as the sea started to return. 'Come on mate, we'd better get a move on. We need the A-frame and tackle so we can lift this blighter out before we get wet.'

Rankin jogged across the firm sand, scrambled up the ladder and walked to the lorry. He swung himself deftly over the tailgate and, in a few moments, was hurrying back with timber, rope and blocks. Throwing them down on the sand, he quickly followed and a wooden frame was soon set up over the bomb. A loop of stout rope was wrapped round the fins of the missile and connected to the gun tackle, suspended from the frame.

'Right-ho!' Valiant said. 'Let's get this blighter out of the putty.' Together they threw their weight on to the tail-end of the rope and heaved. Nothing happened. 'Again!' he commanded. They heaved and again… nothing. 'Damn. We're going to have to dig the bloody thing out. Where are those two men? We could do with a hand.' 'Captain Salt!' he yelled towards the quay.

The landowner's bearded figure peered over the edge. He'd been watching their efforts and instinctively knew what they needed.

'Okay, I'll get the boys. Wally! Stan!' he called, cupping his hands round his mouth. 'Over here, at the double!' The two had been skulking behind the boatshed but knew better than to delay. They walked quickly over to Salt. 'Right lads, they need you to help digging.' Seeing the dubious looks on their faces he added: 'Don't worry, it's safe now, but if you don't get a move on we'll have to wait for the next tide.'

Working quickly, the four had soon dug out enough sand and shingle to expose more than half of the metal casing of the bomb. Then, with all of them heaving on the rope, it came out of the ground with a sucking noise, like a very wet cork being pulled from a bottle. They managed to manhandle the deadweight across the sand to the bottom of the quay. Rankin backed the lorry up to the edge and they used the hoist to lift the bomb up and over the quay wall and into the back of the truck. It wasn't a moment too soon as the incoming tide was already starting to fill the hole where the bomb had lain.

Salt watched as it was made secure in the back of the truck. 'What sort is it?' he asked the army captain.

'Jerry designated it an SC fifty. A Heinkel HE one-eleven could carry 40 of these 50 kilogram jobs and each one contained 25 kilos of TNT. Despite their relative small size they could cause quite a blast. Not only that, but the exploding case would send lethal pieces of shrapnel, flying off in all directions - at about 7000 miles an hour.'

Salt screwed up his face and winced. 'Nasty.'

'Quite,' Valiant said. 'Luckily this one didn't go off. Possibly the pilot ditched it on the way back from a raid. It happened a lot. Once they'd dumped their bombs on London they high-tailed it back across the channel as quickly as they could, usually pursued by Spits and Hurricanes. Then they'd get rid of as much weight as possible. This one's been sitting in the mud and silt, covered up, ever since.'

After apparently enjoying this lengthy explanation, the captain's manner became brusque and military. 'Anyway,' he said, 'better get on. Lots to do.' With that, he turned on his heel and climbed up into the truck.

Stan and Wally dismantled the barrier so the lorry could leave.

'Blimey, Mitch, that could have been nasty,' Wally said. 'Bloomin' good job it wasn't live.' Mitch could only nod his head in agreement.

After all the excitement, the day gradually returned to its normal, steady routine. Salt headed off on his rounds, Mitch found work for his men and Jack sauntered out of the Shipwrights Arms, ready to ply his trade as ferryman, despite having already sunk a couple of pints.

∼O∼

Some distance offshore, the bundled object bobbed, neither above nor below the surface of the sea but somewhere in between. As the tide turned, so the bundle turned and moved slowly, but inexorably, back towards the coast.

∼O∼

Later that day, with the tide high, Jack had a steady trickle of trippers waiting to be rowed across the river to the dunes at Shell Bay. It was warm enough for a few hardy souls to enjoy Alf's ale, pork pies and bread and cheese, sitting outside the pub. Mitch, Stan and Wally had set up a plank on a couple of barrels outside the boatshed and were enjoying their sandwiches, out of the cool onshore breeze, in the weak spring sunshine.

Returning from lunch at his home, farther up the line at Kilnhurst, Salt alighted from the 2.45pm on the platform at Compass Point. A handful of holidaymakers also got off and made their way through the boatyard towards the ferry steps. The sounds of timber being planed and nails being hammered came from the boatshed as they passed.

Jack rowed strongly, angling the boat expertly into the outgoing tide then bumped gently against the steps. With a deft flick, he secured a hanging rope round the sampson post on the bow of his boat. Holding on to a metal ring by the lower steps he helped the next handful of passengers into the boat. Once they were settled, he cast off and rowed purposefully across the quickening tide. At the jetty on the other side he warned: 'Don't forget, last boat will be in 'alf an hour, otherwise it's a long walk back to Collinghurst!'

The sodden object had passed, unnoticed, up the estuary and under the railway bridge where it had snagged on a branch that had snapped off a tree and fallen into the water, itself now held tight against the embankment. It stayed there, captive while the tide turned. As the falling tide gathered momentum it tugged impatiently at the bundle like a mother with a recalcitrant child until, with a rending that left a rag of fabric still attached to the branch, it broke free and flowed with the tide, away from the bridge.

Jack sat on the bench, leaning against the wooden side of his shed, enjoying the warmth of the sun on his face and already looking forward to his next pint. A couple of fishing boats were trawling beyond the mouth of the estuary, each trailing a stream of gulls, eager for scraps thrown overboard as the men gutted fish. There was a ringing from the other side of the river. Jack responded to the sound of the bell with a 'harrumph', rose arthritically to his feet and clattered down the steps to his boat. He had to point the bow even more steeply into the fast running tide but, after a couple of dozen deft strokes, the bow was bumping against the wooden jetty. The trippers were pleased to see him back and clambered down into the boat, chatting happily as they did so. But, halfway across on the return journey, the cheerful mood changed when one of them rose suddenly to his feet and called out: 'What's that?'

'Sit down,' Jack rasped, 'you'll bloody well have us all in the drink!'

'But look!' the man continued. 'What an earth is it?' All eyes turned to follow the line of his arm as he pointed. Bobbing in the water but coming steadily closer was a long cylindrical bundle. It appeared to be wrapped in some sort of dark coloured fabric and was secured with lengths of thin rope, which were tied into many knots. Jack turned the boat and the object bumped alongside. Hands reached over the side to grasp it and, with a few strokes, boat and bundle were against the stone steps. Jack secured the boat, threw a rope over the object and shooed the trippers up the steps where they stood at the top, gawping down at Jack, the boat and the alien object.

'Hey, one of you go an' fetch Mitch from the boatshed. An' don't waste no time!' He had a bad feeling about the bundle and didn't want to deal with it by himself.

The trippers had soon returned along with Mitch who appeared at the top of the steps, quickly joined by Stan and Wally.

'What's up, Jack?' Mitch asked. 'Have you caught something?'

'I'll say,' Jack said, in a low voice, 'You'd better come an' 'ave a look.' As requested, the three men made their way down the steps and, with Jack's help, got the bundle partly on to the lowest slab which was wet from the falling tide and slippery with weed.

'I don't like the look of this,' the old ferryman said, in a voice unnaturally soft for him.

'Hmm,' Mitch said, 'me neither.' He turned to Wally. 'You'd better go and get the Captain. I think he needs to be here.' And, as an aside, he muttered: 'Someone knows how to tie knots.'

Without a word, Wally made his way back up the steps and ran across to the pub where he knew he would find Salt.

'Right-ho, let's get organised.' Salt soon took charge. He had the bystanders moved back and quickly arranged for the police to be called. 'And ask for Inspector Russell. I've met him before, he's a good chap.'

He then asked Stan to get the crane as the swiftly falling tide had left the steps too treacherous to manhandle the object up safely. The machine stood in the corner of the yard, more rust than paint, the tyres cracked and soft. It barely looked as if it could move, let alone be capable of lifting anything. Stan clambered up into the cab, the engine turned laboriously over several times until, with a blast of sooty smoke, it burst into life. Stan manoeuvred it gingerly to the edge of the quay and began lowering the cable. Jack had secured the length of rope around the bundle and once it was close enough, he attached it to the hook. 'Take her up,' he said and Stan winched away. Jack made sure the boat was safely tied up and made his way slowly to his hut, shaking his head as he went.

A tarpaulin had been thrown over the bundle and the trippers had been moved away. The 4.15pm train had come and gone, taking most back to Collinghurst. Names and addresses of witnesses had been noted, although a couple still lingered, curious to know what the odd shape was.

Thirty minutes later a black Wolseley skittered to a halt, dust rising from the disturbed shingle, a metallic pinking coming from the cooling engine. Detective Inspector 'Sonny' Russell and a DC, Johnny Weeks, climbed out. A small, rough-coated, tan and white terrier trotted at the Inspector's heels. Russell was a short man, tending to the rotund, nattily dressed in a blue chalk-stripe suit and dark tie. His hair was neatly Brylcreemed, his jutting jaw was clean shaven and a smile played around his lips. These he pursed and whistled a snatch of the *Harry Lime* theme. As he came to a halt, the small dog sat obediently at his side looking up at him, her head tilted to one side. Weeks was younger, his suit less well cut, a mop of dark curly hair tumbling over his boyish face.

'Captain Salt?' Russell beamed, shaking the other man's hand. 'What have we got here?

'You'd better see for yourself,' Salt said gravely. 'We've not touched anything, it's just as it was found.'

Stan and Wally peeled back the tarpaulin. Russell removed a large white handkerchief from his pocket and bending, placed it on the shingle, then kneeled to examine the bundle. The terrier looked on with interest.

'Well, well, well,' the DI said, 'I'm sure you've guessed what this might be.'

'A body?' Salt volunteered.

'Possibly.' Russell's normal cheerful demeanour was replaced by one of resigned sadness. 'And tied up by someone who knew what he was doing, judging by these knots.'

'Told you so,' Mitch mumbled to Stan.

'I think we'd better have some photos, Weeks, before I start untying this parcel.' His assistant went back to the car, opened the door and reached into the back, returning with a camera and flash gun. He took a number of pictures from different angles then Russell began trying to untie one of the knots. 'Mmm, the seawater has locked this solid. Has anyone got a….?' Before he could finish, Mitch held out a seaman's knife with the marline spike open. 'Thanks.'

Russell smiled wanly up at him and started working at the knot. With some difficulty he succeeded in loosening it, and then began on the next one. There must have been a dozen knots in all, expertly tied, but after the DI had undone five or six, the package started to come apart. It appeared to be wrapped in some sort of loosely woven felted material.

'Looks like carpet underlay, Sir.'

'Mmm, I think you're right, lad.' Carefully, trying to avoid getting water on his suit, he parted the sodden fabric, revealing a different material. 'What the…?' he exclaimed. With the help of his constable he peeled the rest of the fabric off to reveal a piece of Paisley patterned carpet. Carefully, they unrolled it and the body of a man came into view, his face unmarked but his clothes strangely shredded. A gasp escaped from one of the onlookers. Russell quickly covered the dead man's face.

'Right,' he said, as he rose from his knees, deftly shaking the dust from his handkerchief and replacing it in his pocket. 'I think we need the fingerprint boys and the doc here before we go any farther. Salt, please keep everyone back, and don't touch anything. Constable, ring the station and ask them to send the team down.'

While his orders were being carried out, Russell started walking slowly along the edge of the quay wall, whistling quietly and looking around him. With his dog at his heel, he gradually moved away from the steps and on towards a little used area of the yard. After a dozen paces he paused as the small terrier began to tug furiously at something, her tail wagging excitedly. Taking his handkerchief out of his pocket again Russell bent down and, using the cloth to cover his fingers, picked up a piece of the same grey felt that had been used to wrap up the body. It had obviously snagged on a splinter of wood.

'Well *done*, Aggie!' he said, patting her. 'Clever girl!' Rising, he turned and called out: 'Captain Salt. Here if you please.' Salt joined him. 'Did the body come straight out of the water to where it is now?'

'Why yes. Spratt brought it to the bottom of the ferry steps and it was lifted out there,' Salt said.

'And it definitely hasn't been anywhere near this spot?'

'No, Stan used the crane to lift it off the steps and straight on to the quay. Why?' He looked perplexed.

'Mmm,' Russell said, 'then how did this get here?' He held out the piece of material. 'I think we'd better seal off this whole area so we can search it thoroughly.' He started scanning the ground near to where the dog had found the scrap of cloth, then crouched and looked closely at a patch where the shingle was thinner, exposing an area of sand. 'Captain Salt,' he called out to the retreating figure. Salt turned. 'Could you send Mitch over, please?'

'Certainly.' The captain went over to the boatshed and in a few minutes Mitch appeared.

'Yes, Inspector?' he said.

'Have any vehicles been over here today, as far as you know?'

Mitch pushed his cap up and scratched his head. 'I don't think so. In fact I'm pretty sure they haven't. Let me see. Jack arrived on his motorcycle combination, but he parks it over there, by his shed.' He pointed to the ferryman's hut. 'Stan drove the crane, but that was only from the shed to the steps. You can see it's still there.'

Russell looked up to see the crane, the hook on the end of the cable swinging gently. 'Is that it? No other vehicles?'

'I don't think so. The rest of us come in on the train,' Mitch said slowly. 'No, hang on. I forgot.' He groaned and put the heel of his hand to his forehead. 'What with all this bother with the body,

I clean forgot. We had a bit of excitement this morning. The lads uncovered a bomb and a couple of chaps from the army barracks came in a small lorry and took it away.'

Russell stood up. 'Ah. So did they park it here?' he asked.

'Oh no, it all happened up the farther end of the quay.'

'Can you show me where?'

'Of course, follow me.' Mitch led the way along the quay to where Valiant and Rankin had lifted the bomb into the truck. 'Here's where they parked. They didn't go anywhere near the other end, just turned round and headed back over the level crossing.

'Mmm, very interesting... Thanks, Mitch. Can you let me know when the boffins arrive?' Again Russell crouched and examined the ground.

The shingle had been churned up by the lorry, presumably executing a three-point turn, but he was able to distinguish a distinctive tyre-tread pattern in the sparse areas of sand. There was also a fresh patch of black, sticky oil. He retraced his steps to the far end of the quay where Aggie had found the scrap of fabric. Sure enough, there was the same pattern made by a tyre, a patch of oil, although this one had soaked into the sand and... he bent again and could make out footprints. One set was large - at least a size 12 boot, he reckoned - but he was puzzled by the other set. Although they showed very clearly in a patch of smooth sand, they were most unusual. One footprint was virtually flat and had no distinctive tread whereas the other had a well-defined heel and sole. Also, they were very small, almost like that of a child.

He stood for a few minutes, considering this, stroking his chin. Then something else caught his eye. A small clod of earth. No - not earth he realised. Bending down, he could see that it was buff-coloured clay, impressed with the print of a shoe, or boot. He found that particularly curious, as there was no clay in the area, only shingle and sand... He would make sure it was collected as evidence.

~O~

A team arrived from the police station to examine the body. As it was still in good condition John Crooks, the pathologist, had estimated that it had been in the water for between 12 and 20 hours. 'What do you think was the cause of death?' Russell asked. Crooks thought before answering.

'Somehow I don't think it was drowning,' he said slowly. 'But I won't be sure until we've done the post mortem.'

'Any identifying features?'

'Close-cropped grey hair, smooth skin on his face and hands, an old scar on the left cheek and a tattoo on the right forearm. Could be an anchor? It's too faded to be sure at this stage. But look at this.' He lifted the dead man's left arm and pointed to a spot just below his armpit. There was a faint, but definite '0'. 'What do you make of that?' Crooks asked.

Russell shrugged. 'No idea. Have you?'

The pathologist smiled. 'Yes, I have, actually. It shows the blood group of members of the Waffen-SS.'

'So he was a member of the *Nazi* party?' Russell raised his eyebrows and whistled slowly.

The pathologist went on briskly: 'Age, less than 40, but looks older. Though I don't think he's had a tough life. However, there's something very odd about this one. You saw that the clothes had been ripped?' Russell nodded. 'Well there also appear to be multiple lacerations to the body and limbs.'

'Is that what did for him?' Russell asked.

'No, I don't think so. I haven't had a good look - that will have to wait until we get him back to the lab - but none of them appears deep enough to have caused death. I'll be able to tell you more after we've done a proper examination.'

Russell gave him a smile. 'I'm sure you will, John.' Soon the body had been loaded into a black van and was heading back to town.

~o~

DI Russell had set up an interview room in the bar of the Shipwrights Arms. Although the weather was mild, Alf had lit the fire and logs crackled in the hearth. The terrier lay happily asleep in front of the fire warming herself, paws twitching as she chased phantom rabbits. Russell sat on one of the wooden chairs with Weeks next to him, a notebook open on the table, pen poised. The DI began by talking to Captain Salt, who sat opposite them. 'Well, this is a fine pickle,' he said. 'Not going to do a lot for your ideas of tourism, eh?'

'I fear not,' Salt said. 'I expect the only trippers we'll get for a while will be rubberneckers, and other ghoulish characters wanting to gawp at the spot where the body was found. Have you any idea who the man is?'

'None at all at the moment. I was hoping you'd be able to help. You saw his face, didn't you?'

Salt nodded. 'I did, but I've no idea who he is. I know most of the people round here and he didn't look at all familiar. I wonder where he came from?'

'Hopefully Crooks and his team will come up with some clues. Look, keep this under your hat, but I reckon this is where the body was dumped in the water.'

Salt raised his bushy eyebrows. 'Really? Here at Compass Point?'

Russell explained about the fabric scrap, tyre tracks and footprints and said: 'I've a sneaky suspicion that the same lorry that took away your bomb this morning was used to bring the body here, probably last night. But please don't say anything until I've had a chance to talk to the lads at the barracks.'

'Of course not.' Salt paused. 'You don't think the Army is involved in some way, do you?'

Russell shrugged. 'It seems incredible, but who can say? From what we know already I'm guessing the body was dumped in the water sometime late last night. It was high tide then wasn't it?' he asked.

'Just about. 11.20, or thereabouts, I believe,' Salt replied.

'So, the body was carried out as the tide fell, swirled around out there...' The DI gestured towards the estuary, 'Then came back on the flood and didn't reappear until the tide turned again... I wonder how far up the river it went?' he added, almost to himself. 'I'd better get the lads to search along the banks. See if they can find anything.'

'I don't suppose there's any chance you could keep this quiet?'

Russell looked sadly at the Captain. 'I doubt it old chap. Even if I could, enough people know what happened for it to get out. I think you'd best prepare yourself for the press. They have a nose for these things. Hopefully we'll clear this up quickly and they'll soon get bored and move on to something else.'

'So, Mitch, what can you tell me about the body?'

Salt had left and now the boatbuilder was sitting opposite the detective. He sat, relaxed, in a faded fisherman's smock and old corduroy trousers, so worn there was barely any texture on them.

'Not much. One of the people Jack had brought over from Shell Bay came and got me when they returned. I helped to get the body on to the lower step and stayed with it until the crane lifted it on to the quay.' He breathed out loudly through his long thin nose and pursed his lips, making the hairs of his walrus moustache stand out straight.

'Tell me about Jack.'

Mitch looked surprised at the policeman's sudden change of tack. 'What do you want to know?' he asked.

'Well, apparently he didn't come out this morning when they found the bomb and he didn't seem bothered, once the body had been lifted on to the shore. He took himself off to his hut and hasn't been seen since. It doesn't seem to add up.'

'That's not unusual. He spends a lot of time in there. Even sleeps there when he's had a row with his wife, and that happens more often than not.'

'Hmm,' said the detective. 'I think it's time I had a chat with him. Could you send him in please?'

~o~

'I understand you spend a lot of time in your shed, Jack?'

'When I'm not in 'ere or out on the boat, that's right,' he replied, looking suspicious.

'I also understand you even sleep there?'

Jack looked down and picked at his thumbnail. 'Sometimes,' he mumbled.

'I don't suppose you were in there last night?' Russell stared at Jack who looked up, then quickly looked down again at his hands.

'Might 'ave been.'

The DI reached across the table and grasped the other man's wrist. 'Well were you or weren't you?' he asked, his usual easy-going tone replaced by an uncharacteristic menacing growl. Aggie looked up, her ears twitching in surprise at the unusual sound.

Jack snatched his hand back. 'All right, I was. What's it to you?' He stared at the detective with a look that was both sheepish and defiant. With a deep sigh the dog settled down in front of the fire again, her chin resting on her paws.

Russell sat back. 'That's better. Now did you see or hear anything suspicious?'

'Like what?' Jack was still being belligerent.

'That's what I'm asking you, 'Russell said patiently, as if talking to a child. 'Now, can I have a straight answer?'

'Oh I don't know. I'd 'ad a few pints so I went out like a light.' Russell still didn't think he was telling the whole truth.

'If you drank so much you must have had to get up for a pee.'

'Fair enough, I did,' Jack said resignedly.

'And?'

'And what?'

'Look, I'm getting fed up with this. You saw or heard something and I want to know what it is. Now tell me or I'll have you up for obstructing the police!'

'Oh, *all right*. There weren't no moon, so it were pretty dark. I'd gone out to relieve meself when a lorry turned up at the far end of the quay.' He waved vaguely towards the window.

'And then what?'

'As I said, it were dark but I think I saw two figures carryin' sommat an' chuckin' it in the water.'

'Why on earth didn't you tell me this before?' Russell was quite angry now.

'I dunno.' His voice tailed off.

'Is there anything else?'

'No, that really is all I can tell you. Except…' he paused.

'Yes, go on.' Russell encouraged

'Well, it sounded like that Bedford that came for the bomb.'

Thursday

Sheepshank – a type of knot used to shorten a rope or take up slack.

JUST OUTSIDE Collinghurst, inside a high security fence topped with nasty looking coils of barbed wire, was the barracks of the local Royal Engineers unit. It consisted of a group of plain buildings in regimented rows, surrounded by lawns of neatly cut grass. A Union flag flew from a tall flagstaff. A red-and-white-striped barrier blocked an opening in the fence that led to a Tarmac road which wound between the buildings. A small cabin provided shelter for the guards.

Early the following morning Weeks drove the Wolseley up to the barrier and a corporal with a rifle slung over his shoulder walked round to the side of the car. The DC wound down the window. 'Yes Sir, can I help you?' the soldier asked.

Russell leant across so he could peer out of the open window. 'Er… yes: DI Russell to see Captain Valiant.'

'Right you are, Sir, he's expecting you. Drive to the end of this road and his office is on your right.' The corporal walked back and raised the barrier.

Weeks parked the car outside a single-story, brick building. 'Stay,' Russell commanded Aggie. She let out a long, loud sigh and slumped resignedly on the back seat. Getting out of the car Weeks mounted the single step and knocked on the plain green door. 'Enter,' a voice rapped from within. He and Russell went in.

The room was quite small. One wall was dominated by a large-scale map of the area, marked with coloured flags. A single window looked out on to a neat lawn and the fence beyond. Valiant sat behind a wooden desk, bare but for a telephone and a pristine blotting pad with a fountain pen lying perfectly parallel with the top edge. Sapper Rankin stood stiffly at ease to one side, his rumpled uniform at odds with his rigid stance. There were two chairs in front of the desk and Valiant gestured for the policemen to sit.

'Hello gentlemen, how can I help you?' he asked smoothly. 'I presume you've come about that bomb at Compass Point?' The two men sat down.

'Not exactly,' Russell said. 'Although it does involve the Point. 'What I'm more interested is your Bedford lorry.' The captain looked at him quizzically. 'Did you hear that a body was found in the river yesterday?' He noticed a slight movement from the private, almost imperceptible, but definitely there.

'Yes, I heard something about that. Wasn't it near where we collected the bomb?'

'That's right. The thing is, it looks like the body was taken to the Point the night before and dumped in the water at high tide.'

'I don't see how this affects us.' Valiant leant back in his chair placing his hands in his lap.

Russell leant forward and put his elbows on the desk. 'Well I'll tell you. We have reason to believe your lorry was involved.'

'How come?' Valiant sat up, interested now.

'We found tyre tracks that match those of your truck. Also a witness heard the noise of an engine that night and recognised it as being the same as your lorry. Apparently it's quite distinctive.'

Valiant looked at the private. 'Rankin,' he said, 'do you know anything about this?' The sapper appeared perplexed.

'I'm not sure, Sir, although, come to think of it, there was something that's been puzzling me.'

'Would you care to elaborate?'

'Um… well, Sir, when we set off yesterday I was surprised that the needle on the fuel gauge showed that the tank wasn't quite full. I tend to keep it topped up so it's ready when we need it. And I always leave it in gear. I don't trust the handbrake. But when I got in it was in neutral. We haven't had a shout for a few days, so the lorry's just been sitting there.' The private's voice was coarse and his speech stilted, almost as if he was reading from a report or prepared script.

'Mmm,' Valiant murmured. 'Do you think someone else could have used it?'

'I don't see how, Sir. This is a secure area after all.'

'How do you account for the used fuel and gearstick then?'

Rankin shrugged. 'Dunno, Sir.'

Russell, who had been quietly observing the discourse between the two soldiers, spoke softly: 'I think we'd better take a look at this lorry, Captain. Is that okay?'

He and Weeks were led out of the building and round to the back where a number of military vehicles were parked. Valiant stopped by a truck with distinctive red mudguards.

'I'm afraid we haven't had a chance to clean it up gents,' he said. 'All we've done is taken the bomb out and put it in the sandpit.'

Russell was pleased. 'That's good news. There may still be some evidence. Mind if we take a look?'

'Be my guests,' Valiant said. 'Give me a shout if you need any help.' He turned and Rankin followed him back to the office.

'Gloves on, Weeks - and try not to disturb anything. Let's see if we can preserve any evidence there might be left inside.'

They undid the catches and gently let down the tailgate. The back of the lorry was a jumble of filled and empty sandbags, coiled ropes of various thickness and length, chains, canvas bags and baulks of timber. It didn't seem as if Rankin was as conscientious about keeping the truck tidy as he was about making sure the fuel was topped up. Cautiously the officers climbed into the back, carefully stepping over the contents. Standing and slowly scanning the interior, Russell took in the details. 'Not sure what we can find, it's all bit of a muddle. I think we'd better get the team from the station to have a look.' He was just about to get out again when he stopped. 'Hang on a mo. What's this?' He reached down to where the tailgate hinge was exposed. There was a sharp edge and a piece of grey fabric was caught on the metal. 'A-ha!' he exclaimed, holding it up for Weeks to see. 'Looks like the same stuff the body was wrapped in.'

Russell had requested that uniform send some men to have a look around Compass Point for more clues. Two PCs were despatched along the railway embankment. They could have stayed on the level and no one would have been any the wiser but, to their credit, they stumbled and slithered down the uneven causeway to look under the bridge. There they found the branch, wedged against the bridge abutment and still clinging to it was a scrap of grey felt. However, all this proved was that the body had floated as far as the bridge before it started heading back out to sea. Despite their thoroughness, nothing else was turned up.

Russell was back in the police station, sitting behind his desk. His arms were folded across his chest. His eyes were half closed and his lips were pursed, whistling quietly. He sat like this for some time before speaking. 'What have we got, Weeks?' he asked the constable, seated across from him.

'Well Sir, a washed-up body, wrapped in carpet and underlay; an army Bedford apparently used to move the body; some scraps of fabric found on the quay, in the back of the truck and under the bridge... but not a lot else.'

'Not bad, constable,' Russell smiled, unfolding his arms and leaning forward. He put his elbow on the desk and rested his chin on his closed fist. 'But what about those expertly tied knots, the odd footprints and the lump of clay?'

'Oh yes, of course,' Weeks replied bashfully.

The DI continued: 'The knots suggest a seaman, or at least someone connected with boats or the water.'

'And what about those strange footprints, Sir?'

'Hmm, they were pretty small. A child?' He shook his head. 'No I don't think so. And the fact that although the same size they were so different in pattern. Why would one be smooth and the other more defined?' Russell leant back in his chair and folded his arms once more.

'Sounds like a built-up shoe,' Weeks said quietly.

Russell sat up. 'What was that?' His sudden movement alerted the dog under the desk and she pricked up her ears.

'Could be a built-up shoe, Sir.'

'*That's it*! Well done.'

'Really, Sir?' The constable was puzzled. The dog settled again.

'Listen Weeks, let's say someone had polio and one leg developed more than the other. He'd have to wear a built-up shoe, wouldn't he?' Weeks nodded. 'And possibly, he never grew fully so he stayed small, hence the shoe size. So we're looking for a little man.'

'Or woman, Sir.'

'True, or a woman. With an orthopaedic shoe. Mmm… now, where we do start?' He settled back into his chair again, deep in thought.

After a while Weeks spoke: 'And what about the lump of clay, Sir?'

Russell came out of his reverie. 'Presumably it had been caught in the wheel arch of the Bedford and when it stopped, the lump fell out. I wonder if our boys are still at the barracks.'

The telephone was picked up on the third ring. 'Russell here, can you tell me if the fingerprint team is still with you?'

'Hang on a mo…' Valiant said,' I'll just take a dekko.' Russell heard the phone clatter on the desk and waited. In a few moments Valiant was back on the line.

'Yes, they're still out there, it looks like they're packing up.'

'Oh good. In that case, could you ask them to look under the wheel arches for traces of clay, please?'

'Sure thing,' the captain said. 'Anything else?'

'No, that's all. Thanks for your help.'

Friday

Keelhauling – a form of punishment meted out to sailors at sea.

THE NEXT day Russell was sitting alone in his office, trying to make sense of what he knew already, which, he admitted, didn't amount to much. The way the body had been carefully wrapped and tied and the fact it hadn't been weighted didn't make sense. If it had been it surely would have sunk without trace. As it was, by ensuring that it stayed afloat it made it look as if it was meant to be found. What did that mean? Perhaps a warning of some kind? Was it meant to set an example? It was certainly puzzling.

There was something else bothering him. Rankin had said that the lorry was kept in a secure area, so how did someone from outside gain access to it? ... if it was someone from outside. He was just deciding that he needed to have another chat with the soldiers when the phone rang. It was the pathologist. 'Crooks here. Wondered if you wanted to come over to the mortuary to see what we've found?'

'Anything interesting?' Russell asked.

'I think you'd better come over and take a look for yourself.'

'Okay, I'm on my way.' He got up from his chair, left his room and as he entered the outer office he called out: 'Anyone seen Weeks?'

'Here, Sir.' Weeks's tousled head popped up from behind a teetering pile of files.

'Come on, lad, we're wanted in the mortuary.' Weeks grabbed his coat and followed Russell out to the car park.

The Wolseley slowed to a halt in front of a large, austere, red-brick building on the edge of Collinghurst. The façade had the scale and proportions of a stately home but not the gravitas. Something about its bulk rendered it utilitarian and everyday, not special. The mortuary was part of this forbidding looking Victorian complex that had once housed an asylum but was now an annexe of the town's hospital. The two detectives got out and walked up the steps to the front door. Passing the receptionist, who was engaged in an involved telephone conversation, they turned left and walked down a long corridor. It was painted two-tone, in colours far from jolly - dull institutional green below the dado rail and bilious beige above. They hurried along the uninviting length, pushed through the swing doors at the end then in through a door marked PATH LAB – ONLY AUTHORISED PERSONNEL TO ENTER.

There was a small, plain anteroom containing just a row of filing cabinets and a pair of straight-backed chairs - cold comfort for those unfortunate enough to be waiting to identify a body. At the opposite end from where they had entered was another door marked PRIVATE. Russell knocked then pushed the door open.

'Ah Sonny,' Crooks said, walking towards them, a green, ankle-length gown stretched tautly across his generously padded frame. A face mask, the chords looped over his large ears, hung under his jaw but failed to conceal his multiple chins. 'I think you'll find this most interesting.' He led the two police officers across the room to a metal table where a body was stretched out, covered by a light sheet. He walked up to the head of the table and pulled it back. The man's pale face looked calm and serene. Russell was always surprised at how the faces of those in death rarely reflected the trauma they had suffered in life. Crooks pulled the sheet back farther and the naked man's body came into view. It was criss-crossed from chest to toe with small scratches, some short and some long - none very deep.

'Ouch!' Russell exclaimed. Weeks looked away and swallowed noisily. 'You okay, son? Russell asked, concerned. The DC swallowed again.

'I think so, Sir. Just a bit of a shock.'

'You're right. It's not a pretty sight.' He turned to the pathologist. 'How on earth did that happen, John?'

'It puzzled me initially. I expect you remember that the clothes were ripped too?' Russell nodded. 'The scratches are so random I thought at first he'd been dragged through the proverbial hedge backwards. But on closer examination I could find no traces of thorns or other plant material, which I would have expected, had that been the case. But, what I did find....' He walked over to a side table and picked up a kidney-shaped, stainless-steel dish. '...was this.' He held it out for the policeman to look at.

It contained a number of small grey flakes and some short strands of greenish, almost translucent, material. Russell frowned.

'Yes, it had me vexed at first, too,' said Crooks. 'So we had a closer look at his clothes and we found more of the same. 'Do you know what it is yet? He cocked his head to one side waiting for a reply. Both the detectives shook their heads. 'It's barnacles!' he said, triumphantly, 'Barnacles and seaweed!'

'Well I'll be jiggered! How on earth did that happen?' Russell was incredulous.

'Ah, well, this is very interesting...' In common with others in his profession Crooks took an almost morbid delight in his work. Like his colleagues he'd seen so many strange things during the course of his working life that little shocked or surprised him. However, this latest revelation had obviously awakened his curiosity and he was determined to make the most of it. 'Have you heard of keelhauling?' he said.

'Keelhauling?' Russell's brow furrowed even deeper. 'I thought that was stopped centuries ago.'

'Well not *so* long ago,' the pathologist explained. 'And for the benefit of those who don't know...' - he paused and looked at Weeks - 'keelhauling was a practice used as a punishment in the 17th and 18th centuries, meted out to sailors at sea, although officially only the Dutch navy used it. It involved tying ropes round a man and dragging him under the ship, from one side to the other. If the ship hadn't been out of the water for some time, the bottom would be covered with barnacles, so the man could be ripped to bits, or, if kept under water for too long, he'd drown. Either way it was a pretty horrific punishment, I think you'll agree. Surprisingly the Dutch only banned it in 1853, a mere one hundred years ago.'

Russell looked again at the body. 'Do you really believe that's what happened to this chap, John?'

'Well not quite as severe, as that's not what killed him, but something like that.'

Russell thought for a moment. 'Could he have been dragged under the hull of a smaller vessel, say a fishing boat?'

'That's what I thought. Enough to frighten the life out of him, but not to finish him off.'

Weeks had regained his composure. 'What did finish him off, Sir? You said when you first saw him on the quayside that he didn't drown.'

'That's right, there was no trace of water in his lungs so he was dead before he went in the drink. Have a look at this though.' He bent down towards the man's chest and pointed to a spot, a couple of inches below his left nipple. 'We missed it at first, what with all the scratches.' The two detectives peered at the place he indicated. There was a line, more pronounced and deeper than the scratches, of a darker hue, more purple than red.

'Looks like someone stuck a knife in him,' Russell said.

'That's it, that's what did for him. Up between the ribs and into the heart.' Crooks stood back and placed his hands on his hips. 'So, keelhauled as a frightener, then stabbed with a thin, narrow-bladed knife. Trussed up like a chicken and dumped in the drink. What a way to go. Any idea who he is yet?'

'None at all. I was hoping you'd be able to help,' Russell said. 'We looked through the missing persons files for the past couple of months but nothing turned up so we went back even farther, to the middle of last year. Still nothing. Either no one reported him missing or...' he thought for a moment, '...he's not from round here. Perhaps he's from another country.'

'Sadly I can't help you with that.'

'That's okay. What you've given us so far is very useful ... thanks.' Crooks proceeded to cover the body again. The policemen were just about to leave when he called out: 'By the way, would you like to know what he had for his last meal?'

'Go on,' said Russell

'Shellfish. Most likely whelks and cockles.'

'Captain Valiant. I think we need another talk.' Weeks had driven Russell back to the barracks and they were in the officer's room again.

'Oh really?' the officer drawled. 'I thought your boys had done their work with the lorry.'

'Yes they have, but, there are still one or two unanswered questions. I need to speak to you, and also to Private Rankin.'

'What more can he tell you?' Valiant sounded a little terse.

'That's what I'm hoping to find out. Would you mind getting him for me please?'

'Very well, although I don't see what help he can be.' The captain lifted the telephone handset and dialled a number. 'Yes, can you put me through to the mess?' There was a pause. 'Hello, Valiant here. Is Rankin there?' another pause. 'He is? Good. Can you ask him to come to my office?' Pause. 'Now please.' He replaced the handset. 'He's on his way. Now what did you want to ask?'

'I think we'll wait until he's arrived, if it's all the same to you.' It clearly wasn't and Valiant made his feelings known without speaking. He linked his fingers and rested his hands on the desk, his mouth a thin grim line and his brow furrowed with suppressed anger. The two policemen stood quietly and they waited in uncomfortable silence until the door opened and Rankin appeared.

'Sir?' he said to Valiant, and nodded to the policemen.

'They want to ask us some more questions – apparently,' the captain said, sarcasm clear in his voice.

Russell ignored his manner and said pleasantly: 'It's about the lorry.'

'We guessed as much.' The captain was doing little to disguise his annoyance.

'Ahem,' Russell said, carrying on, 'You said you were surprised that someone may have used the Bedford.' He said this directly to Rankin.

'Yes, Sir, that's right.'

'Would any of the other personnel here have used it?'

'That's very unlikely,' the Captain interrupted, 'Not only is it a bit old and ropey, but it has to be ready at a moment's notice in case we have an emergency.'

'I see.' Russell looked thoughtful. 'And you said it's kept here, in this secure area all the time?'

The soldiers exchanged a quick glance. 'That's right, Sir,' the private said.

'Then how could it have been taken?'

Rankin shrugged.

'You can see the dilemma I'm in,' Russell said, now looking at the captain.

The captain was still starchy but his mood softened a fraction. 'Yes, I see what you mean.'

'Perhaps we could have a word with the guards at the gate on the night it was used. Maybe they can shed some light.'

'Yes, of course.' The captain, although still not over-eager to assist, seemed to realise that the sooner he helped Russell the sooner he would leave them alone. 'I'll find out who it was and let you know. Meanwhile, is it okay if Rankin goes back to his duties?'

'Yes, that's fine. We've finished with him... for the time being. However, I'd like to see those two other men now, if possible,' Russell said firmly, not prepared to wait. Valiant got on the phone and asked for the guards' roster.

Two soldiers entered the office. With Valiant and the policemen, it was becoming uncomfortably crowded. Russell stood up, pushing back his chair, preferring to meet the two men at eye level. Weeks stood up next to him. Valiant, still seated, spoke. 'These are privates Don Dunne and 'Swing' Lowe. Ask them any questions you wish.'

Russell nodded to the captain. 'Thanks.' He turned to face the men, standing just a few feet away. 'I understand you were on guard duty the night before last.'

'That's right, Sir.' Lowe, the rounder and elder of the two, spoke. His speech was clipped, more like an officer from Sandhurst. 'We were on duty from 10pm until six in the morning.'

'Can you tell me if there was any traffic, in or out, that night?'

'Very little, Sir.' He turned to the taller man next to him. 'Can you remember who we saw, Don?'

Dunne furrowed his brow. When he spoke his voice was guttural, almost rasping.

'Them officers came back from some do in the Landy. That was about midnight. Apart from that, I fink it was quiet all night.' Dunne's speech was far less eloquent.

'Are you sure?' Russell asked. The two men pondered.

Valiant cut in: 'Haven't you got a log for the vehicle movements?'

Lowe looked sheepish and cast his eyes down. 'Er, not exactly, Sir,' he mumbled.

'What!' the captain exclaimed.

'Well, we didn't fill it in then, Sir. We was goin' to do it later today. Sorry, Sir.' Dunne looked crestfallen.

'But you're supposed to do it as it happens!' Valiant said, almost shouting. 'You do realise this is a chargeable offence?'

'Yes, Sir,' the two men said in unison.

Russell broke in: 'Anyway, this isn't getting us anywhere. Please try to remember what other traffic went through the gate. It was only two nights ago, after all.'

Dunne appeared to have a thought, his dull face lighting up. 'Oh yeah,' he said. 'That lorry come through about midnight – remember, Swing?'

Lowe looked baffled for a moment, then realisation dawned. He looked directly at Valiant. 'But it was your truck, Sir.'

'Yes we know that. But who was driving?'

'Dunno, Sir,' Dunne said. 'Wasn't it Rankin, who's usually with you?'

'I was tucked up in bed and I assume Corporal Rankin was too,' Valiant said defensively.

'Well someone wiv a uniform on was drivin'. We didn't take much notice cos we're used to you rushin' out at all times of day and night.'

'So it was a soldier then?' Russell asked.

Lowe turned towards him. 'I'm pretty sure it was Sir. Although it was dark, the area by the barrier is pretty well lit.'

'And presumably you were still on duty when it came back?'

'Oh yes, Sir.' Lowe was eager to help now. 'I remember that because I said to Don - Dunne that is, Sir - that I was surprised to see them back so soon. They could have only been gone for an hour or so.'

'If you'd kept the log up to date you could have been more precise about the time, couldn't you?' Valiant said sternly.

'Yes, Sir.' Again the men spoke in unison.

'We'll discuss this later. If you've nothing else to add, you're dismissed. For now...' the captain added. The two soldiers saluted and left the room.

~O~

Back at the police station, Russell sat in his office and pondered the new information. Unless Rankin was lying - and he hadn't ruled that possibility out - another soldier, or someone impersonating a soldier, had driven the Bedford out of the camp, returning an hour or so later. This meant that either there was a rogue or corrupt squaddie in the camp or, somehow, someone from outside had got into the camp undetected and taken the lorry. The more he thought about it the more that seemed unlikely. So, most probably, it had to be an inside job. Russell knew enough about the Army to know that they were very likely to close ranks and protect their own so finding out who it was could be tricky. He started whistling *Cherry Pink and Apple Blossom White*. After a few bars he stopped and returned to his pondering.

The other puzzle was the lump of clay. The fingerprint team had searched the underside of the lorry's mudguards and chassis but could find no trace of it, just loose soil and sand. However, they had found some dry smears in the passenger footwell. He was still sitting thinking about this when the phone rang. He picked up the receiver. 'DI Russell.'

'Russell, John Crooks here. How's the investigation going?'

'Not great, I have to say. Things keep cropping up to muddy the water. We know the how but as to the why and by whom ... your guess is as good as mine.'

'I'm afraid I might be about to muddy the water even farther...' He paused for a moment, then added: 'Or perhaps not.'

'Go on,' Russell said, giving him his full attention.

'You remember when you came to look at the body and I showed you the wound where a knife had gone in?'

'Yes.'

'Something was bothering me. I'd found the scraps of barnacle, which explained the scratches, but I decided to have another look at the wound and guess what I found?' Crooks said, enigmatically.

'Go on.'

'Fish scales.'

'Really?'

'Yes, only fragments, and pushed into the wound, but definitely fish scales, although don't ask me what type of fish. Does that help?'

An idea was forming in Russell's mind. 'Mmm, that's sounds very interesting. Thanks, John.'

'You're welcome. Glad to be of help.' The pathologist rang off.

It was just starting to get dark and Russell decided to call it a day. Aggie was sitting expectantly at the side of the desk. 'Yes, you're right, time to go home.' He picked up his jacket from the back of his chair and headed out into the main office. He stopped to speak to Weeks, whose desk was still piled high with files. A single Anglepoise lamp formed a circle of soft light on the page he was reading.

'You still here, son?' Russell asked. Weeks leant back, stretched his arms and yawned.

'Just about to pack up and go home, Sir.'

'Can you give me a lift then?'

'Sure.' Weeks switched off the lamp, shrugged his arms into his coat and followed his boss out of the police station.

The Wolseley bumped slowly along the stony track and the DC brought it to a stop outside Russell's home, the headlamps picking out a swirl of dust rising into the air.

'Thanks, lad,' the DI said. 'Can you come and get me at eight in the morning? We're going to have a look at the fishing boats at Compass Point before the tide comes in. And make sure you bring your wellingtons, it could be a bit sticky underfoot.' He climbed out of the car and opened the gate.

Picking his way in the evening gloom up the stepping stones between the clumps of seakale and Red Valerian, the dog trotting ahead, Russell walked through the shingle garden to the front door of a converted railway carriage. This was one of several redundant Victorian coaches along the track, originally placed there as holiday homes although he had chosen to live in his permanently. A farther carriage had been placed close behind the first with a flat-roofed extension beyond that, making a perfectly adequate home for him and Aggie. Once inside he opened the front of the coal stove in the living room, raked the embers until they glowed then threw on a handful of sticks. Once these were blazing merrily he added a shovelful of coal and shut the door.

Next he filled the kettle, lit the gas with a match and set it to boil. Then he opened a tin of food for Aggie which he tipped in a bowl and placed on the floor. The small dog set to with gusto. Looking in the larder, he found a slice of cheese and onion pie. He bent, sniffed, and deciding it was still okay, placed it on a plate. He added a spoonful of chutney from a jar and took it over to the armchair and switched on the standard lamp. Before eating he slid a disc of the Bavarian Radio Symphony Orchestra's live version of Mahler's 5th out of its sleeve. Carefully he put it on the radiogram knowing that the soaring strings would calm his nerves and bring a sense of tranquillity. Then he settled down with his notes.

He read through the details he and Weeks had managed to amass about the dead man and the manner of his death. It didn't amount to much. It seemed likely that it involved sailors or fishermen. The barnacle scraps and weed; keelhauling (he shuddered); the fish scales in the knife wound, and the knife - a thin blade perhaps. They all pointed in that direction. At first he assumed a stiletto but the more he thought about he wondered if it was, perhaps, a fish filleting knife. And then the expertly tied knots... He hoped the morning would offer up some more substantial clues as to the why and by whom. After a while the soothing heat from the crackling stove took effect. He put the papers aside on a small table next to his chair, the dog jumped on to his lap and they both dozed in the warming room.

Saturday

Clay - a fine-grained natural rock or soil material that combines one or more clay minerals, with traces of metal oxides and organic matter.

'**I HOPE** you remembered your wellies, constable,' Russell said.

It was just after 8am and they were driving along the track to Compass Point. Weeks slowed the car and it bumped over the railway level crossing and came to a halt in Mitchell's boatyard. All was quiet. No one had yet arrived to start work. Boats of differing sizes and colours stood about the yard, some resting upturned on blocks of wood or trestles, others sitting on the stony ground shrouded in green canvas. Lengths of timber leant against the boatshed, coils of rope and piles of chain cluttered the ground, creating hazards for the unwary. A thin haze hung over the estuary, obscuring the horizon. Unseen oystercatchers called as they searched for food and the mournful cry of a curlew came from some distance away.

They climbed out and after changing from their shoes and into wellingtons, crossed the yard and started to descend the iron ladder to the sand and shingle bed of the estuary, damp from the outgoing tide. Aggie looked down on them from the quayside and whined, upset at being left behind.

'What exactly are we looking for, Sir?' Weeks asked.

'Well…' Russell mused, as they walked towards the first of a line of fishing boats, 'one of these,' - he pointed at a boat - 'with plenty of growth on the bottom.' When they drew close, they circled the hull. 'Not this one. The bottom's too clean. Barely any weed - must have been out of the water recently. Let's look at the next.'

There were a dozen boats in all, small inshore fishing craft, 20 to 30 feet long, some with trawling gear, others festooned with marker poles topped with cotton flags that were flapping lazily in the gentle breeze. Each had a line or chain running from the bow to a stake in the bank and another from the stern. All had the local registration letter CP, followed by a number on the bow. The two men worked their way along them. Each one had surprisingly little growth on the hull.

'Looks like we've drawn a blank, Sir,' said the DS, disappointed that they hadn't found what they'd hoped to find.

'It's very odd,' Russell said, scratching his head. 'I felt sure the likely candidate would be here.' He put his hands on his hips and looked slowly from one side of the estuary to the other and frowned, then he looked again and his face brightened. 'Ah ha! Look over there,' he said, nodding towards the farther bank. 'There's a mooring buoy but no boat. I can't read the letters on it from here, can you?'

Weeks shook his head. It was not possible to cross over directly to the spot as a rivulet, a good 15-feet wide, and probably deep too, ran out from under the bridge to join the sea. There was nothing for it but to climb back up the slimy ladder and make their way through the yard, along the railway track and over the bridge to the other side, the terrier now jumping delightedly along in front of the two men. They clambered down the overgrown embankment and on to the sand. The imprint of where the boat normally sat at its mooring was quite clear in the shingle and sand of the estuary bed. A spherical metal buoy attached to a length of anchored chain, with crudely painted numbers and letters on its side, rested next to the indentation.

'CP13,' Weeks said triumphantly.

'That's the number,' Russell nodded. 'Let's go and see if Mitch knows whose boat it is.'

Mitch had arrived at work while they were down on the sand examining the boats. 'Ah, CP13 - that's *Moonshine*,' he said. They were standing in his office in the boatyard. Shelves were crammed with books on the sea, charts and nautical almanacs, loose screws and bolts and sundry yacht fittings. In between were hung pictures of boats. The floor was littered with odd shaped pieces of metal and wood that may once have had a purpose. The desk was piled high with all sorts of paperwork: letters, receipts, invoices and scribbled notes. 'Scuse the mess,' he said, his full moustache bristling as he spoke.

Russell dismissed the apology with a wave of his hand. 'D'you know who owns it, Mitch?'

'Up until recently it belonged to old Ted Spencer, but he was finding the fishing too strenuous and his two sons weren't interested. His father and grandfather had both been fishermen before him but he just couldn't persuade them to take it on, so reluctantly he sold it a few weeks ago. I acted as broker.'

'Who did he sell it to?'

'That's the odd thing,' Mitch went on. 'She was an old boat but still in fair nick. He'd looked after her really well. The only thing he hadn't done was haul her out for a good clean and paint on new anti-fouling, like the rest of the boat owners had done, so she was pretty weedy.' The policemen exchanged a glance. 'But it wouldn't take much to sort that out. We've got all the facilities he'd need here in the yard.'

'So who did he sell it to? You said it was odd.'

'Jack Spratt - I think you've met him - he bought it.'

Russell raised his eyebrows. 'The ferryman? How could he afford it? I doubt he makes much of an income?'

'That's what I wondered, but he said he was buying it for someone else. Paid cash too.'

'Who was this someone?' Russell asked.

'That I don't know. It was all very mysterious. Jack wouldn't say, just that he was acting for a friend.'

'When was this?'

Mitch went to his desk and starting shifting piles of papers. Finally he found what he was looking for. 'Yes, I know it looks like a mess, but I really do know where everything is.' He grinned, holding up a diary. 'Now let me see.' He riffled through the pages. 'Here it is, end of March.'

'And did whoever Jack bought it for carry on using it for fishing?'

'No. And that's odd too. Once we'd sorted the paperwork out, Ted ended up with a wad of cash and a big smile and Jack scuttled off back to his shed. I didn't see him again that day, and by the next the boat was gone.'

'So that's just over a month ago. Have you seen the boat since?'

'Not a sign. I assumed they'd be back, as the mooring went with the boat, but I haven't seen hide nor hair of it, let alone the new owners, come to that.'

'I think it's time we had another little chat with Mr Spratt. Come on Weeks.' He thanked Mitch and the two policemen left the office, Aggie trotting importantly behind.

Jack Spratt's shed was on the far side of the yard, next to the Ferry Steps. It was a black, tarred structure, with a rusty, corrugated-iron roof. Raised off the ground on heavy baulks of timber, the space beneath was cluttered with ropes, lengths of chain and assorted pieces of wood. A clinker-built dinghy, undergoing repair, sat on a pair of trestles and various tools were scattered about. A crudely painted sign on the side of the shed announced:

FERRY, OPEN ALL DAY, 10 – 5

This sign was more than optimistic as Jack only rowed across to the dunes when he could tear himself away from the Shipwrights Arms and only then when there was enough water in the river. Russell mounted the steps and rapped on the closed wooden door, ignoring the large FERRY CLOSED sign hanging from a nail.

'Go away! Can't you read?' growled a voice from within.

'We don't want the ferry; we want to talk to you.'

'I don't care; I'm 'avin' a nap.' Russell lifted the latch and opened the door. 'Don't you understand English?' Jack began, then seeing who it was said: 'Oh, it's you, what do you want now?'

'We'd like a little chat - about *Moonshine*.' Russell peered in the gloom of the shed and could just make a figure stretched out on a narrow bench. The terrier stood beside him, growling quietly.

'What if I don't want to talk about it?' Jack said, sitting up.

'That's up to you Jack. We could always take you down to the station.'

The ferryman reconsidered. 'Oh, *all right*, give me a moment an' I'll come out.' Russell backed down the steps and Jack emerged, scratching his chin and grumbling under his breath. 'What about Moonshine?'

'I understand you bought it on behalf of a third party,' Russell said.

'Well what if I did? There's no law against it, is there?' Jack continued, belligerently.

'Maybe not, but we'd like to know who paid for it.'

'S'pose I don't want to tell you?'

The DI was beginning to get annoyed. It showed in his voice. 'As I already told you,' he said slowly, 'we can continue at the station. Now,' - he pushed his face close to the ferryman's - 'are you going to tell me or not?'

Some of the bluster went out of Jack. He sighed. 'All right, I'll tell you.'

Russell leant away from him gratefully. The smell of stale beer coming from his breath and the dank reek of his clothes was less than pleasant. 'That's better.'

'It was two brothers; not that you'd think they was related.'

'What do you mean?' Russell asked.

'Well, one was built like a brick shithouse - over six foot tall with huge shoulders an' a face that 'ad been round the block a few times.'

'And the other?'

'Wolfgang? Couldn't 'ave been more different. Little an' weedy - more like a child. Funny thing is, 'e was definitely the one in charge. The big brother, Ludwig, 'ardly said a word, just stood there with 'is chin on 'is chest, wringing 'is cap in his 'ands.'

'Wolfgang and Ludwig? Foreign names. Were they German?'

Spratt shrugged. 'Who knows?'

'So how come they got you to buy the boat for them?'

The ferryman considered, then spoke, 'All right, I'll tell you. You'd better sit down.' Russell and Weeks made their way to the bench along the side of the shed, Aggie jumping up beside them. Spratt perched on an upturned fish box.

'It was like this,' he began. 'I was getting me boat ready for the season, touching up the paintwork an' doing a few little repairs. I was working away quite happily. In a world of me own - truth be told - when this great shadow comes over the sun. I turned round to see what it was, an' there was this 'uge bloke standing right behind me; didn't even hear 'im come up. Next to him was this little bloke; noticed straight away there was something wrong with 'is leg.' Spratt was silent for a while as he remembered the meeting.

'I was a bit taken aback an' asked what they wanted, scaring a bloke like that. I was a bit sharp but they didn't seem to notice. The big bloke just stood there, looking down. It was the little one who did the talking.'

'"We'd like you to buy us a boat," 'e said. Just like that. 'Oh yeah,' I said, 'why 'ave you come to me?' "We heard you could be discreet," 'e said 'An, what's in it for me?' I said. "Don't worry about that," the little bloke said, "we'll make sure it's worth your while". He 'ad a funny, squeaky sort of voice - more like a schoolgirl.'

The two policemen had been sitting, listening intently. Then Weeks spoke. 'What sort of boat did he want?'

'Oh, 'e was quite definite about that. It 'ad to be about 30 feet long, 'ave a good size cabin, a decent turn of speed an' be capable of easily crossing the channel.'

'Did he say what they wanted it for?' Russell asked.

'I asked 'im that. Said did 'e want it for trawlin' for dabs an' plaice or for shooting crab pots? "Neither", 'e said. "Just get us a decent boat and we'll see you're all right". Then he give me 20 quid an' says: "This is your retainer, when you've found a boat, we'll give you the money to pay for it, plus something extra". An' with that, he turned round an' walked away with the big bloke following 'im.'

The three of them sat in silence for a few moments. The only sounds were of rigging ticking on a nearby mast, the distant cry of gulls and the gentle lap as the tide crept in. Then Russell spoke. 'You mentioned their names, Wolfgang and Ludwig and that they were brothers. How come you know all that?'

Jack looked down at his calloused hands, his brow furrowed for a moment.Then he looked up. 'I think the only thing the big one said was something like: "Make sure it's fast Wolfgang". An' the little one, Wolfgang, said: "All right, brother"'.

'What about Ludwig?'

'Oh yeah, I remember, as the little one turned to leave 'e said, in 'is 'igh- pitched voice: "Come on Ludwig, time to go". That's when they left.'

'You said the little one had something wrong with his leg.'

'I noticed it wasn't right when I first clapped eyes on 'im. But when they walked away, I could see 'e 'ad quite a limp, almost dragging one leg.'

'Anything else?'

'Yes, 'e 'ad one boot with a big thick sole an' heel.' Weeks looked pointedly at his DI.

'And so you set about finding a boat?'

'I didn't 'ave to look far as I knew old Ted Spencer wanted to get shot of *Moonshine* an' it fitted the bill. It was 30-foot long, with a decent cabin. 'E'd 'ad a new Gardiner diesel engine fitted not long ago an' that meant she could shift along at a good speed. I went round to see 'im the next day an' 'e was delighted. The money 'e wanted was pretty fair. I reckon 'e could have asked for more, so I bumped the price up an' we split the difference.'

'Ah. So that's why you've been looking a bit flush,' Russell smiled.

Spratt thought for a moment then spoke again. ' 'Ere, you ain't gonna tell the tax people are you?' He sounded rattled.

'Don't worry, we're only interested in the two men,' Russell said. He continued: 'When did you see them again?'

'The next day I was sat 'ere, putting the finishing touches to me dinghy, when the sun was blotted out again. I knew what it was this time so I turned round an' smiled. They smiled back at me - well the little one did - the big one just scowled. "Have you found a boat for us yet?" Wolfgang says. 'Yes,' I says, 'd'you want to ' ave a look?' "Yes", 'e says, so I says: 'Follow me.' An' we walked over the bridge an' down to the mooring.

'The tide was out so we 'ad to cross the wet sand to get to it. The little one was 'avin' trouble; 'is boot kept getting stuck an' Ludwig all but carried 'im across to the boat. I knew it quite well so I was able to climb on board fairly easily an' lower a ladder down the side so they could follow.'

'What did they make of the boat?' Weeks asked.

'They seemed to like it. 'Ad a good look round, poked about in the cabin then asked if I could get rid of the fishing gear. I didn't answer straight away an' Wolfgang said: "We'll make it worth your while". I couldn't refuse as I knew I'd be able to sell it on, so I said yes.'

Russell spoke this time. 'Were they all right about the price?'

'Yeah, didn't say a thing. Seemed almost surprised it was so cheap, even with the extra I bunged on.' He scowled. 'Could've asked for more.'

'When did they pay you?'

'There and then. Wolfgang turned to the big bloke an' held his hand out. Ludwig reached into 'is jacket pocket, pulled out a great wad of notes an' handed them to 'im. The little bloke counted them out, gave some back to Ludwig an' handed me the rest.'

'Did you count them?'

'You bet. An' it were all there, plus extra for gettin' rid of the other gear. I went an' got a barrow an' they 'elped me get the stuff they didn't want over the side. I 'ad a look round the boat an' the only things that were left was the navigation stuff, a few tools and a couple of knives.

'I asked if they needed me to show them 'ow to use the engine and 'ow to work the boat but Wolfgang smiled, shook 'is head an' said that they would manage. So I left them to it, no handshakes or nothing. After telling Mitch it was sold I went straight round to Ted with 'is share. 'E was delighted of course, then I come back here. I got on with me boat but kept a weather eye on the tide an' as soon as there was enough water I 'eard *Moonshine*'s engine start. I could see the big bloke casting off the mooring, the boat reversed away from the shore, turned an' 'eaded out of the estuary. It was all done so neat like, I reckon they knew what they was doing.'

'Did you see them again?'

'No, that was the last I saw of them, and of *Moonshine*. They haven't been back since.' Jack folded his arms across his chest and exhaled noisily. It seemed that was all he was going to say.

Russell rose from the bench. 'Is that it?' He raised an eyebrow and waited. Jack shrugged and remained silent. 'We'll leave you in peace then - for now.'

The two detectives had returned to the station and were sitting in the DI's small room, Russell leaning back in his chair, hands characteristically clasped behind his head, whistling quietly. Weeks sat opposite, his tousled head bent over a notebook open on his lap. The clatter of a typewriter and the occasional murmur of voices came from the larger outer office. Russell spoke. 'Let's go over what we've got so far.'

'Well,' Weeks said, slowly running his finger down the page, 'a body gets washed up at Compass Point. It's been in the water for less than a day although drowning wasn't the cause of death. That was a knife wound to the heart. However, the victim had been rather gruesomely tortured, sometime before.'

'Mmm,' the DI murmured. 'That's the victim and cause of death, now who were the killers?'

'We're pretty sure the body was taken to the Point in a lorry belonging to the bomb disposal unit. But we don't know who drove it out of the camp.'

Russell leant forward.

'If only those lazy sods had done their job properly we might have some idea. I'm still not sure about that soldier, Rankin. There's something about his explanation that doesn't add up. I think we should get him in - on his own - and ask some more questions. As charming as Captain Valiant is, I have a feeling that he would protect his man if he could.' Russell sighed. 'Anyway, carry on.'

'Yes, Sir.' The DC returned to his notebook. 'The fingerprint team went over the lorry thoroughly but the only ones they found belonged to Valiant and Rankin.'

'As you'd expect.' Russell leant back again.

'They found nothing else in the lorry to suggest any other person had been in or around it, apart from the clay dust in the footwell. However, there were those footprints. The boys didn't find them anywhere else, going to or leaving the scene, just there on the quayside...'

'So we can assume only that whoever made them came and went in the truck.'

'Exactly. And there's that piece of clay.'

'Yes, that is a puzzle. Now where would you find clay soil in an area where the terrain is predominantly sand and shingle? I suppose if you dug deep enough you might find some.' Russell pursed his lips and stared at the ceiling.

'A building site?' Weeks suggested.

'Mmm, that's a possibility. Where are there any houses being built round here?'

'There aren't many, Sir. There's still a chronic shortage of materials since the end of the war. All they seem to be building locally at the moment are those prefabs and they come in on the back of a lorry...' Weeks's voice trailed off.

'Still, I suppose they have to dig foundations for those, don't they?' Weeks nodded. 'Get on to the county council and find out what building work is going on.'

The DC looked alarmed. 'Couldn't we limit it to a certain area, Sir? If we have to scour the whole county it'll take forever.'

'Point taken, constable. Let's try to narrow it down. Let me think...' Russell put his elbows on the desk and steepled his fingers, resting his chin on the tips. After a few moments thought he spoke again. 'Now if, and it's a big if. *If* Rankin was telling the truth then how much fuel had been used? Couple of gallons perhaps?'

'I guess so.'

'And what does one of those lorries do to the gallon?'

'I dunno, Sir. Ten miles to the gallon, 15 at the most?'

'That sounds about right. So, let's assume whoever took the

lorry drove it between 20 and 30 miles altogether. How far is it from the army camp to the quayside I wonder?'

He got up from his chair and pulled a road atlas from a shelf and put it on the desk. He riffled through the pages and laid it open at a large-scale map that showed Collinghurst and Compass Point. Looking at the scale at the bottom, he measured the distance with his finger and thumb. 'It's got to be about 10 miles, hasn't it?'

'Looks like it, Sir. Also, you remember what that guard said?'

'What was that, lad?'

'He said he was surprised that the lorry was only gone for an hour or so.'

'Yes, that's right. So there wouldn't have been enough time to do much more than a return journey.'

'Exactly, Sir.'

'Now we're getting somewhere.' Russell was showing signs of excitement.

'Sir?' the DC enquired, not catching on.

'Don't you see? According to the amount of fuel used, if the lorry could only be driven from the barracks to the Point and back, wherever they picked up the body had to be on the direct route, or very close to it. Presuming our squaddie is telling the truth.'

He slumped back into his chair, deflated. 'That's the trouble, it all hinges on what he said.' He sat up again. 'Okay. We'll work on that assumption for now. What we need to do is follow the route and find out if there are any building sites nearby. Right, get on to the council and see what you can come up with. Meanwhile, let's get Rankin in – on his own.'

Rankin was sitting opposite Russell in the small office, Weeks was standing to one side of the desk. The soldier appeared quite calm, his face blank and impassive. The DI sat staring at him for some minutes. As the time passed he could see a minute tic begin by the sapper's right eye and a slight bloom of sweat appear on his forehead. Then, almost imperceptibly, Rankin rubbed his fingers along the seam of his baggy khaki trousers. He spoke. 'Are we going to sit here all day without speaking?' Then added: 'Sir?'

Russell leant forward. 'I'm not sure you've told us the truth, have you?' he asked quietly.

The soldier folded his arms defensively across his chest. 'Don't know what you mean.'

'You said,' he consulted the notebook open on his desk, 'that… "I was surprised that the needle on the fuel gauge showed that the tank wasn't quite full as I tend to keep it topped up so it's ready when we need it. Also, I always leave it in gear, don't trust the handbrake, but when I got in it was in neutral".'

'Yes, I think that's what I said.'

'I can assure you it was. My constable is very accurate when it comes to taking notes.' He nodded to Weeks.

'Well then, I did.'

'Mmm, it might be what you said, but we don't think it's what actually happened, do we constable?'

'No we don't,' Weeks confirmed.

Russell continued: 'The chances of an outsider getting into the barracks, unnoticed, taking your lorry from the compound and driving it out unchallenged are virtually nil.' Rankin made to speak but Russell held his hand up and continued. 'And also I don't think any other soldier would be likely to take your Bedford. Your officer said,' - he looked down at the notebook again - 'and I quote: "Not only is it a bit old and ropey, but it has to be ready at a moment's notice in case we have an emergency".'

'That's right' Rankin said.

'So no-one is going to take it, just in case you need it in a hurry, are they?'

'I suppose not.'

'Of course they wouldn't. Knowing your Captain Valiant he would make sure that all hell broke loose if it wasn't there when you needed it.' Russell had leant right forward and almost spat out the last words. The soldier was visibly shaken.

'No, Sir,' he said quietly.

The DI sat back and he too lowered his voice 'I suggest that it was you who used the lorry that night.'

'What?'

'And that you were paid to.'

'You're joking!' Rankin blustered.

'What if I said you were seen by a witness?'

'I'd say they were lying.'

'A very *reliable* witness.'

'Who? Tell me who?' Rankin gripped the sides of the seat.

'And they saw you with two other men in the lorry.'

'You've got to be joking!'

'Am I?' Russell said mildly and leant back.

The soldier thought for a moment. Russell could see that the sweat was starting to trickle into his eyes. He wiped the back of his hand across his forehead. He coughed. He looked ready to confess. Russell sat quietly waiting to hear how he would respond. The silence stretched. Then Rankin suddenly stood up and took control of himself, and when he spoke, it was with confidence. 'I don't believe anyone saw *me* as I wasn't there. As Captain Valiant said, I was tucked up in bed. You can tell your *reliable* witness that they were mistaken. Now, if there's nothing else, I need to get back to barracks, I've got work to do.' With that he turned on his heel and left.

Weeks and Russell looked at each other. The DI spoke: 'Now if that wasn't the action of a guilty man, I don't know what is.'

'One thing puzzles me, Sir. Who was the witness who saw him? You didn't mention it before.

Russell gave a snort. 'There wasn't one. I was just calling his bluff, and it almost worked. Sadly he failed to rise to the bait so we're back to square one. Now if you've got that list of building sites I think we'd better go and have a look.'

The first project they came to consisted of a handful of completed dwellings, half a dozen plots where bases had been poured and the same number where the ground was prepared ready for the concrete footings. Standing next to them were prefabricated wall panels, with openings for doors and windows. Nearby a large cement mixer was steadily turning, its single-cylinder petrol engine thumping out a regular beat as concrete slopped around inside.

A small crane was lowering one of the panels on to a base, with three or four men, all wearing flat caps, manoeuvring it into position. Russell waited until they had completed the task then went over to speak to them. 'Hello,' he said, 'is the foreman around?'

The nearest man was wearing a suit jacket that had seen better days. He took an unlit roll-up out of his mouth and said: 'Over there,' pointing to one of the completed prefabs. 'They're finishing off the inside of that one.' He put the cigarette back between his lips and turned away.

'Thanks,' Russell said to the man's back. He and Weeks picked their way over the uneven ground to the building.

As they walked in they could see that the prefab had a fitted kitchen and through a door was a bathroom with man-sized bath and flushing toilet, a luxury for those used to outside conveniences and tin baths. Two men were touching up the magnolia paintwork on the interior wall. 'Can I help you?' one of them asked, turning towards them, paintbrush in hand.

'We're looking for the foreman. I'm Detective Inspector Russell and this is Detective Constable Weeks.'

The man spoke. 'I'm George, the foreman. If it's about the materials that were nicked from the site last week I've already spoken to your lot.'

'Er, no,' Russell said, 'it's not.'

The foreman looked puzzled. 'Then why are you here? I'm afraid we've got a lot to get done today.'

'I was wondering if you'd be able to help with something else.'

'I'll try.' The man was anxious to get on.

'Can you tell me what sort of soil there is here?'

'That's a strange sort of question. Why do you want to know?'

'Oh, it's just a routine enquiry.'

'Oh, well,' the man sighed. 'You'd better come and take a look.' He put down his paintbrush and led the two detectives out of the building and over to the nearest freshly dug plot. 'There you are, see for yourself,' he said.

Russell crouched down and looked in the excavated hole. 'Looks like very sandy soil and some sort of rock. Am I right?'

'You certainly are. It's sandstone and it's a bugger. The holes either collapse when you're digging them or you have to use a pickaxe to get through the rock. It means we have to use a lot more concrete than usual.'

'So there's no clay then?'

'If only. You can see what we've dug out there.' He pointed to a pile of spoil. Russell stood up and walked over to examine the heap. It consisted of lumps of soft rock and loose sand. 'See?'

'Yes, you're right. Sorry to have bothered you.' They were just making to leave when Russell suddenly stopped and spoke again. 'Do you know of any other sites round here where they're digging in clay?'

George thought for a moment. He reached up with his hand and scratched the back of his head, pushing his cap up at the same time. 'I can't think of any. The soil is pretty much the same from here to Collinghurst. You could try up at Kilnhurst. There's quite a bit of building been going on there but I think they've almost finished.' Russell thanked the man who grunted an acknowledgment and made his way back to the prefab, still scratching his head.

~o~

The site at Kilnhurst consisted of a street of solid-looking, two-storey, semi-detached houses. They appeared to be nearing completion and fresh Tarmac was being laid to provide a road for them. A tipper lorry had dumped a load of the black stuff and a group of men with rakes and shovels were spreading it on a prepared base. A steam roller was trundling slowly along the new road, vapour rising from the hot Tarmac and a strong smell of tar filling the air. Weeks parked the car and as they got out he smiled, tilted his head back and breathed deeply. 'You like that smell, lad?' Russell asked, joining him.

'Love it, Sir,' he grinned.

Russell shook his head and grinned back. 'Takes all sorts.' They made their way to the nearest house, which had curtains in the windows. The door stood open so they walked into the hall and entered the first room they came to. It was fully furnished, complete with wallpaper and pictures. There was even a trio of plaster ducks flying in formation up the wall. A plush sofa and two armchairs were arranged around the tiled fireplace. Surprisingly the floor was bare boards. Seated in one of the chairs was a man smoking a cigar. He wore a dark suit with a broad chalk-stripe, the jacket open but with the waistcoat buttons straining over his stomach. His thinning hair was swept back from his forehead and he had a small, neatly trimmed moustache, almost lost in his jowly face. As he rose to greet them he removed the cigar and beamed.

He extended a pudgy hand towards Russell. The handshake was limp and warmly damp. 'Hello, gentlemen. Have you come to buy one of our fine houses?'

'I'm afraid not,' Russell said, and explained who they were. The man's smile vanished as quickly as it had appeared.

'I'm sorry we haven't come to buy one of your houses….' Russell said, sweeping his arm in an arc to encompass the room, '….Lovely as they are. I just wanted to ask a question about the soil.'

For a moment the man looked baffled, then smiled. 'Oh, for the flower beds. We're going to bring in some quality topsoil…'Russell held up his hand.

'No, I'm sorry. You misunderstand Mr…?'

'Soffit.'

'Mr Soffit. We're police officers. We need to know what the soil is that the houses are built on. Is there any clay?'

'No there bloody isn't. It's all sand and rock, that's why we're having to pay a fortune to bring in decent soil.' He looked dejected. 'These blasted houses have cost far more than I'd budgeted. Nobody'll want to buy them at the price I'll have to ask…' Russell almost felt sorry for him….Almost.

'They were just about to leave when Soffit said: 'I thought you'd come about the break-in.'

'Break in?' Russell echoed.

'Yes, someone broke in here a few days ago and stole a roll of carpet. We hadn't even had time to lay it, that's why we've got bare boards.'

Russell looked interested. 'Why didn't you report it?'

'Didn't think it was worth it; the house was unlocked and that's all they took. Oh, that and some underlay.'

'I don't suppose you've got any of it left?' the DI asked.

'I think there's a bit under the stairs. Why?'

'It could be linked to an investigation we're carrying out. Can we see it?'

Soffit opened the understairs cupboard and pulled out a roll of grey felted underlay. Weeks and Russell exchanged a glance. It was the same as the material the body had been wrapped in.

'Could I take a piece?'

'Help yourself. We'll have to get a new roll anyway.' The man walked away and sat back in his chair and clamped the now extinguished cigar between his little pointed teeth, a picture of dejection. Weeks tugged a small corner off the roll and put it in his pocket.

'At least we know where the carpet came from.' Weeks turned to his superior. He was slumped in the passenger seat of the Wolseley, a look of frustration on his face. 'What's the matter, Sir?'

Russell took a deep breath then exhaled noisily through his pursed lips. 'It still doesn't get us any farther with clay and I'm sure that's important in solving this case. How many more building sites are there on the route?'

'Two, Sir.'

'Doesn't seem much point though, does there lad?'

'I guess not, Sir.'

'Amazing, wasn't he?'

'Who's that, Sir?'

'Our "friend" Mr Soffit. Fancy building houses so well that he can't sell them. Much better to put up those cheaper prefabs instead of building with brick.' The DI had slumped even lower into his seat as he spoke. He pulled back his cuff and looked at his wristwatch. 'Time's getting on. Better head back to the station.'

Weeks switched on the ignition and pressed the starter button. The engine coughed into life. He depressed the clutch and put the car in gear. He was just about to pull away when Russell suddenly sat up. 'Bricks!' he said. Weeks put the gearstick back in neutral.

'Bricks?'

'Yes, bricks. Where did he get them from, lad?

'A brickworks, I presume, Sir,' the DC said flatly.

'Exactly!' he exclaimed. Weeks looked perplexed. 'And what are bricks made from lad?'

'Clay?' Weeks said hesitantly. Then more forcefully, 'Clay! From clay, Sir!' He looked jubilant.

'So where is the nearest brickworks?'

Now Weeks slumped back into his seat. 'I don't know, Sir.' He looked deflated. 'Can't think of any brickworks around here.'

'Well, let's go and ask the man.'

'Oh, it's you again. What do you want now?' Soffit didn't even bother to get out of his chair this time. Russell ignored his rudeness and knowing the developer probably wouldn't have the answer, asked for the site manager. 'Harris? He'll be down there somewhere.' He waved vaguely in the direction of the other houses. 'Can't miss him - little bloke wearing a brown overall and a trilby.'

Nodding his thanks, Russell left the house and he and Weeks picked their way round the piles of rubble, carefully avoiding the freshly laid Tarmac. Harris was at the end of the road, holding a clipboard and talking to a workman. As they drew near the man nodded then walked into the nearest house and the site manager turned to face them. 'Can I help you, gentlemen?' His voice was high pitched and nasal.

'I'm DI Russell and this is DC Weeks.'

'Yes?'

'Can you tell me where your bricks come from?'

'What a strange question.' The man frowned. 'Oh, well, if you must know...' he appeared reluctant to help, 'They come from The London Brick Company in Bedford.' He paused, puzzled. 'You don't look very pleased.'

'Sorry,' a dejected Russell said, 'I was rather hoping you'd tell me they came from closer to hand.'

'No.' The man's voice became even more nasal. 'There's nowhere round here anymore. Used to be a brickworks up the road towards Collinghurst but that's long gone. The clay was worked out and it closed before the war.'

'What's happened to the site?' Weeks asked.

'Nothing as far as I know. I expect it'll be developed at some time; it was quite big, even had its own railway siding.' Then, suspicion creeping into his voice: 'Why do you want to know?' Harris realised that he had been more helpful than he'd intended.

'Oh, just a case we're working on. Can you tell us how to get there?'

~o~

Weeks pulled the Wolseley off the road and bumped down a rutted track. After 200 yards he stopped the car in front of a pair of tall, iron-framed gates, covered in battered, chain-link fencing. A high rusty fence continued for some distance in both directions, weeds growing waist deep along the bottom. They climbed out of the car and walked up to the gates. Beyond was a group of low industrial buildings surrounded by more undergrowth. The gates appeared to be chained and locked. Russell took hold of the padlock and gave it a vigorous shake. He was surprised when the chain flew apart in his hands. 'That's a stroke of luck, Weeks.'

'Or someone's been here already?'

'I think that goes without saying.' They pushed one gate open, the bottom scraping on the ground, and squeezed through the gap.

'Hang on a minute.' Russell grabbed Weeks' arm and stopped his progress. 'Look down there.' He pointed to the ground a few feet in front of them. 'They're the same tracks we found at Compass Point.' The marks the tyres had left led downhill towards the first building. They walked carefully along the side of the track until they reached it.

The building was single storey with low brick walls and a long, shallow, pitched, tiled roof. Many of the tiles had slipped or were missing, the north-facing slope covered in moss. They walked up to a weathered wooden door, being careful not to scuff any possible foot prints. The door was not locked, but creaked eerily when Russell pushed it open. They sidled into the building, shafts of light from the holes in the roof spotlighting broken wooden benches and derelict machinery, strangely lit as if part of a giant stage set. 'Look!' said Weeks, pointing. There was a roll of grey carpet underlay leaning against the nearest bench.

'Bingo!' the DI said. 'We'd better get the fingerprint boys here before we disturb anything. Go back to the car, ring the station and get them to send the team over. I'll stay here and have a look around.'

'Right-ho, Sir.' Weeks carefully retraced his steps.

Russell stood still for some time, slowly observing and taking in his surroundings. He whistled a snatch from *Love Letters in the Sand*. Then he crouched and examined the floor where he detected footprints in the dust. He was pretty sure he could make out a very small pair, one smooth and the other with a defined sole and heel. Also, he was pleased to see lumps of buff-coloured clay dotted about, some softened by the rain that must have come through the rents in the roof.

The fingerprint team arrived at the entrance to the brickworks in their green Morris J-type van. After photographing the tyre marks along the track they opened the gates fully and drove down to the buildings. Flash photographs were taken, surfaces dusted for fingerprints and plaster casts of footprints made. They looked round the other buildings in the complex but these were untouched, the dust of a dozen years remaining undisturbed.

Russell was back in his home. The coal stove in his living room had been stoked up and was blazing merrily. Aggie was stretched out on the rug, blissfully happy, soaking up the heat. Her owner was far from blissful. Even the sound of Rubinstein's Chopin preludes in the background couldn't lift his mood. He walked over to the radiogram and lifted the needle off the record and switched off the power, the warm glow of the lights on the dial slowly fading. He needed silence. He was disturbed and dejected. It had been three days since the body was discovered and there were very few leads. And as to why the murder had been committed…he just didn't have a clue. Revenge? Punishment? The result of some sort of turf war? And how did the two odd brothers fit into it? Wolfgang and Ludwig. Were they their real names even? Perhaps their mother had a liking for German composers, he thought. No, stop being flippant.

Then the manner of the death, well, the torture leading up to it, was something he had never come across before. It seemed certain that they had stolen the carpet and underlay from Soffit's show house and that they had been at the brickworks where they had finished off the poor sod who had been keelhauled. And why dump the body in a way that made it almost certain it would be discovered? A mystery he just couldn't begin to fathom. Not yet, anyway.

He thought back to another case, at the end of the war, nothing like this one, but just as puzzling. A man had been found dead in a derelict warehouse. He was tied to a heavy chair, bound and gagged. Russell was still haunted by his first sight of the man. His eyes were open and staring and when they untied the gag, his lips were curled back in a rictus of terror. The ropes had cut deeply into his wrist and ankles, as if he'd been trying to force them off by sheer pressure and his fingernails had bitten deeply into his palms, which were caked with old dried blood. The autopsy revealed that a very unpleasant and extremely toxic dose of poison had been administered and he had died a particularly horrific death, all of which explained the state of his body and terrified expression but not why. At first they were unable to find a reason for the killing, let alone track down the perpetrators and it looked like it was going to remain in the unsolved crimes file. Then they had a breakthrough.

The warehouse stood on a disused part of the dockside at Nottery Quay, not far from Kilnhurst, on the coast. In fact, most of the dockside was derelict after being a regular target for German bombers during the war. There were moves to reinvigorate and rebuild it, but the necessary government funds were slow in being approved so it lay in a state of decay for many months. But the lucky break came when an off-duty policeman, taking his dog for a late walk along the quayside, was surprised to see a boat motoring slowly up the estuary, in the dark. His suspicions were aroused as the boat showed no lights, and apart from the soft putt-putt of the engine and the gentle swish as the bow cleaved the water, all was quiet. He slipped into the shadows, holding up a warning finger to quieten the dog and watched as the boat came up to an old stone staircase and stopped. A group of shadowy figures then proceeded to carry an assortment of bundles and packages up the steps, across the quay and into one of the ruined buildings. After a few minutes, they returned and repeated the exercise. In all, he reckoned they made half a dozen journeys. Then, just as quietly as they'd arrived, they departed. Needless to say, the officer hot-footed it back to the station and reported what he had witnessed.

The next day the warehouse was searched and a pile of black market contraband was discovered, tucked away in a dingy corner, under a pile of ragged tarpaulins and broken timber. This nondescript heap looked like a natural part of the collapsing building so would have been easily overlooked under normal circumstances. It was decided to leave the pile undisturbed, as they found it, but to mount a surveillance. So, every night, two officers hid in the shadows, keeping watch. After a week, there was much muttering as, although they were being paid overtime, it was a cold miserable existence. The senior officer in charge was on the verge of giving up when, on the eighth night, a lorry came bumping slowly along the quayside and backed up to the doorway of the warehouse.

Undecided what to do, the constables watched for a while and were astonished to see a second truck arrive. Almost immediately, all hell broke loose as the two gangs slugged it out between them. Unwilling to get involved with so many tough nuts brawling amongst themselves, one of the policemen continued to keep watch, while the other ran the two or three hundred yards to a nearby phone box and, panting breathlessly, called the station, which was only a couple of streets away. Within minutes, constables and patrol cars had surrounded the area. One of the lorries tried to drive off at speed but was forced to swerve by a car driven by an enterprising officer and ended up crashing into a wall, crumpling the bonnet. A plume of steam shot out sideways and the horn sounded as the driver was thrown against the wheel. The brawl continued, with the police sustaining injuries but eventually, most members of the gangs were rounded up, handcuffed and carted off for questioning.

It took three Black Marias to transport them and the numbers had to be split between two police stations. In time it was learnt that they were rival gangs, both involved in the post-war black market and it turned out that the man they had originally found, lashed to the chair, was a member of the second gang. He had been treated in such a sadistic way as a warning for his colleagues to keep clear of the first gang. Russell remembered how complicated it had all seemed at the time but the top brass had been pleased with the final outcome, when several ruthless characters were put behind bars for very long stretches.

This case had a whiff of the same unpleasant odour about it. The man they'd found had been tortured in a most macabre way and he wondered if this too was a warning. It seemed likely that the two Germans, if they were indeed German, lay at the heart of this. He needed to find out who they were and the only person who'd seen them was the ferryman. Time for another visit.

Sunday

*The Maronibrater boot - originated as working boots
for mountain farmers and woodsmen. Made in Vienna
from dark brown calf leather with a band of grey
melton wool around the top.*

ON SUNDAY Weeks had the day off so Russell decided to catch
the train down to Compass Point. The line ran close to the end of
the unmade track where he lived so it was a short walk to the low
wooden platform by the narrow gauge railway line. He stood in
front of the simple shelter, waiting for the 10.15. He was whistling
Freight Train. Aggie sat obediently at his feet looking up at him in
the hope of a treat. Russell kept a supply of her favourite biscuits
in his pocket and she didn't mind at all that they were sometimes
covered in fluff or tasted vaguely of cough candy twists.

The three-foot gauge branch line had been completed in 1895
in a flurry of optimism for traffic that never materialised but it
had soldiered on, just about breaking even, until the outbreak of
the Second World War. Then, requisitioned by the military to help
with the war effort, it received a much welcome cash injection
that allowed the infrastructure and rolling stock to be upgraded
and renewed. Thus, when it was handed back at the cessation of
hostilities, it was in much better heart.

Within a few minutes a smudge of grey smoke appeared on the near horizon and he could hear the steady beat of the engine. As the train drew closer he could see it was hauled by the little red Bagnall locomotive, Cardinal. He preferred this engine to the more basic petrol railcar that often provided the service, but realised economics meant it was more expensive to run on regular trains. However, he knew Captain Salt, who owned the narrow gauge railway, liked to use it at weekends, when there were more tourists.

The train drew to a halt, its single wood-panelled carriage level with the platform. Russell opened the door and climbed aboard. He was just sitting down when, with a single toot from the engine's whistle, it drew away from the halt, jerking him into his seat. He had a handful of happy trippers for company: parents with straw hats and picnic hampers and excited children holding buckets and spades. The flat landscape seemed to float past the window as the carriage rocked along the rickety track at a stately 15 miles an hour. After 10 minutes the train was pulling into the station at Compass Point.

It was a beautiful spring day. The tide was in, boats bobbed on the sparkling water and gulls mewed softly. However it did little to lift Russell's spirits. Even the terrier, sensing his mood, was subdued, trotting closely at his heel, seemingly uninterested in any possible new scents.

Russell had slept badly. His dreams had been filled with visions of a club-footed man, stomping across a sandy beach, leaving giant footprints, which, however hard he tried to avoid them, he kept tripping over and falling into. And as those images faded they were replaced by ones of a huge man wielding a long knife, mercilessly pursuing him across a barren landscape. The more he tried to escape, the heavier his legs became, until he could feel the giant's breath on his neck. Just as his pursuer was about to plunge the knife into his back he would burst into wakefulness, covered in a cold sweat. Then he would lie awake for long minutes, trying to control his breathing, until he fell into another uneasy slumber. He spent the night alternating between short periods of troubled sleep and long bouts of restless wakefulness. He was in no mood for a confrontation and hoped Jack would be approachable.

As it transpired, the ferryman was in a good mood. He'd already rowed a boatload of sunseekers across to the dunes at Shell Bay, some of whom had tipped him, and was just returning from the trip. He pulled strongly to the foot of the steps, effortlessly tied the boat to a mooring ring and came up the stone staircase at a speed that belied his age and penchant for beer.

'Morning, Inspector,' he exclaimed loudly, before Russell could speak. 'I'm glad you've turned up. I've got summat for you.' He rummaged around in his trouser pocket and, with a flourish, produced a crumpled piece of paper. ''Ere,' he said, offering it. 'Dunno what it means though.'

The DI unfolded the paper and smoothed out the wrinkles as best he could. The writing was neatly done in blue ink. It was smudged and had run in places but some of the few words were reasonably clear, although not all:

Fl*t. Freitag 05.35
**ell-Buch*
versteinerte *ald

Russell looked up from the paper. 'Where did you find this?'

Jack grinned. 'S'funny. I was pokin' about under me shed earlier, lookin' for a bit of tackle I wanted, an' there it was, just below the steps. I was rackin' me brains, trying to figure out where it might 'ave come from. Thought at first it'd been dropped by one o' they trippers but then I remembered…' he paused and appeared to think deeply.

'Yes?' said Russell, encouragingly.

'It was that little bloke.'

'What, the one who wanted you to buy the boat?'

'The very same. I remembered t'was when 'e gave me the first 20 quid. I saw somethin' flutter down - when 'e took the cash out of 'is pocket - an' fall between the steps. Didn't think nothin' of it at the time.'

'You are certain it was this piece of paper?' Russell held it out towards him.

'As sure as I can be. Why, d'you think 'tis important?'

Russell was reluctant to let the man know it was the first solid piece of evidence he had, so just shrugged and said: 'Thanks, it might help me with my enquiries.'

Jack, disappointed there wasn't more enthusiasm for his find, lost some of his jollity and was about to turn away when he stopped and spoke again.

'Oh, I nearly forgot. The little bloke, Wolfgang, paid me in onesers. I didn't notice at first but when I counted them again I found this tucked in between the pound notes.' He held out a banknote, printed in blue. In bold, across the centre, it said:

EINE
DEUTSCHE
MARK

'It's German, ain't it? Don't suppose it's worth anythin'?' he asked, hopefully.

'Sorry, Jack. A few coppers, that's all. I'll tell you what, as you've been so helpful, I'll treat you to a pint or two.' Russell reached into his inside pocket and opening his wallet produced a crisp 10-shilling note. Spratt looked at it and smacked his lips in anticipation.

'But...' Russell continued, holding it just out of reach, 'Before I give it to you, I need a bit more information.'

'Thought there might be a catch.' Jack's mood was turning sour.

Russell, keen to keep him sweet, went on quickly: 'Oh, it's not much. I just need to know a bit more about the two brothers.'

Eager for his reward Spratt asked: 'Go on then, waddya want to know?'

'I could do with a bit more information about them - what they looked like and anything else you can think of.'

'I told you, Wolfgang was little wiv a gammy leg an' 'is brother was 'uge.'

'Yes, I remember that, but can you recall, for instance, how they were dressed?

Jack screwed up his face, gurning in the attempt to think back. 'Blimey, you're askin' somethin' aint yer? It was ages ago.'

'Anything you can remember could help,' Russell encouraged.

Spratt's face became even more contorted as he tried to dredge the information from the depths of his booze-addled brain. After a time the creases unfolded, he smiled and held up a finger. 'Ah!' he said. 'I remember! Ludwig, the big bloke, 'ad one of them thick blue jumpers on. You know, named after some island...'

'A Guernsey?' Russell offered.'

"Yeah, that's right, with a jacket over the top. And 'is boots...'
'Yes?'

'They was kind of brown leather at the bottom but with a sorta woollen bit on the top 'alf, an' a little strap an' buckle on the side. I 'adn't seen nothin' like 'em before.' He shook his head uncomprehendingly.

'Can you remember if he had a hat?' the DI asked.

Jack brightened. 'Yes! It was a blue cloth cap. Like them Dutch bargees wear. I remember, when is brother was talking to me, 'e'd taken it off an' was holdin' it an' kept turnin' it round in 'is 'ands.'

While he was talking he had walked across to his hut and had sat down on the bench along the side. Aggie trotted over and sat in front of him, looking up at his face.

'That's very helpful, Jack, but I could do with some more info about his brother,' Russell said.

'What, Wolfgang?' The DI nodded. 'I dunno,' the ferryman said. 'It was difficult not to look at 'is gammy leg.'

'Tell me about that then.'

'As I said, 'e seemed to 'ave this skinny leg wiv a built-up boot on 'is foot. An' there was the iron…'

'*What*?' Russell asked. 'You didn't mention that…'

'Yeah well, I must 'ave forgot. Anyway, it were one o' them leg irons. You know, the ones they put on kids what can't walk proper like.'

Russell looked heavenwards in exasperation, but managed to say calmly: 'Well, that is quite unusual. Anyway, can you remember anything about his clothes?' Jack screwed up his face. Russell waited for a few moments. 'Anything at all?'

Again Spratt's face brightened. 'Oh, yeah,' he said, 'e 'ad an odd sort of jacket.'

'How do you mean, odd?'

'Well it weren't like yer normal suit jacket, it were almost, well, sort of, like military.'

Russell was impressed with Jack's recall. He'd underestimated the man's memory and was pleased with the information he was now being given. 'Can you describe it?

Jack was in full flow now. 'Yeah, it were a sorta greeny tweed with a buttoned-down collar. Not seen one like that afore so I noticed it.'

Russell held out the 10-shilling note. 'You've earned this old fella. I expect you're dry after all that talking.' Jack's eyes twinkled and a grin spread across his face.

'Thanks guvnor. You know where to come if you need to know anythin' else.'

The DI's mood was considerably brighter than it had been when he arrived. 'Come on, Jack,' he said, gently taking the other man's arm, 'I think I'll join you.' The ferryman beamed - but Russell had an ulterior motive for visiting the Shipwrights Arms.

'Hello, Captain,' Russell said, tapping the seated man on the shoulder. Salt turned, half rising from his stool at the bar. 'No, stay where you are. Same again? he said, pointing to the empty rum glass.

'Go on then. It is Sunday after all. Twist my arm,' Salt said, chuckling. He sat down again. 'What brings you in here at,' he pulled his fob watch from his pocket and consulted the dial, '… just after 11 in the morning?'

'Ah well, I have a puzzle for you,' Russell said mysteriously. Seeing Alf looking expectantly at him he said: 'Oh, a half for me and the same again for the Captain.' Then aware of Jack at his elbow he added: 'And one for this fine gentleman too.' This brought smiles from the other three men. The drinks were served and the DI perched on the remaining stool at the bar. 'Now Captain, what do you make of this?' he said, taking the piece of paper from his pocket and laying it in front of Salt.

*Fl*t. Freitag 05.35*
***ell-Buch**
*versteinerte *ald*

The Captain reached into an inside pocket and pulled out a pair of gold-rimmed, half-moon spectacles, which he perched on the end of his nose. He peered intently at the smudged writing for some minutes before speaking. Then he turned to Russell and raised an eyebrow. 'Ah, you knew I read German?'

'I had heard.'

'You're right, but I'm not sure how much help I can be.'

'Oh?'

'I can tell you the bits I can read but can only hazard a guess at the rest.'

'Start by telling me what you can read then,' Russell encouraged.'

'As I said, not much. The first bit is straightforward; it can only be flut, that is high tide and *Freitag*, Friday, presumably at five thirty-five am.' He paused, concentrating. 'The next word could be anything and *Buch* means book. Unless there's an 'e' on the end, then *buche* means beech.'

So it could be high tide on a beach somewhere then?' Russell asked eagerly.

Salt shook his head, 'Sorry, not that sort of beach, rather the tree kind. And the last bit, **versteinerte** means fossilised and the last word, something – **ald**, could be **bald**, which means soon.'

'So, high tide on Friday, early morning, perhaps written in some sort of book and then something is soon fossilised. Doesn't make much sense, does it?'

'Apart from the tide, not really,' Salt agreed. 'And that could be high tide anywhere. Let me copy this down, as I presume you want to keep the original?' Russell nodded. The Captain reached into his jacket pocket and pulled out a notebook and a pencil. As he wrote he spoke: 'Leave this with me and I'll give it some more thought. If I come up with anything I'll let you know.'

Russell had half an hour to kill before the next train back up the line. He wandered down to the quay and perched on a barrel, looking out across the estuary, the little terrier sitting patiently at his feet. He could see the white sails of a dinghy, heeling over in the gentle breeze. The boat rounded a buoy, the helmsman put the tiller over, the sails shook, changed sides and the boat headed off on the opposite tack. He watched, engrossed as it worked its way up the river, tacking back and forth. Whoever was in the boat was obviously skilled as they let the bow almost nudge the bank, before they put it about and set off for the other side. Watching the craft and its manoeuvres kept him completely engrossed and he spent several pleasant minutes until the toot of a steam whistle alerted him to the arrival of the train.

'What are we going to do with this one, Wolf?' the big man asked, looking down at the lifeless body, lying on the blood-splattered bed.

'Something different from last time. Maybe leave him on the building site somewhere.' The little man stroked his chin, deep in thought. 'Perhaps not here though. What about that other site?' The big man grunted. 'Okay, we'll get him trussed up first.'

Together they rolled the corpse up in the carpet underlay then bound and tied the bundle with rope, the smaller man tying the knots in a skilled and meticulous fashion.

'Right, let's get him outside. I'll ask Rankin to back the lorry up to the door.'

He set off down the stairs, his awkward gait creating a syncopated rhythm on the wooden treads. The big man heaved the bulky package effortlessly over his shoulder and followed his brother down to the front door of the house.

Monday

The constrictor knot - one of the most effective binding knots. Simple and secure, it is a harsh knot that can be difficult or impossible to untie once tightened.

IT WAS Monday morning and Russell was sitting in his office. There was a knock on the door. 'Come in,' he said. It was Lewis from the fingerprint team. 'Please sit down.' Once the other man was seated the DI continued: 'Did you turn up much evidence at the brickworks?'

'Sadly, I think it will confirm only what you know already. Apart from a number of scuffed boot marks, we couldn't find much else. There appeared to have been plenty of activity but we found no prints – they must have worn gloves.' Russell looked crestfallen. 'But, we did find traces of blood.' The DI brightened. 'Not a lot,' Lewis went on, 'just some scattered droplets in the dust on the floor.'

'Could you get that over to Crooks in the path lab?'

'Already done.'

'Good, thanks.'

'We had a look round the rest of the site, but judging by the thick, undisturbed clay dust everywhere, that first building was the only one they went in.'

'Ah well. It's as I suspected. They took our poor friend in there to finish him off and truss him up, then left.'

Lewis nodded his agreement. 'We also went to the house on that first building site you visited to dust for prints. Blimey, that Soffit's a slimy character.' he chuckled. 'I wouldn't want to buy a house from him.'

'Did you find any prints there?' Russell asked.

'Too many. The place has been crawling with tradesmen. There were dozens of different prints all over the place, but not so many on that cupboard under the stairs. So, if we concentrate on that, we *may* come up with some evidence. But don't hold your breath. However, I have got something you might be interested in.'

'What's that?'

'You know that the body was securely tied with chord?' Russell nodded. 'We'll I've done a bit of research and it seems that whoever did it had a thorough knowledge of knots.'

'Oh really? I know the ones I untied were locked almost solid. I assumed it was because they'd been in the water.'

'That was partly the reason.' Lewis added.

'What else then?'

'A variety of expertly tied knots were used, including properly tied reef knots, which you'd expect, but there was also a fisherman's knot and even a sheepshank.'

'What on earth is that?' Russell laughed. 'Sounds positively perverse.'

'Not really,' the other man chuckled, 'It's a method of shortening a rope. You'd only know it if you were a sailor – or a keen Boy Scout.'

'Doubt if we're looking for the latter,' Russell smiled.

'But the most curious one is called a double constrictor knot. It's quite unusual and apparently is generally used when you don't want something to come undone, which - whoever tied it - didn't.'

'So what does this tell us?' Russell asked.

'That whoever trussed up that body was not only well versed in knot tying - a sailor or a fisherman perhaps - but also...' he paused.

'But also what?'

'It was almost as if he was trying to say something.'

'What do you mean exactly?'

'Difficult to explain. I just have a feeling that the way those knots were tied contained some sort of message. I might be completely wrong, but they were almost like a signature.' Russell was thinking about this when the door opened suddenly.

'Bad news I'm afraid, Sir.' Weeks was standing in the doorway, his tie askew and his hair wilder than usual. The two men looked towards him.

'Tell me the worst, lad.'

'They've found another body.' Russell groaned. 'Not in the water this time though.'

'Where was it then?'

'You know that first building site we visited?' Weeks asked.

'Where they were putting up the prefabs?'

'That's right. The foreman, George, has just rung. He was in quite a state.'

'Let's get over there then.'

~O~

They were gathered by the concrete mixer, the subdued workmen standing in a huddle a short distance away. George was visibly shaken. His voice quivered as he spoke. 'The men turned up at eight as usual to start work and were getting ready to pour the footings for the next base. One of them fired up the concrete mixer, ready to do the first mix, and could see that something was already in the drum. He was surprised because they always clean it out at the end of the day. When they've finished the last mix, they chuck in a bucket of water and a couple of half bricks to knock any lumps of set mortar out, let it run for a few minutes, then empty it.'

'And this is what he found,' George nodded. 'I think you'd better go and sit down. Get someone to make you cup of sweet tea,' Russell said.

It was another felt-wrapped parcel, similar to the first, but instead of being soaked in salt water it was only slightly damp, daubed with smudges of mortar. Like the one they had found at Compass Point, it was bound with cord and neatly tied. This time the pathologist, plus Lewis and his team, were already on hand to take photographs and make notes before they started unwrapping the package. Again, the knots proved awkward to unravel. 'Looks like the same MO,' Lewis said, pointing to one of the knots. 'See? That's another one of those double constrictors.'

'Curious,' Russell observed.

Finally, with the ropes undone, they were able to peel off the felt. This time there was no carpet, just a body. It was a man, perhaps in his forties with dark curly hair and a lightly tanned face. He was dressed in a blood-soaked shirt and trousers but with no shoes or socks. His wrists and ankles had knotted ropes tied round them. The loose ends were cut and frayed. The officers rolled him over. 'My God!' said Weeks. He turned, walked away, then retched emptying his breakfast on to a pile of sand. The man's shirt was shredded and his back was criss-crossed with angry weals, some bloody, others with pieces of felt adhering to them.

Russell breathed out hard. 'My God, indeed,' he said. He turned to the pathologist. 'What do you make of it, John?'

'Well it's not keelhauling this time.' He bent down and looked closely at the wounds. After a moment he turned his head to look up at the DI. 'Do you know what, Sonny?'

'What's that?'

'I think this man's been flogged – with a cat o' nine tails.'

Russell instructed a pale-faced Weeks to get the workmen together and then to ring the station to send some uniform officers to interview them. He was just standing, discussing this latest event with Crooks when the constable came running back, stumbling over the uneven ground. 'Steady old chap!' Russell said, 'you'll come a cropper!'

'Sir!' Weeks said breathlessly. 'There's been a break-in at the other site.'

'Yes, we know about that. Our friend Soffit told us.'

'No, another one. And this one's quite different.'

'Right. Get uniform here as soon as soon as they've finished at the other site and seal off the whole area. Get Soffit into one of the other houses and round up all the workers too. I need statements from everyone.' Russell and Weeks were standing in the furnished bedroom of the showhouse on the housing estate. The sight they were looking at was far from pleasant, No wonder Soffit was sitting downstairs with his head in his hands, groaning. The DC, though still pale, was maintaining his composure. 'Well,' Russell said, 'it looks as though this is where the deed was done.' The bed in the centre of the room was a mess of badly rumpled bedclothes streaked with blood. Its four corner posts had a piece of knotted rope tied round each of them, each with a loose, frayed end, like those on the victim. 'It's pretty obvious how he was restrained. I bet when Lewis comes he'll be able to identify the knots.'

The forensics expert and his team were soon on the scene and the two detectives left them to it. They headed back to the station but no sooner had they arrived than they were summoned to the mortuary. The man found in the concrete mixer lay on the slab. Crooks had pulled back the sheet and they were looking at his naked body. Weeks seemed more composed although his face was still ashen. 'Will you be all right this time?' Russell asked.

'I think so, Sir.' The DC sounded abashed. 'It was just a bit of a shock earlier.'

'I didn't notice this at first,' the pathologist said, pointing to the chest. There was a short, thin red line on the left hand side. 'Same cause of death: a thin blade, up between the ribs and straight into the heart. Death wouldn't have been instantaneous, but pretty quick. However, judging by the severity of the damage to his back, he may well have been unconscious.'

'You mentioned a cat o'nine tails. Do you still think that's what was used?' Russell asked.

'Almost certainly. Let's look.' Crooks signalled to his assistant, who was waiting to one side, and together they rolled the body over. The surface of the man's skin had been cleaned of dried blood and the numerous angry lines were vivid in his flesh. 'Something else that I found curious,' he said. 'See the stripes are crossed diagonally?'

'Is that significant?' Russell said.

'I think it is,' Crooks said slowly. 'I've been reading up on floggings.' Russell could see that the pathologist was revelling in his knowledge. 'It was a regular punishment in navies around the globe. I won't go into the gory details.' Weeks looked visibly relieved. 'But a bit of background might be useful.

'Floggings in the British Navy were meted out as punishment regularly in the 18th century, less in the 19th and not suspended at sea until 1881. They were carried out by a bosun's mate and were supposed to consist of only a dozen lashes unless there had been a court martial.' He paused for breath. Russell made to speak but Crooks held his hand up and continued. 'However, many more were often administered and the transgressor could even be flogged round the fleet. This was where he would be rowed between ships for multiple floggings. It could take as long as a year and often ended in death.' He took another breath but before he could carry on Russell broke in.

'That's all very interesting John, but I don't see the relevance to this case…'

'Ah, I was coming to that. You remember I mentioned the pattern of the stripes?' The inspector nodded. 'It seems that in order to inflict maximum pain, after the first dozen lashes were administered, a second bosun's mate would carry on with another dozen, often applied left-handed. Do you see?'

'Are you suggesting that our victim,' Russell asked, looking down at the body 'was whipped by two different people?'

'Yes, I am. It's possible that one was left-handed. Or he just came at the man from the other side. Difficult to be sure.'

'Now that *is* interesting.' Russell stroked his chin. 'We keep coming back to some sort of nautical or maritime connection.' He stopped for a moment, deep in thought. 'If our two German-sounding brothers handled the boat Jack bought for them as skilfully as he said, then they could be seamen of some sort and may well be suspects.'

'The only ones we've got so far, Sir.' Weeks added.

'Yes, quite,' the DI said. 'The only thing is, there's a huge difference in their stature. Would that show in the way that the punishment was given John?'

The pathologist considered this for a moment. 'Not necessarily as the victim was most certainly lying down when it was done.'

'Could you take a closer look and see if you can find anything else?'

'Okay, Sonny. I'll do that and let you know if I do.'

'As soon as you can please, John. Anything that will stop this investigation from stalling completely.'

'Oh, by the way,' the pathologist added, as the two officers prepared to leave.

'Yes?'

'The blood spatters we found at the brickworks?' Russell raised an eyebrow. 'It's the same blood group as the first body you found.'

Tuesday

Careening- the practice of grounding a sailing vessel at high tide in order to expose one side of its hull for maintenance and repairs below the water line when the tide goes out.

'**WELL WE'RE** starting to put a picture together, although it's still rather sketchy at the moment. That boat Spratt bought for the brothers, I still think it plays an important part. Any joy in tracking down *Moonshine*?' Russell asked. They were sitting in his office, looking at the pathology report and the preliminary findings that Lewis had just given them.

'Not yet Sir.'

'Where have you looked so far?'

'First of all uniform were sent out to look in the nearest harbours east and west along the coast. Nothing. So they looked in all the boatyards along the coast of the county and still nothing. We've asked the forces in neighbouring counties to look too, but there have been no sightings so far.'

'Do you know what I think, lad?'

What's that, Sir?'

'I think it's across on the coast of Europe somewhere. If you remember, they said they wanted a swift boat that could cross the channel. That could be France, Belgium or Holland. That's where we'll find it. I think we'd better have a chat with our friends at Interpol. Could you get the switchboard to set up a call, please?' Weeks nodded. 'And as for *this...*' He tapped the newspaper on the desk in front of him. It was the first edition of the *Collinghurst Chronical.* The banner headline across the front page read:

SECOND MUTILATED BODY FOUND
POLICE BAFFLED

'This is just what we *don't* need.' The DI tossed the paper angrily to one side. 'Salt was worried what it might do to tourism at the Point. Heaven knows what it's going to do to our reputation. If we don't start making some progress soon, the Super will blow a fuse...or worse.'

~O~

'Is that Inspector Russell?' The voice at the other end of the telephone was cultured but with a slight country burr.

'It is,' Russell answered. 'Who's calling?'

'I'm sorry, my name's Captain Clive Bagwall, harbour master at Nottery Quay'

'Ah, away up the coast from Compass Point.'

'Well only about 10 miles by boat, though half that by road.'

'Quite. What can I do for you, Captain?'

'I hope I can do something for you, Inspector.'

'Oh yes?'

'Yes, some of your men were here yesterday looking for a boat.'

'That's right, *Moonshine,*' Russell said, intrigued.

'And they didn't find it...'

'No.'

'But it had been here.'

Russell sat up, excited. 'When?'

'Until the day before yesterday.'

'How come my officers didn't pick up on that?'

'Ah, well, I wasn't there when they asked. My deputy had only just returned from holiday and I'd been away on business so we hadn't had a chance to catch up.'

'So tell me about the boat.'

'It came into harbour - about a week ago - late, just as I was packing up to go home. We had to fill in the usual documentation, where she had come from, how long they were staying and so on. I was a bit perplexed as I knew it was a boat from the Point, but as he didn't offer any explanations I didn't pursue it'

'Who did you deal with?'

'It was a little chap...'

'With a gammy leg?'

'Yes, how did you know?'

Russell chuckled. 'Just a feeling. Please carry on.'

'He said they'd just come over from France and were going to stay at Nottery for a few days. I told him he could remain tied up to the admiralty pier for a week but after that he'd have to find a mooring in the river.'

'Was there anyone else on board?'

'There was. A big bloke...'

'Built like a brick outhouse?'

'Yes, right again. Do you know something about these two?'

Russell decided he should let the other man know a little about the ongoing investigation, so, without giving away too much detail, explained how the two men were suspects. 'I don't suppose you got a full name?' he asked.

'I did. Strange, he said his name was Wolfgang Miller.'

'Do you think he was German?'

'Difficult to say. There may have been a hint of accent but his English was almost perfect.'

'Perhaps too perfect,' Russell mused.

'Anyway, as I said, they'd gone by yesterday.'

'What about mooring fees?'

'Oh, he paid for a week. Cash in advance. So that covered it.'

'And you've no idea where they went?'

'That's the strange thing. He said he wanted to get the hull cleaned as he knew it was foul with weed. I explained that his best bet was Compass Point, where the boat could be lifted. But he said, not to worry, they were going back to France and there was a careening dock in Boulogne harbour.'

'Excuse my ignorance,' Russell said, 'but what does careening mean?'

'Ah, it's a fairly old-fashioned method of cleaning a ship's bottom. With the old sailing ships, they would be taken to shallow water and ropes and tackle would be used to 'heave down', that is, pull the ship over at an angle so the hull was exposed below the water line and could be cleaned.'

'Good gracious!' Russell exclaimed. 'That sounds drastic.'

'Apart from the cost of the rope, which would have to be pretty thick and extremely long, it was cheaper than moving the ship to a graving, or dry dock.'

'Presumably that's not what our friend was talking about though?'

'No, I'm pretty sure I recall that in the inner harbour at Boulogne, there's some horizontal staging that is exposed at low water. He'll manoeuvre his vessel on to that and, when the tide drops, the boat will lean against the quay wall and he can deal with the weed and barnacles.'

'So do you think that's where he is now?'

'Honestly? I don't know, but it's as good a place as any to start looking.'

~o~

'Er, *bonjour*. This is Inspector Russell from the British police. Do you speak English?' the DI said hesitantly.

'*Patientez un instant...*' The line crackled as the receiver was put down. Russell could hear muffled voices in the background, then the receiver was picked up again. ''Allo, Inspecteur Guillaume Bruissement 'ere. 'Ow can I 'elp?' The voice was heavily accented but clear.

'Monsieur Bruissement...'

'Please, Guillaume.'

'Guillaume, it's about an English boat, *Moonshine*, number CP-13.'

'What do you wish to know?'

'We believe she is in Boulogne harbour. Possibly having her hull cleaned.'

'Let me make some enquiries and I will get back to you. *Au revoir.*'

Russell replaced the receiver and slumped in his chair. If *Moonshine* was indeed in Boulogne then a trip to the port might be necessary. However, he wasn't sure what that would achieve. The trouble was, although the case was going nowhere fast, he didn't want to appear to be clutching at straws but it was one of the few leads he had. He supposed it might establish that the Miller brothers were indeed aboard the boat but, without any more proof, he couldn't see how he'd be able to get on board to conduct a search. Perhaps the French police would have some ideas.

He was still sitting thinking about this when he was startled by the phone ringing. ' 'Ello? Inspector Russell?'

'Yes. Guillaume?'

'Yes, it is me. Do you 'ave another name?'

'Everyone calls me Sonny.' Russell smiled to himself.

'Ah, Sonny. I 'ave some good news for you.'

'Yes?' Russell said expectantly.

'Your *'Moonshine'*, she 'is 'ere. And, as you made to suggest, 'aving 'er bottom cleaned.'

Russell was delighted. 'Thank you so much, Guillaume. That is good news indeed.'

'Is there anything else I can 'elp you with?' The Frenchman asked.

'There may well be.' Russell had made up his mind. 'I'm catching a ferry over to Bolougne as soon as I can. Would you be able to meet me?'

'Eet would be my pleasure.' Bruissement seemed genuinely pleased.

'Right, I'll make a reservation. I will find out what time I get in and let you know.'

Russell opened the bottom drawer of a filing cabinet and took out a small overnight bag containing washing and shaving gear, a clean shirt and underwear. He put on his jacket and leant out of his door.

'Weeks,' he called, 'can you come here a minute?' The DC got up from his file-stacked desk. 'I'm going to France to follow up a sighting of *Moonshine*. Can you run me to the station?'

'Certainly, Sir.' Weeks was glad to get away from the paperwork. He stood up and pulled on his jacket.

Russell went over to the Superintendent's office and tapped lightly on the door. He waited a moment but there was no reply so he pushed it open. The room was empty.

He turned to Weeks, who was standing expectantly behind him. 'Can you tell the Super where I've gone? He's not in his office so must be out somewhere. And tell him I'll be back with some new leads.' Russell sincerely hoped that would be the case.

The two went out to the car park, climbed into the Wolseley and made the short journey to the station. On the way they discussed the case. Russell gave instructions on what to do if any more information should come in. He gave Weeks his door key and asked the constable to pop in and feed Aggie.

'Don't worry, Sir, she can come home with me until you get back.'

Russell caught the train from Collinghurst and was in Dover by 3.30pm. He was booked on board the 3.50pm Côte D'Azur. This was the second ferry to carry that name. The first one had plied its trade from when it was launched in 1931 until it was sunk towards the end of the war. The ship Russell was to travel on had been commissioned only a couple of years before so he was looking forward to a luxurious crossing.

He wasn't disappointed. The ship was not only clean and bright but fairly quiet. Few passengers seemed to be crossing the Channel at that time. It was a balmy afternoon and the sea was almost flat calm, promising a smooth passage. As the Côte D'Azur steamed out of Dover Harbour he leant on the taffrail, watching the wake tumbling and foaming, the spring sun lighting up the white cliffs. He found the scene quite soothing and felt the worries of the case begin to fade away, although he knew it would only be for a short while. As the white cliffs of England faded into the distance, he strolled contentedly in to the cafeteria, ordered coffee and a pastry and found a vacant seat next to the window. He had brought his notes but was happy to leave the file closed and enjoy the journey. In little more than an hour the coast of France hove into sight and a voice on the Tannoy announced it was time to prepare to disembark. The carefree mood he had enjoyed during the crossing faded as he prepared for what he feared might be a trying time.

Russell queued with the handful of foot passengers. As he made his way down the gangplank he was aware of a rotund figure, sporting a luxuriant moustache and with a dark mop of well-groomed hair, standing by the barrier. As the man caught sight of his English counterpart he smiled and waved.

'Sonny! Come this way.' The DI walked over and the two men shook hands warmly across the barrier. A French customs office moved towards them. Bruissement quickly produced his identity card and spoke quietly to the man who nodded, pushed the barrier aside and waved Russell through the gap.

'Come this way and you will avoid the wait at the passport control and *douanes*,' Bruissement said. The two detectives made their way through the customs hall, past the passengers queuing with their passports, and out on to the quayside where the Frenchman led Russell to a shiny black Citroën traction Avant. They climbed into the back and the driver set off for the town.

The day was fading as Bruissement said: 'I think, for now, we should avoid making ourselves known to the men on *Moonshine* but while we still 'ave the light I will show you where your boat is.' He drove the car out of the docks and over *Pont Marguet* towards the town. Turning left along the *Quai Gambetta*, the driver brought the Citroën to a halt and the two men climbed out. 'Over there,' said the French detective, pointing across the channel to the opposite side. The tide was falling and Russell could see a white fishing boat, perhaps 30 feet long, sitting on a series of substantial parallel timbers, coming out at right angles from the quay. The boat leant in towards the wall and appeared to be well tied up. A large man, wearing a pair of chest-high waders, was playing a hose on the hull of *Moonshine*, the powerful jet sending clouds of spray and debris in all directions. On the deck stood a much smaller man, looking down at the operation. 'That is them, eh?' Bruissement asked.

'It certainly looks like it,' Russell agreed. 'How long have they been there?

'I think they moved the boat round when the tide began to fall, say two hours ago? Then, as soon as it 'ad fallen enough, the big man started the cleaning.'

'How much longer do they have?'

'Oh, several hours of low water but soon the light will fade and they will 'ave to pack up.'

'Mind you,' Russell said, 'the speed he's working at it won't take long.'

'Don't forget 'e still 'as to do the other side an' they will 'ave to turn the boat round for that.'

'When will they be able to do that?'

'Let me see...' The Frenchman thought for a moment. ' 'Igh tide is about two in the morning but there will be enough water to float the boat in a few hours. Then they will 'ave to wait until the tide goes down, so the earliest 'e can start is about six *heures*.'

'Six in the morning, eh?' Russell pondered. 'Do you think they're likely to do it then?'

''Oo knows?' Bruissement gave a shrug. 'As I said, I think we should tread very carefully. We don't know why they are 'ere, or what they are planning to do. I think we should wait until the morning, and then go on board. We could say we were making some general enquiries and not raise a suspicion, *oui*?'

Russell was troubled. 'I suppose that's a good idea, although I don't like the thought of them going before we have a chance to look at the boat.'

'Don't worry,' Bruissement reassured him. 'I can't see them leaving until she has been cleaned completely. If we come back at say, seven in the morning, the boat will still be on the bottom.'

'Maybe you're right...' Russell still felt uneasy.

'Let us go to the Commissariat de Police and you can explain what information you 'ave already.'

They drove to the police station in *Rue Perrochel*. Bruissement's office was much like his own, Russell thought: a small room, off a larger office. His too had a single desk with a comfortable-looking chair behind and two upright seats in front. The difference was that there was a pervading smell that he recognised as coming from the almost ubiquitous French cigarettes, *Gauloises*. As a non-smoker, Russell normally found the stench of tobacco smoke distasteful but - he couldn't explain why - he didn't mind either pipe smoke or this very French fragrance.

'Please to sit down, Sonny,' the Frenchman said, waving him to one of the chairs and taking his place behind the desk. He too had a single filing cabinet but when he reached over and opened the bottom drawer, he produced a bottle of cognac and two glasses. 'I think the sun, as you say, is over the yardarm, *oui*?'

Russell smiled. 'Yes, I think it is.' The two men settled down and after toasting each other Russell proceeded to explain why he was there. Bruissement sat quietly, occasionally sipping his drink and listening without comment. It took some minutes to explain the whole story until finally, Russell said: 'You see, although Wolfgang and Ludwig are our only suspects, we have very little evidence. Certainly nothing that would stand up in a court of law.'

'*Oui*, I see your problem.' Bruissement leant back in his chair and linked his hands behind his head. A gesture, Russell realised with amusement, was something that he was prone to do himself. 'Why do you think the two men were killed? And tortured in such a way?'

'I really don't know. I can only imagine some sort of gang rivalry where they overstepped the mark and had to be punished.'

Bruissement took his hands from behind his head and, leaning forward, laid then on the table, palms down. 'What if it 'ad something to do with smuggling? Many things are still 'ard to get 'old of since the war. You still 'ave some rationing in England, *mais ouis*?'

'Yes, that's true. But I can't think what would be so important to cause two deaths.

Bruissement shrugged. ' 'Oo knows? I am constantly amazed at man's inhumanity to man as your poet Robert Burns would say. Now let us find you your bed for the night then we must eat. I would let you stay in my *appartement* but it is *tres* small so you will stay in a nice little hotel run by a friend of mine.'

The hotel was located a little farther along the *rue Gambetta*, near where they had stopped earlier. Although a modest affair, it was warm and welcoming, as were Bruissement's friend, the *patron* and his wife. Russell was shown to a first-floor room that had a view across the fishermen's quay, with colourful boats tied up along its length. After he'd freshened up he met Bruissement in the little lobby and they set off for a nearby restaurant. 'This place is not, 'ow you say, fancy, but it 'as a very good chef who offers the best of the local cuisine.'

He was obviously ready to show off his town but Russell needed to warn him of something. 'Um, I don't like to sound ungrateful but I don't eat meat or fish, so that may cause a problem.'

'*Pas de problem* my friend,' Bruissement said, taking the sudden announcement in his stride. 'You can see that I take food very seriously,' - he patted his ample stomach and winked - 'so you will 'ave the very best *omelette aux champignons*, I promise you!'

They walked companionably through the new part of the town, the Frenchman pointing out places of interest, and up through the cobbled streets to *la Haute Ville*, the old walled citadel. The restaurant, which overlooked one of the squares, was a plain but homely affair. The evening was too cool to sit outside but they were given a seat in the window. Bruissement ordered for them both and Russell wasn't disappointed. The mushroom omelette came with crispy French fries and a good green salad; the wine flowed, as did the conversation. They talked of cases they had worked on, comparing notes and toasting successes; they touched on family life, or lack of it - both were bachelors, wedded to the job. It was late by the time they started on the cognac.

'I think I'd better get back to my hotel,' Russell said, feeling slightly bleary. 'We have an early start.'

'Yes, you are quite right,' Bruissement agreed. Russell offered to pay for the meal but the Frenchman was quite insistent that it was his treat so he backed down graciously, promising to return the compliment when Bruissement came over to England. After farewells to the chef and *patron* they headed back, through the quiet streets to Russell's hotel where they bid goodnight to each other and Bruissement headed off to his apartment. Russell's head was spinning as he laid it on the pillow. He'd had more wine that evening than he had had for a long time and hadn't realised how much he had drunk as the atmosphere had been so relaxed. Ah well, he thought, I dare say I will pay for it in the morning.

Wolfgang leant over the gunwale of the fishing boat, holding on to the corner of the wheelhouse to steady himself. 'Have you finished yet?' he shouted down to the other man.

Ludwig looked up, paused, then turned off the stream of water jetting from the hose. 'Eh?'

'How much longer will you be?'

'Oh, maybe another 20 minutes.'

'Good. We must get going as soon as there is enough water.'

Within an hour the boat was swaying as the tide lifted it off the timbers and they made ready to set sail. Wolfgang entered the wheelhouse and started the engine while Ludwig climbed the ladder up to the quay and prepared to cast off. When he heard the shout from his brother, he untied the last warp and let it drop. Climbing down the ladder, he gave the boat a shove away from the quay wall and jumped on to the deck as the vessel moved downstream, against the tide. Once outside the harbour entrance Wolfgang pointed the bow south and they headed down the coast towards Saint Valery.

Wednesday

Tide tables – *used for tidal prediction and to show the daily times and heights of high and low water, usually for a particular location.*

MORNING CAME all too soon, and with it a hangover headache. Russell sluiced cold water over his face and felt a little better. Downstairs he was glad the breakfast consisted of just good coffee and crisp rolls. After he'd eaten, he felt a little more human. Just before seven Bruissement arrived. He looked glum. 'I am afraid I 'ave some bad news, *mon ami*. The boat, it 'as gone.'

'*What*?' Russell was flabbergasted – and very angry. He'd come all this way and was now no farther forward. 'But you said they'd have to turn the boat so would still be here this morning,' he said sharply. 'What the *hell* happened?'

Bruissement looked sheepish and unhappy. 'You recollect that I thought they had just started the cleaning of the boat?' Russell nodded. 'It seems that what we saw yesterday was them cleaning the *second* side. One of my colleagues saw them turn the boat earlier in the day. Unfortunately, he only told me this morning. I am so sorry.'

'I don't suppose you have any idea where they have gone?'

Bruissement shrugged. 'It could be anywhere. Maybe back to *Angleterre*?'

Russell's thoughts were instantly transported to the events at home. He took a moment or two to calm down, pondered for a second or two then said: 'Guillaume…'

'Mm?' The Frenchman had been deep in thought too. '*Oui*?'

'I don't suppose you speak German?'

'A little,' he said, surprised. 'Why do you ask?'

Russell reached into his pocket and took out the paper that Jack Spratt had found under his shed. 'I wondered if this means anything to you.' He passed the paper to Bruissement.

Fl*t. Freitag 05.35
**ell-Buch*
versteinerte *ald

'A colleague in England suggested that the first line is probably the time of a high tide on a Friday.'

'*Oui*,' Bruissement said, 'I would agree with that.'

'But the second line…' He paused. 'Maybe something to do with beech trees, if that's an "e" on the end of "Buch".'

Bruissement studied the paper. 'But what if it's a "t"?'

'What would that make it then?' Russell asked.

' "Bucht" means bay in English. Don't you 'ave a place near you that is called 'Shell Bay'?'

'You're right,' Russell said enthusiastically. 'Just across the river from Compass Point, where the first body was found. But what about the last line? Captain Salt said '*versteinerte*' meant fossilised and '*bald*' meant soon.'

'Ah, but what if the last word is '*wald*', then it could mean petrified forest.'

'That's *it*!' Russell exclaimed. 'There *is* a petrified forest at Shell Bay. A whole forest of petrified trees is exposed when the tide is out.'

'Then all you 'ave to do is find out when there is an 'igh tide there and see what is going on.'

Russell sighed. 'Ah, well, I suppose that's something.' He sighed again. 'Do you know what time the next ferry back to England is?'

~o~

'Right. We've got two unidentified bodies, badly mutilated; *possibly* an army Bedford with an anonymous driver; *possibly* a fishing boat, currently on the high seas somewhere and two *possible* suspects, *possibly* German, but who knows? I've had an angry Mr Soffit on the phone, demanding to know when we're going to let him have his show house back plus another developer wanting to know when he can get on with building his homes. And you go off on a jolly, without authorisation, and come back empty handed.' The Superintendent paused for breath and Russell made to speak. His superior held up his hand. 'Let me finish!' he growled. '*And* I've had the Chief Constable giving me grief, demanding to know when we're going to make some progress on this case. *Now* you may speak.'

Superintendent Vic Stout was sitting bolt upright in his leather swivel chair, his fleshy face glowing pink with suppressed anger, his eyes bulging and his fists white-knuckled on the pristine desk, uncluttered except for a pair of telephones and a crisp, unmarked blotter. Russell stood, hands clasped in front of him, head slightly tilted forward and the corners of his mouth drooping, saying nothing. 'Well?' Stout demanded.

'Er…' Russell began hesitantly, 'We've got a note…'

'Oh *yes*,' the super replied sarcastically, 'A note with a *possible* time and a *possible* location of a *possible* high tide. Not much to go on, is it?'

Russell stood crestfallen. 'No, Sir.'

'No Sir indeed.' Stout's face softened. 'Listen, I've trusted you in the past when things have looked black and you've come up trumps so I'm prepared to stick my neck out again. But…I need something more concrete - and fast. You've got 48 hours to produce some decent evidence or I'll have to bring in another team. Understood?'

Russell nodded. 'Yes, Sir. Thank you, Sir.'

'Now, get on with it.' The DI nodded dejectedly, turned and left the office, closing the door quietly behind him.

Russell was back in his own office, feeling suitably chastened. Weeks was sitting across the desk from him. The DI had gone over what he had gleaned from his trip to Boulogne, such as it was, and reiterated the scant details of the case. 'So,' he said, 'any idea where we go from here?'

The constable had a puzzled look on his face. Then it cleared. 'What about the note? If we work out when and where it relates to, that might be a start.'

'Yes,' Russell said slowly. 'That may be something. Have we got a set of tide tables?' Weeks got up and went into the outer office. In a few minutes he came back with a slim book. 'Here, Sir,' he said, handing it over to his superior.

The DI riffled through the book, then stopped, smoothing the pages open. 'Look at this,' he said suddenly, swivelling it around. Weeks looked at where Russell's finger was pointing.

'Oh yes, Friday oh-five-thirty-five. What's the date?'

'This Friday. That's the day after tomorrow!' Russell exclaimed. 'I think we should be there, and see if anything happens.'

'How are we going to get there at that time in the morning? There's no proper road, just a rutted dirt track, which is why there's a ferry across from Compass Point. Besides, if we take the car there'll be nowhere to hide it. There are no trees, just scrubby bushes, and the dunes would hardly conceal it.' The normally reticent Weeks had surprised himself with his eloquence. 'Sorry,' he muttered, looking down.

Russell smiled and waved away his apology. 'Don't worry,' he said. '*Mr* Spratt owes us a favour. He can row us and a couple of constables over. And anyway, he often sleeps in his shed so it shouldn't be too much of a hardship for him. We'll drop by on the way home and arrange it. Meanwhile, tomorrow, I want to have another look at the brickworks, see if the backroom boys have missed any clues. I've got to come up with something or Stout will take the case away from us.' He looked at his wristwatch. 'Time to knock off I think. Let's go and visit Mr Spratt.'

The two set off for Compass Point, bumping along the stony track, over the level crossing and into the boatyard. It was after five, so Mitch and his workers had finished work and all was quiet. Spratt's boat was tied up by the ferry steps, its pale-blue hull reflected in the water that lapped a few feet below the top of the quay. As the two policemen walked towards the shed, the sound of a ringing bell drifted across the water and Jack appeared in the doorway of his hut. He stopped and a look of surprise crossed his face as he saw the two policemen. Then he smiled, probably remembered the 10-shilling note the DI had given him.

'Ah, gen'lemen,' he said, beaming hugely, 'just let me collect them grockles from t'other side, then I'm all yours.'

He walked the few yards to the quayside, bandy legged with a rolling sailor's gait, descended the two or three visible stone steps and then, climbing over the gunwale, settled himself on the forrard thwart. Weeks and Russell sat down on the bench at the side of Jack's hut and watched him row strongly across the river. It was almost high water so there was very little tidal flow. Spratt brought the boat against the wooden jetty on the other side and the two people who had been waiting stepped aboard and, within a few minutes, they were back at the ferry steps. The two detectives rose as Jack came towards them.

'Now gen'lemen, 'ow can I 'elp you?'

'We need you to take us across to Shell Bay,' Russell said.

'Right you are.' Then his smile faded and his face clouded. 'Why didn't yer say before? I could 'ave saved meself a trip!' he said tetchily.

'Oh, not now, Jack. Friday morning.'

'Well, that's all right then. Let me think.' He screwed up his face. 'Should just catch the last of the tide by about nine.'

'No, Jack, earlier than that. We need to be there before five.'

'In the *morning*?' Spratt was incredulous.

'That's right. There'll be four of us.'

'Not sure about that… Bit of a cheek, ain't it?' Jack rubbed his chin, the rasping audible as his hand worked across the stubble.

Russell decided that a bit of blackmail would come in useful. 'I don't suppose you want to declare that cash you got for buying the boat do you?' he asked.

Spratt looked deflated. 'I s'pose not,' he grumbled. 'When d'yer wanna go then?'

'Let's say about four-thirty, shall we? I presume you'll sleep in your shed?'

'I guess I will. Not very comfortable though...' he muttered, his voice trailing off. Then he appeared to have a thought. 'The ferryman looked puzzled. ' 'Ere. *Why* d'yer wanna go?'

Russell tapped the side of his nose. 'Ah, afraid I can't tell you that.' Spratt grunted and raised his eyes heavenwards. 'We'll see you then.' The policemen walked back to the car, got in, and set off for home.

Weeks dropped the DI at his railway carriage and headed off, agreeing to pick him up early the following morning. Russell wasn't ready for his evening meal. He needed time to think, so he set off along the path that ran above the shingle beach towards the distant Compass Point. Aggie trotted happily in front of him, delighted to be going on a long walk. Normally, they would have walked along the strip of exposed sand below the shingle ridge, the dog playing in the shallows but, as the tide was full and the waves lapped against the stones, they stayed on the narrow path.

A lot seemed to have happened in the past 24 hours. Russell replayed it in his head. The trip to Boulogne: although it had yielded little, he had enjoyed meeting Bruissement. He hoped their paths would cross again before too long. The carpeting from his Superintendent: to be fair, Russell appreciated that he too was under pressure from his superiors to produce results. In the circumstances he felt he'd got off quite lightly. But if he didn't start producing results pretty damn soon, another team would take over and, probably, get all the glory if and when the case was solved.

He was pretty certain the German brothers were involved with the murder of the two men in some way but still couldn't work out how. Also, why did they need the boat and what was the connection with Boulogne? He plodded on hoping the steady rhythm of his footsteps would help to put his thoughts into some sort of cohesive order. The trouble was, the more he tried to make sense of it the more the thoughts fluttered round his head, like so many moths flying round a candle flame, until all the disparate strands seemed to unravel, taking him back to his original muddled ideas. Shaking his head, he looked up and realised the sun had long gone down; he had walked much farther than he had meant to and it was a long trek in the dark back to his house. He stopped and Aggie looked up at him. He could read her thoughts: where the devil was her dinner?

'Yes, I know, I'm ready for mine, too,' he told her, giving the small dog a sympathetic pat. With a sigh, he turned and retraced his steps.

Thursday

AWOL- military absence without leave; absent from one's post or duty without official permission but without intending to desert.

WHEN RUSSELL arrived at the police station the following morning the desk sergeant called to him: 'There's a pair of soldiers waiting to see you. I've put them in your office.'

'Any idea what they want?' The DI was puzzled.

'Sorry, none at all. They wouldn't say.'

As Russell walked into his office, the two squaddies stood up and turned towards him. 'Do you remember us, Sir?' the shorter one asked.

'It's Lowe, isn't it? And er...'

'Dunne, Sir,' his taller colleague said.

'Ah, the guards from the barracks?'

'That's right, Sir.'

'What can I do for you? Please sit down.' Russell gestured to the chairs while he took his place behind the desk.

'Well, Sir,' Lowe began hesitantly, 'something's been bothering us since last week when you came to interview us.'

'Oh yes?' Russell was intrigued.

Dunne continued: 'We weren't gonna say nothin', but then that rat mucked us about...'

He trailed off and his companion took up the story, 'It *was* Rankin we saw that night, driving the Bedford,' he said, his voice more cultured than his lowly rank of private would suggest. 'And it wasn't the first time.'

'Really?' Russell looked incredulous.

'Yes, he took the lorry a few days before. He said he'd pay us if we'd keep quiet and not let on it was him. Then it happened again.'

'When was this?' the DI asked.

The two soldiers looked at each other. Dunne spoke. 'It was last Sunday. We was more than surprised because 'e was on his own like before. 'E promised he'd pay us double if we kept our mouths shut again... But 'e ain't paid us yet an' it don't look as if 'e's gonna. That's why we decided to split on 'im. Never liked 'im very much anyway.'

'Or trusted him either,' Lowe added.

'Hmm, that's very interesting. Would you be prepared to sign a statement to that effect?' Again they exchanged glances, then nodded in unison. 'Good. Just a minute, wait there.' He got up from his seat and went to the door. 'Weeks,' he called.

The constable looked up from his desk.

'Sir?'

'Can you come and take statements from these two gentlemen, please?'

The soldiers went over what they had already said and Weeks wrote it down. When he'd finished, and they had checked what he had written, they signed the statements. After telling them he'd be in touch, Russell wished them goodbye.

'That's a turn-up for the books, Sir,' Weeks said. 'What next?'

I think we should drive to the barracks and *request* that Rankin helps us with our enquiries or we'll bring him in for questioning.'

'When, Sir?'

'No time like the present, lad. Let's get going.'

~o~

As the Wolseley drove up to the barrier at the army camp, they were recognised straight away and waved through. Stopping outside Captain Valiant's office, they got out of the car and mounted the step to the door. Russell knocked. 'Come,' said a voice from inside. And, as they entered: 'Ah, the detectives. How can I help you *this* time?' The Captain was sitting behind his desk, a tense expression on his face.

'We'd like to talk to Private Rankin.'

'I'm sorry to inform you that you've had a wasted journey then.' Valiant looked embarrassed.

'Why is that?' Russell asked.

'I'm afraid Rankin has gone AWOL. Absent without official leave, to state it in full.'

Russell started. '*What*? How…?'

'And not only is he missing but he's taken the lorry too.'

'How on earth could that happen? I thought your security was tight here…'

'I don't know. Security *is* tight. His disappearance has caused me all sorts of problems.'

'I can imagine.' Russell paused. 'Also, I have to inform you it's not the first time he's taken the lorry without permission.'

The captain cocked his head to one side. 'How so?'

'It seems your guards were rather economical with the truth. You remember when we first asked about the Bedford going out late one night?

'Yesss…' Valiant said slowly.

'We now have signed statements from the two soldiers concerned, Lowe and Dunne, admitting that it was indeed Rankin who took it.' The captain looked even more despondent. 'Not only that but he took it on other occasions. So, we're pretty sure he's involved in the case we're working on.'

'This is more serious than I imagined. I was hoping to contain it but I shall have to tell the CO now.'

'I think that's probably wise,' Russell said. 'It's gone beyond being an internal affair.'

He and Weeks left the barracks, with Valiant promising to do what he could to find out what had happened to Rankin. He assured them he would alert them as soon as he had any information. Now he had made a decision and had the task in hand his initial hangdog demeanour had been replaced by one of determination. Russell could see how he made an excellent UXB officer.

~O~

Driving away from Collinghurst the two men soon reached the turn-off for the brickworks. The gate had been secured with a new padlock but Russell had brought the key with him. He climbed out of the car, Aggie trotting behind him, unlocked the padlock and, with some effort, opened the gates. He waved Weeks through, and he and the dog followed the car down the rough track.

When they reached the first building they started looking round the room where they'd found the carpet underlay. The fingerprint team had obviously been thorough as they found no more clues, so moved on to the other buildings. There were store rooms, still with filled sacks, covered with years of dust; a making shed, with long benches cluttered with battered, wooden brick moulds and discarded tools. Broken, unfired bricks lay about the floor and everywhere was thick with more clay dust. Next they entered one of the kilns.

They had to stoop to go through the low doorway into a sooty, brick-lined room, littered with the broken pieces of clay uncleared from the last firing years before. Despite their efforts they failed to turn up anything interesting but, just as they were making their way out of the kiln, Weeks coughing from the soot they had disturbed, the terrier ran round to the back of the building, barking.

'Aggie'! Russell called, 'come back here!' The dog didn't show. He called again, more forcefully this time. 'Aggie!!' She still didn't appear so he walked round to the side of the kiln. At first he thought the bushes and weeds had grown naturally, creating an impenetrable barrier behind the building. Then he realised that cut brushwood and branches had been forced into a gap. The dog must have wriggled through somehow. He dragged some of it aside and pushed his way through the rest of the undergrowth between the kilns and saw her jumping up excitedly at the door to a small building. Reaching forward he turned the handle and the door creaked open. He just managed to grab the terrier's collar before she shot in. 'Stay!' he said sternly, holding up his finger. The dog sat reluctantly.

Russell peered into the room and, as his eyes became accustomed to the weak light coming through a grimy window, he could just make out a pair of mattresses on the floor. Looking round he could also see a makeshift table with a primus stove, kettle, mugs, tins and packets on it.

'Well, well,' he said quietly to himself. Then more loudly: 'Weeks, come round here, and bring a torch.'

Judging by the number of empty tins, the room had been occupied for several days. And also quite recently, Russell reckoned, as there were only slight traces of mould on one or two of them. Weeks had gone back to the car to ring the station to alert the fingerprint team. They were now on their way. Meanwhile, Russell picked his way through the detritus of primitive living, carefully handling various objects with a handkerchief, or moving them aside with a pencil. By the light of the torch he could see that instead of what he at first thought were mattresses, whoever had been sleeping there had been lying on large, straw filled sacks. The bedding consisted of grey army blankets which looked quite new. As he peeled one of them back he could see that the sack had lettering on it. A noise in the doorway made him turn round. It was Weeks. Taking the torch from him, he shone it on the sack.

'Ah, lad, what do you make of this?' Stencilled in black were the words, **PARK FARM - KILNHURST** above the profile of a rearing horse. He pulled the blanket back farther to reveal the year **1950**.

'It's a hop pocket, Sir. I did some farm work when I was a kid. I remember they filled them with dried hops and they were sent off to the brewery'

'Just what I thought,' Russell agreed. 'I wonder how they came by them?' The pillow was nothing more than a rolled-up sweater and when the DI moved it, he disturbed a photograph that had been concealed underneath. 'Aha!' he exclaimed. 'What's this then?'

Carefully picking it up by a corner he took it to the doorway so he could see the image more clearly. In the photograph were three young men, still in their teens. They were standing with their arms round each other's shoulders, smiling happily at the camera.

What was noticeable was that the one on the right of the picture, although the same sort of age, was much bigger than the other two. The one on the left seemed to have a perfectly proportioned body whereas the central figure was skinny and as Russell peered at the picture, he could see that he had an iron brace strapped to one leg. Looking more closely he could see that all three were wearing shorts. Indeed, he realised, not just shorts, but lederhosen.

'What's that in the background?' Weeks asked, peering over his shoulder. 'Mountains?'

'You're right. Looks like it could be the Alps.' Russell turned the photograph over and they could see written on the back, faded but still legible:

Innsbruck 1936. Franz, Wolfgang & Ludwig. Frohe Feiertage!

Russell beamed. 'Our missing German mariners, Weeks! They've definitely been here.'

'But who's the one on the left?'

'Who indeed? I wonder if he has an important part to play in the solving of this case? Let's have a *careful* look round to see what else we can find.'

The two detectives moved methodically around the room, gingerly lifting blankets, pushing aside boxes and peering in corners.

Weeks was crouching down, looking under the table. 'What's this, Sir?' He stood up, holding a small grubby canvas duffle bag, the kind that sailors use for their personal possessions.

'My, my...' Russell murmured, a big grin lighting up his face. He loosened the tie around the neck and feeling inside pulled out a slim bundle of papers. Unfolding the top sheet he peered at it. 'German,' he said. He flicked through the rest of the sheets. 'All in German lad. Best find Captain Salt. He'll be the best person to translate these I reckon. I wonder what else there is?'

He reached into the bag and brought out two oval metal discs. Each was dull silver in colour with a hole in the corner through which was threaded a length of chain. On the front was an embossed German eagle, its wings outspread above a swastika. On the reverse it read:

GEHEIME
STAATSPOLIZEI

Weeks gasped. 'Gestapo!'

'So it seems,' Russell agreed. 'I think we'd better get these papers dusted for prints pronto, before we get them to Salt.' Just as he was speaking a vehicle come to a halt on the rough ground outside. 'Sounds like the cavalry has arrived. Right on cue.'

As soon as Lewis, the fingerprints man, saw the papers, he declared he would need to take them back to the lab for detailed examination before he could release them. Meanwhile he set to, carefully examining the room and its contents. The photographer took pictures, the whumph of the flash making the interior brighter than the daylight outside and leaving a blurred, stark black and white image burnt into Russell's retina. He blinked, shook his head and, mumbling a goodbye, stumbled out into the open air.

On the drive back to town Russell slumped in the passenger seat, deep in thought. Weeks knew better than to disturb his boss in that mood. At long last things were starting to come together. The statement from the two guards that implicated Rankin and then his disappearance pointed incontrovertibly to his involvement. The discovery of the hideaway at the brickworks, coupled with the German papers and Nazi identity tags, proved beyond doubt that the two Miller brothers were up to their necks in it. But up to their necks in what? Black marketeering? Gun running? Both possible but none seemed quite right. Maybe the visit to Shell Bay in the early hours of the following morning would make things clearer. Russell really hoped so, as there was very little left of the 48 hours before Stout brought in another team.

When they arrived at the station Russell entered with heavy heart. Weeks too was downcast, especially when he sighted the mountain of paperwork, still to be sorted, on his desk. Russell quietly shut the door to his room, sat down in his chair, linked his hands behind his head and leant back, thinking. He remained like this for some time before, sighing deeply, he stood up, stretched and wandered along the corridor to Lewis's office. Tapping lightly on the door, but not expecting a reply, he pushed it open and was surprised to see the fingerprint man sitting behind the desk.

'Oh, you're back already?' he said.

'I am. I left the lads at the brickworks; I'm picking them up later. I wanted to have a good look at these.' He tapped the papers in front of him. Russell recognised them as the ones they had found in the duffle bag. 'I believe you were going to show these to Salt, once we'd finished with them?'

'That's right. He reads German so he seemed to be the man for the job.'

Lewis smiled up at him. 'You didn't know?'

'Know what?' Russell was perplexed.

'I spent part of the war in a German POW camp, quite a lot of it in the cookhouse. Surprising what you pick up if you keep your eyes and ears open. *Ich spreche sehr gut Deutsch und ich lese es noch besser.*'

Russell grinned. 'I'm not entirely sure what you said, but it sounded pretty good. What do you make of the papers?'

'Well I haven't had time to look at them thoroughly, but it seems they are the identity documents of two members of the Waffen-SS – low-ranking Nazi officers. The two discs confirm this.'

'So are these the absent Germans?

Lewis frowned.

'I don't think so,' he said slowly. 'The papers contain brief descriptions of the men but they're nothing like your two fugitives. They're both of normal height and build, not big and small like the Miller brothers.'

'Well who are they?' Russell asked.

'Can't help you there. I'm afraid that's something you'll have to find out for yourself.'

Friday

Petrified wood - *the name given to a special type of fossilised remains of terrestrial vegetation. It is the result of a tree or tree-like plants having completely transitioned to stone by the process of permineralisation.*

THE CROSSING in the dark from Saint-Valery-sur-Somme had been uncomfortable. The short seas were choppy, the wind, force five gusting six, made the boat pitch and roll awkwardly. The man trussed up in the shallow fish hold, although unconscious for most of the passage, had been rolled about and now his clothes were soaked with seawater and his own filth. As they neared the English shore he struggled to sit up, but a well-aimed boot from Ludwig sent him sprawling back, groaning.

Soon they were nudging the sand in the shallows and as the keel scraped along the bottom, Wolfgang killed the engine and the boat slid to a stop.

Just before 4.30am the Wolseley was once more bumping down the track to Compass Point, only this time in the grey dawn before the sun rose. The car crunched to a halt on the shingle and four figures climbed out, quietly closing the doors behind them. Weeks mounted the steps to Spratt's hut and knocked lightly on the woodwork of the weathered door and waited. Nothing happened so he rapped louder. Still nothing. 'Go and wake him!' Russell hissed.

The DC turned the handle and pushed the door open. He shone his torch to reveal an interior crammed with a jumble of nautical gear and a rumpled blanket on the narrow wooden bench, but no sign of the ferryman. 'He's gone, Sir!' Weeks exclaimed.

Russell pushed past so he too could confirm that the shed was, indeed, empty. 'Well I'll be....The old bugger's run out on us. Let's see if he's taken his boat.'

One of the constables, PC Lee, jogged across to the steps and shone his torch down.' He turned and in a stage whisper said: 'It's gone, Sir.'

'Oh that's just wonderful,' Russell said. 'What are we supposed to do now?'

'We could find another boat and row ourselves across,' Weeks suggested.

Russell sighed. 'I suppose so. Right, spread out and see if there's anything suitable. This is a *boat* yard after all. And keep the noise down!' he hissed, as they blundered about, tripping over timber and ropes.

After more than 10 minutes of fruitless searching they reconvened. The only boats any of them had found were either being repaired or beyond repair. Besides, even if one had proved seaworthy, there were no decent oars to be found. Presumably they were locked up in one of Mitch's sheds. 'Damn!' Russell said. 'What's the time?'

'Ten to five,' Weeks said, shining his torch on his watch. 'What do we do now, Sir?'

'Damn and blast it!' his boss said, exasperated. 'We'll have to drive over there.'

'But by the time we've driven back up to the bridge, crossed over the river and bumped down that awful track it'll be well after five, Sir,' the other PC, Beaumont, said.

'I know that, *constable,* but what alternative do we have? If we're to be there by high tide it's the only thing we can do.' Russell exhaled noisily, showing his frustration. Turning on his heel he headed back to the car. 'Come on, let's get going.' They piled in, Weeks started the engine and they set off.

With four on board they couldn't go too fast along the uneven track without causing serious damage to the vehicle's springs so it was a frustrating quarter of an hour before they even reached the bridge. Once over, Weeks had to drive even more slowly along the other side of the river, partly because he had only side lights to guide him but mainly because the track was so rutted. Russell, hanging on to the grab handle to stop himself being bounced out of his seat, snapped: 'This is ridiculous! It'd be quicker to walk!' The constables Lee and Beaumont, bouncing around in the back, would have agreed but knowing the DI's mood, kept quiet.

'I'm sorry, Sir,' Weeks said, wrestling with the spinning steering wheel. It threatened to jerk out of his hands at any moment, and send the car into the soft sand at the side of the track. 'I'm doing the best I can.'

Russell was conciliatory, 'That's all right, lad, I know you are. It's that bloody Spratt! When I get hold of him I'll….' He was cut short as a particularly vicious bump bounced him in his seat, his head connecting with the roof. 'Arghh!' he cried. The torture continued for what seemed an age until at last, the timber of the jetty at Shell Bay came into view. Weeks brought the Wolseley to a halt and turned off the engine. In the moments that followed, the four officers sat in silence, their ears ringing and their muscles aching. Then Russell spoke in a whisper: 'What's the time now?'

There was a brief flash of light from the back and Lee said: 'Twenty past, Sir.'

'Ye gods and little fishes! It's high tide any time. I thought we'd be in place by now. How long's it going to take us to get to the beach with the petrified forest?'

'Should be there in about 10 minutes, Sir,' the PC said.

'Come on then, we'd better get going and we *might* make it in time.'

As they walked quickly past the jetty Russell stopped in his tracks, Weeks almost crashing into him. 'Well would you believe it….' he said, pointing. There, tied to a timber post was the ghostly shape of Spratt's boat. 'Where is the old rogue? If he's compromised this investigation…' His voice trailed off as he turned and made for the beach.

The sky in the east was getting lighter by the minute so they were able to move quickly through the sand dunes. The spot they were heading towards was obscured by the forbidding bulk of a Martello tower. This large conical stone structure dated from the time of the French Revolutionary Wars. Several of its companions stood farther along the shore, marching into the misty distance. In the few minutes it took to reach the tower the sun had risen enough to give them clear visibility as they rounded it and could see the curve of the bay, with the tide high on the sand. Also, clearly visible, close inshore, was a fishing boat.

'It's *Moonshine*!' Weeks exclaimed.

'You're damn right it is,' Russell said.

On the deck of the boat there was a sudden flurry of activity. 'Wolf!' shouted the big man, pointing to the shore. '*Guck mal*!'

'*Scheisse! Die Polizei!*' In a moment there was a roar from the diesel engine, a cloud of spray was thrown up by the propeller and the boat moved backwards gaining momentum, until suddenly, as the helm was swung, it turned through 180 degrees, the engine was put in forward gear and it headed off, out to sea. As the bow cut through the still water, plumes of spray rising from either side, there was a loud yell and a splash. Someone was in the water. As the boat powered off towards the misty horizon a panic-stricken voice shouted: '*Help!*' PC Beaumont ran towards the gently lapping waves, peeling off his jacket as he ran. Throwing it to the ground, he waded waist deep, then dived into the sea. He was a strong swimmer and within a dozen strokes had reached the figure, bobbing in the water. The other three policemen stood at the water's edge as the constable brought the man into the shallows.

'Well I'll be....!' the DI exclaimed. 'If it isn't Jack Spratt...!'

Sure enough, it was the ferryman, but in a sorry state. They dragged him up on the beach where he lay, water running off his sodden clothes. He was panting heavily and spluttering as he coughed up mouthfuls of dirty liquid. Russell noticed his hands were caught behind his back.

'He's tied up. Quick, loosen the ropes!'

Carefully they rolled him on his side and Weeks tried to get the knots undone. He struggled for a few moments then said: 'I can't shift them, Sir. I reckon it's another one of those double-constrictors. Anyone got a knife?' Constable Lee, who had been standing on the shore, reached in his pocket and produced a clasp knife and handed it to him. Opening the blade Weeks worked at the cords until, with a grunt and an oath, Spratt was able to bring his hands round to his front where he proceeded to rub his wrists, all the time alternating between muttering and spitting out seawater.

Sitting up, he held his head between his hands and groaned.

'Cor! I thought I was a gonner back there!' He coughed, spraying the ground, his face florid with the effort.

Russell carefully crouched down in front of him.

'Once you've recovered I think you owe us an explanation,' he said.

'Blimey, give us a moment. I almost drownded.'

Standing up again, Russell nodded. 'Okay.'

Until this point, all eyes had been turned seaward, watching the rescue of the ferryman and the boat disappearing into the morning mist. Weeks was the first to turn and peer inland.

'Sir! *Look*!' he said suddenly, pointing.

All eyes turned. In the distance, tucked behind the Martello tower, its nose just visible, they could see the distinctive shape of the Bedford lorry, the red mudguards gleaming dully in the weak sunlight.

'Well blow me down. Now I'm really confused,' Russell said, scratching his head, a perplexed frown on his face. He turned back to Spratt whose breathing was becoming less laboured. 'You feel up to talking now?'

'I s'pose so. What d'yer wanna know?' The DI sighed. 'I thought that was pretty obvious, Jack. What you're doing here, when you were supposed to row us across, for starters.'

'Let me think.' Spratt screwed up his face as he tried to dredge up the details. 'Oh yeah, I was fast akip when I was woken by a ringin' sound. Nothin' usually wakes me but I s'pose I was a bit on edge cos I knew you was comin' an' the sound of a bell means I'm needed on t'other side. Anyhow, I gets up an' the bell rings again. I opened the door an' it was still a bit dark but I knew it wouldn't be long before the sun come up. Then I 'eard the bell agin, an' it *was* from t'other side.

'I thought it were strange but reckoned you'd changed your plans an' needed me over there. There was just enough light for me to get into the boat an' row over. The tide was slack so I just 'ad to go straight across an' in a few strokes I was bumpin' agin the jetty.' He paused, then added: 'An' that wasn't the only bump.

'I'd just got on to the jetty an' was tying up the boat when somethin' hit me 'ard across the back of me 'ead. As I fell I sorta spun round an' caught a glimpse of a giant figure before I passed out. Next thing I knows, I'm sitting on *Moonshine's* deck, wiv me 'ands tied behind me back an' wiv a thumpin' 'eadache startin'.

'Anyways, I didn't let on that I'd come to, just kept me eyes 'alf closed. I could see them two brothers and they was deep in conversation with some squaddie.'

'Rankin,' the two detectives said in unison.

'Eh? I don't know about that but they were right pally. 'Well, to start with anyhow.'

'What do you mean?' Russell asked.

'At first they was chattin' like old mates. 'E was askin' 'ow long they were plannin' to be there. The little one said somethin' like, "as little time as possible". They chatted away for a while, as if they was discussin' some sort of pleasure trip or jolly. The army bloke then asked what they wanted 'im to do. The little bloke said 'e wanted 'im to go to some brickworks or other and get some stuff they'd left there. Then the squaddie started gettin' all uppity. 'E said there was no way 'e could go back, on account of the fact that 'e'd pinched the lorry and gone AWOL an' they'd all be out lookin' for 'im. 'E said 'e thought the brothers had come to take 'im away.

'Wolfgang started to get real angry then. 'Is face went kinda red like and 'is voice got louder and 'e even used some foreign words. German I think. Funny thing was, the soldier shouted back at 'im, an' 'e was speakin' in foreign, too. 'Is brother Ludwig 'ad been standing back but when the little one got angry, 'e moved forward, real quick like, and grabbed the soldier by the throat. That seemed to calm 'is brother down. 'Is voice got quieter and 'e told the big bloke to let 'im go. Which 'e did.

'The squaddie coughed a bit, then said: "What about 'im?" an' pointed forrard, into the fish 'old. I looked, an' blimey, if there weren't some poor sod trussed up lyin' there - 'e looked scared stiff. They was standin' there quietly starin' at this wretched bloke when you lot turned up. That's when Ludwig jumped into the wheelhouse and banged the engine in reverse. Wolfgang shouted somethin' and I made me move. I just got to me feet an' fell backwards over the rail into the water, praying someone would get to me before I drownded.'

'Lucky for you this gentleman is a strong swimmer then,' Russell said, jerking his thumb towards Beaumont, who had draped his jacket round his shoulders but was starting to shiver. 'Better get you somewhere warm, lad. D'you reckon the keys are still in that lorry?'

They made their way over to the Bedford and the keys were indeed still in the ignition. Russell and PC Lee climbed over the tailboard into the back, while Beaumont and Spratt got into the cab. Weeks clambered up into the driver's seat, fired up the engine and put the heater on full blast. The lorry had moved forward only a few feet when Weeks happened to glance out to sea and stamped on the brake. 'Hey!' a shout came from the back, 'what the hell's going on?!'

Weeks was throwing the door open and clambering down from the cab. 'Sir! I think they're coming back.' Russell and the two constables tumbled out of the lorry and they stood, staring as the shape of *Moonshine* grew larger as she approached them. When the vessel was 30 yards off the shore, the engine was cut and she slewed round sideways. They could see movement on the deck and a plank being run out over the bow. After a few moments a figure was seen stumbling along it, shoved from behind by a much larger one.

'What the...?' Russell said. 'I don't believe it...they're making him walk the plank!'

With that, the man teetered to the edge of the narrow board, which projected a couple of feet over the gunwale, and fell headlong into the water. Then, with a roar, the boat reversed a few yards, spun round, and headed out to sea again. Beaumont, still dripping from his previous dunking, was just shrugging off his jacket when Weeks yelled: 'It's too far to swim,' and ran for Spratt's boat, followed by Lee. They jumped down from the jetty into the dinghy. The constable cast off and Weeks slotted the oars into the rowlocks and pulled strongly towards the figure that could just be seen, bobbing in the water. Russell watched as they reached the man and heaved him into the boat. He could see it took quite an effort as he looked to be more than six feet tall and heavily built.

After a few minutes they had returned. Willing hands lifted the man on to the jetty. He was unconscious and barely alive. Again, Weeks worked at his bonds with the knife and once free of the tightly knotted ropes, the constable, using the Holga Nielsen method of resuscitation, started pumping the man's chest. Nothing happened for a few moments, then he coughed, bringing up seawater, his eyes briefly opened then closed again, his breathing steady, though ragged.

'We'd better get him to hospital...quick,' Russell said. They carried him to the back of the lorry and laid him on the pile of sacks, the rest of them getting in as before.

With Weeks driving they bumped across the sand until they reached the parked Wolseley. Russell and Lee climbed out of the back of the lorry and transferred the prone figure to the back seat of the car. They then set off in convoy to Collinghurst. At the hospital, nursing staff helped the victim out of the car. 'You stay here with him,' Russell said to the constable, 'and let me know the moment he wakes up.' Protesting that he was all right, Jack too was taken inside for a check-up. Russell got back into the car and they set off for the police station.

The sun was just cresting the horizon as they drove into the car park. The day shift was yet to clock on so, apart from a sleepy desk sergeant, the station was empty. The kettle was soon coming to the boil and Beaumont had changed out of his wet clothes and into a spare uniform. Russell went into his office and sat in his chair. Looking down at the desk he saw there was a hand-written note on his blotter. It was from the forensics man, Lewis.

Dear Sonny,

I had a good look through those papers you found and I think you might have struck lucky. I had a conversation with John Crooks and we discussed the two men whose bodies you found. From the descriptions it seems the papers belonged to them. However, it's quite probable that they were forged. The men who had them had most likely been in the Gestapo. The identity discs seem to confirm this.

During the war they were possibly SS officers working for the Reich Administration Main Office. Briefly, this dealt with the belongings of Jews and other people the Nazis deemed unwholesome and undesirable. I will go into more detail when I see you but basically, they stripped their captives of all their wealth in life and in death. They were most unpleasant characters. No wonder they were dealt with so horrifically at the end. I just wonder how it came about.

I'll get in touch when you've returned to the office. I hope the nocturnal visit went well.

Lewis

Russell sat back in his chair, linking his hands behind his head. Despite having had very little sleep, he was intrigued by this note. His 48-hour deadline was fast approaching and he needed something definite to tell Stout. The confrontation on the beach had not turned out as he had planned. He just hoped that the man they had rescued would be able to provide some much-needed information. He also had the discovery of the brothers' secret hideout at the brickworks and the uncovering of the identity papers and SS discs but he wondered if that would be enough to placate the Super. He looked at his wristwatch. Ten minutes to seven. It would be a while before Lewis came in - he allowed himself the luxury of a nap.

~o~

'Russell?' Russell slowly opened his eyes and Lewis's concerned face swam into focus.

'What time is it?' the DI asked, through a yawn.

'Just after nine. Thought I'd better wake you before Stout came along.'

Russell was alert. 'Why? Is he on the warpath?'

'Not yet, but I suspect it's only a matter of time. However, I think I've some information that might just appease him. You saw my note?' Russell nodded. 'While you were having '40 winks'...' he paused and grinned, 'I've been busy. I felt sure there must be some sort of connection with France. After all, the brothers seem to go back and forth across the Channel quite regularly. I took the liberty of telexing the details to your friend Bruissement. I hope you don't mind?' Russell shook his head and waved away any objections. 'He came back to me pretty quickly. What he had to say was very interesting.'

'Go on,' Russell said.

Lewis took a deep breath and continued. 'Apparently, he has an American friend who works with the German police in Berlin and as soon as he saw what I'd wired over he got on to him straight away. This American is an expert on the SS and spends his time tracking down those who went to ground at the end of the war. We know that a large number of them escaped to South America but many, after going into hiding, returned to Germany under false names and continue to live there.'

'How on earth is that possible?' Russell asked, perplexed. 'I thought they would have been rounded up.'

'Far from it. A large proportion of the worst of them had been planning their escape from expected persecution months before the end of hostilities.' The DI raised an eyebrow but made no comment. 'They could see the writing was on the wall as the Americans moved across Europe and the German Army was suffering crushing defeats at the hands of the Russians. SS officers were making plans to disappear while forcing the regular army, the Wehrmacht, to carry on fighting a war that was already all but done. As the war reached its conclusion many of the Gestapo just quietly disappeared and few were tried for war crimes.'

'But what about the Nuremberg Trials?'

'They were high profile certainly, and many of the most senior

Nazis were tried and sentenced but a huge number of SS officers - and men - had already melted away. They'd formed an organisation called ODESSA, which aided their members in escaping via a system called ratlines. And...' he paused, '...they were even helped by the Vatican!'

'*Really*?!' Russell was incredulous.

Lewis looked down at his notes. 'Yes, in particular, a certain Bishop Aluis Hudal helped dozens of senior Nazi officers escape capture and almost certain trial and subsequent punishment.'

'But how can that be possible?'

'I know, it's incredible, isn't it? But, he actually believed that the SS men were being wrongly pursued, saying that they were victims of allied propaganda. He considered saving German and other fascist officers and politicians from the hands of Allied prosecution, a "just thing".'

Russell shook his head sadly. 'But how on earth could he justify it?'

Lewis read from the notes on the pad in front of him. 'He said he did "what should have been expected of a true Christian", adding: "We do not believe in the eye for an eye of the Jew".'

There was silence for a while as he thought this new information over. Then Russell spoke: 'So our two corpses are quite possibly SS officers who had been in hiding since the end of the war and somehow, they'd been discovered.'

Lewis nodded. 'Not only that, but whoever found them tortured them in bizarre ways before finishing them off and dumping the bodies, one in the sea and the other in a mixer.'

'And our elusive Miller brothers are probably responsible.' Again Lewis nodded his head. Russell exhaled noisily. 'I don't know whether to despair or to congratulate their actions.'

'It certainly makes you wonder,' Lewis agreed.

Russell thought for a moment, then sat up in his chair. 'Nevertheless, we can't have people going around the countryside committing murder, even if the victims are war criminals. We need to find these two brothers before they kill anybody else.'

As he finished speaking Weeks put his head round the side of the doorway. 'The Super wants to see you, Sir,' he said, 'and he doesn't look very happy.'

'Thanks, lad.' Russell turned to Lewis. 'Come on, hopefully the information you've got will cheer him up a bit.'

~o~

It was just after 10 am when they sat down in the Superintendent's office. 'So you reckon our German brothers are somehow involved in tracking down and executing ex-Waffen-SS officers?' Stout said, evenly. When they had first walked into his office his anger was barely suppressed, but as Lewis began to outline the information he had received from the American via Bruissement, he grew gradually calmer and more attentive, his initial ire abated and he appeared almost chastened as Lewis's explanation drew to a close.

'It seems that way, Sir. As they were holed up in the brickworks down the road, there are obviously connections with this area. Also, it's pretty certain that the squaddie, Rankin, is tied up with them too. Some wartime connection perhaps...'

'Tell me again about your 'operation' on the beach.' Stout leant back in his chair and folded his hands in his lap.

'Well it wasn't quite as I'd planned, Sir.'

'So I understand.'

'First there was the problem with getting across to Shell Bay, owing to the absence of the ferryman.'

'Couldn't you have rowed yourselves across?' Stout asked.

'We would have done but there wasn't a useable boat to be had, let alone oars to row with.'

The superintendent grunted.

'This meant that we had to drive back up the track to the bridge that crosses the estuary, which cost us more time. Then, drive down the track to Shell Bay, which was even more rutted so we had to go slowly. However, I'm not sure we'd have been able to do much more if we had been there earlier. It seems that the soldier, Rankin, had been on board the *Moonshine* for some time. At least we managed to save Spratt from a particularly nasty death and rescue that poor blighter who's in the hospital now.'

'Any news from there?'

'Nothing yet. We've got PC Lee waiting outside his room so we'll know as soon as he comes round.'

Stout grunted. 'Good, let me know the minute you hear anything.' He paused, deep in thought. 'What I don't understand is why Rankin was there? Why did he purloin the lorry? Any ideas?' Stout held his hands out, palms upwards.

'Not as yet, Sir,' Russell said.

'I've got my men going over the lorry with a fine-toothed comb, Sir,' Lewis added.

'Well, let me know when you have anything, however slight.' Turning to Russell he went on: 'I think you'd better find out what you can about the two dead men: where they've been living, how they escaped capture at the end of the war and if there's any connection with the Miller brothers. Also we need to know more about Rankin. Not only have I got the Chief Constable breathing down my neck but the press are hammering on my door, wanting to know what we're doing about the deaths and asking if there are going to be any more.'

'I hope not,' Russell said, quietly.

'So do I,' the Superintendent said. 'So do I.'

'Right, son.' Russell was in his office with his constable. He was leaning back in his chair, hands clasped behind his head and Weeks was bent forward, his mop of hair tumbling over his forehead as he jotted down notes on his pad. 'The Super has given us a breathing space so we'd better make the most of it.'

'Yes, Sir.'

'Lewis and his men are going over the lorry. Maybe they'll pick up some clues from it this time. You get on to Valiant at the barracks. Find out all you can about Rankin. I'm going to speak to Bruissement and, hopefully, his American friend.' Weeks nodded. 'Right, let's get cracking.'

'Oh well, thank you anyway. Please let him know I called.' Russell put the handset back on the receiver. 'Damn!' he said quietly. Getting a call through to the Commissariat de Police in Boulogne had proved troublesome. First the operator had struggled to make his opposite number in France understand who Russell wanted to speak to. Then, when it was eventually clarified, the connection was lost and it took some time to reconnect. Finally, once they were back in touch it was discovered Bruissement had left the office, hence his frustration.

Russell sat back in his chair and massaged his temples with his knuckles. He was getting a headache. The weather, which had been fine and dry for several days, was on the change. It was becoming increasingly oppressive and there was thunder in the air. Russell realised it was getting dark outside and checked his watch. Just after 2.30 pm. There must be a storm coming. He switched on his desk lamp, which cast a warm pool of light on the open file in front of him. Leaning forward he idly turned the pages, glancing at them but not really reading the words. Getting to the last page he started from the beginning again, this time looking more carefully. He had almost reached the end when he stopped, turned back a leaf and studied the handwritten note clipped to the sheet of paper. It was the account of Spratt's time on *Moonshine*. Weeks had written it down when they arrived back at the station. Known for his eidetic memory, it was bound to be word-for-word accurate. Something struck Russell as being significant.

Apparently the soldier, Rankin, who had absconded, had shouted back at the smaller brother, 'in foreign', according to the ferryman. Russell sat back in his chair and thought about this. If Spratt had recognised the language that Wolfgang had used as being German, in all probability, it was German that the squaddie had spoken too. Most curious. If the soldier had indeed spoken in German, then the chances were that the relationship was more complicated and involved than it had at first appeared. He hoped that Weeks would be able to shed some light on Rankin's background and that it would offer up some clues. He was just pondering this when Weeks burst into the room. 'Sir! You won't believe what I've found out...' He stopped in his tracks, retreated a pace and tapped gingerly on the door. 'S-sorry, Sir,' he stammered in embarrassment.

'That's all right, lad. Sit down, get your breath, then tell me what it's all about.'

Weeks slid into the chair opposite his superior, took a deep breath and began. 'You know you asked me to find out about Rankin's background?' Russell nodded. 'Well, guess what...?'

'He spent some time in Germany.' Russell sat back and linked his fingers behind his head.

'What? How….?' Weeks stammered. 'How on earth did you know that?'

'I *am* a detective,' his boss chuckled. 'Go on, tell me more.'

Weeks took another breath. 'Well,' he began, 'I spoke to Captain Valiant again, only this time he couldn't have been more helpful. He'd anticipated that we'd be getting in touch to find out more about Rankin's background and had already got hold of his file. He said that he wasn't surprised to discover that the soldier had seen active service in Germany during the war. They hadn't talked much about their backgrounds but the captain had assumed he'd fought over there. What did surprise him though, was that Rankin had lived there for some time in the Thirties so knew the country well and spoke the language pretty well.'

'So is that where he met the Miller brothers?'

'That the captain didn't know. There seems to be a missing period after he left Germany and came back to England to sign up in '39.'

'How long was it?' Russell asked.

'Well, that's the curious thing,' Weeks said. 'Apparently his records show that he was living and working in Germany until the summer, when he went off to do some climbing, then he disappeared off the radar until he turned up in London in early September.'

'So he could have met up with the brothers sometime then.'

'I suppose so. But where and for what reason?' Weeks look perplexed, his dark eyebrows almost meeting in the middle as he frowned.

The boat rocked drunkenly from side to side, the bow dipping and rising gently as it met the oily swell. The late afternoon sky was dark and the still air was heavy with foreboding. The calm before the storm.

The small man spoke: '*Richtig! Wir gehen jetzt*'. He pushed the throttle forward, the engine note rose, the bow lifted and the boat surged forward. The coastline, an indistinct smudge on the horizon, grew larger and clearer as they neared the shore.

~o~

'Any news from the hospital?' Russell was leaning round the doorway of his office.

Weeks looked up from his desk. 'Nothing yet, Sir. PC Lee is still sitting outside the man's room. Do you think we should send someone to relieve him? He's been up a hell of a long time.'

Russell put his hand to his chin and thought for a moment. 'Good idea, son.'

'Do you want me to go, Sir?'

The DI shook his head. 'No, I need you here. Is there anyone else free?'

Weeks looked round the empty office. 'Not that I can think of at the moment. Everyone is busy.'

'Ah well, we'll just have to hope he manages to stay awake.' Russell ducked back round the doorway and settled himself in his chair.

~o~

The small man eased the throttle back and the boat nudged against the stone steps leading up to the quay. 'What are you going to do?' asked the man in the soldier's uniform, standing up and holding on to the mast shroud, steadying himself. He was ignored, so after a moment he tried again: '*Was wirst Du tun?*'

'*Setz Dich hin und bleib ruhig!*' the little man growled. The soldier meekly did as he was told and sat down on a pile of rope, looking deflated. Then the bigger man, who had been standing at the side of the boat, stepped over the gunwale, on to the steps and climbed nimbly to the top. He looked back, his large frame looming over the boat, as he tucked a slim blade into the waistband of his trousers. The little man leant out of the wheelhouse and looked up. '*Ich bin zurück zwischen vier und fünf. Vielen Erfolg!*' The other turned and was gone.

Thunder rumbled in the distance. A flash of lightning lit the horizon briefly, then all was dark again. Although it was still afternoon the lights shone from the hospital windows. The bulky figure had been standing in the shadows of the entrance for some time, patiently watching the woman behind the reception desk. He had seen her make several phone calls, talk to a passing nurse then answer a question from a white-coated doctor. Now she was alone. He looked on as she glanced at her watch and put her hand to her mouth to stifle a yawn. She stretched, stood up, and pushing the chair back, moved out from behind the desk. As she walked across the entrance hall and away down the nearby corridor he made his move.

His speed belied his bulk as he pushed open the glass-panelled door, noiselessly crossed the hall and stealthily climbed the stairs, taking them two at a time. Rounding the corner at the top of the flight he saw a uniformed figure seated to the side of a closed door.

He ducked back, concerned he had been seen but grateful he was in the right part of the building. Breathing heavily he waited for a number of seconds then cautiously peered round the corner again. He could hear the man snoring gently. Tip-toeing silently, he approached the sleeping figure, ready to react if he woke. Just as he reached him, the policeman stirred and let out a sigh. The big man was just reaching for the man's throat when he sighed once more, his chin slumped on to his chest and he started to snore again.

Slowly turning the handle on the door, the large figure pushed it open, entered the room and silently closed it behind him. Moving swiftly now, he crossed the floor to the figure lying in the bed. He looked down and could see that the man's breathing was shallow and his eyes were closed. A tube from a bottle suspended on a frame next to the bed disappeared under a dressing on the patient's left arm. Leaning over the bed, he gently lifted the arm and pulled back the bedclothes to reveal a hospital gown, covering the man's chest. Still holding the covers, he reached under his jacket and withdrew the thin blade from his waistband. Then, with one deft movement, he thrust it upwards, into the sleeping man's chest. The man gasped, arched his back but made no other sound. Then he slumped back, a final breath escaping from between his lips. The big man smiled grimly, pulled the bloody knife out, wiped it on the bedclothes then tucked it into the waistband of his trousers.

As he moved away, his boot caught on something, probably the bed frame. He jerked his leg and it came free. Retracing his steps, he opened the door and stepped into the corridor. Just as he was about to walk away, the policeman stirred and opened his eyes. 'What the....!' he began, and started to rise from the chair. He got no farther as the big man smashed a fist into his jaw, knocking him to the ground. He fell into an untidy heap, groaned, then lay still.

The whole thing had taken only a few minutes and when the large figure reached the bottom of the stairs and crossed the entrance lobby, the receptionist had still not returned. As he pushed open the street door there was a terrific crash of thunder, a blinding flash of lightning and the heavens opened.

'Is that Inspector Russell?' The female voice was shaky but controlled.

'Speaking. Who is this?'

'I'm the receptionist at the hospital. I'm afraid there's been a terrible tragedy.' The DI sat up in his chair. He feared the worst but wasn't sure what it would be. 'Your constable has been injured.'

'Is he badly hurt?'

'The doctor says he's got a fractured jaw.'

Russell relaxed a little. 'Oh? How did it happen?'

The receptionist ignored his questions and went on: 'But that's not all...' Russell tensed again. 'It's the man he was guarding...'

'What?'

'He's dead.'

'*Dead*? How?'

'Stabbed, Inspector.'

She went on to explain that an unknown person had got into the man's room and killed him, then felled PC Lee on the way out. Russell thanked her and put the phone down. He let out a heartfelt sigh and resting his elbows on the desk, cupped his face in his hands. This was all he needed. The Chief was going to be apoplectic with rage and he didn't know what he was going to say to him. He'd been banking on the man regaining consciousness and filling in some details. Now that chance was well and truly gone; another victim had lost his life and Russell was no farther ahead with the investigation. He was starting to think that perhaps it would be better if the Superintendent did hand the case over to another team. They might have better luck than he'd had up to now.

The two detectives stood in the hospital room, rain dripping off their raincoats and leaving puddles on the floor. 'It's the same MO as far as I can tell.' John Crooks straightened up after a cursory examination of the man in the bed. 'A thin blade, expertly thrust up under the ribs and into the heart. Virtually identical to the other two deaths. I'll be able to confirm it when I've got him back to the mortuary.' He paused, then said: 'I don't know whether this will help. Have a look.' He lifted the gown covering the man's chest. A vivid scar ran from his navel, to just below his throat.

'My goodness! What on earth is that?'

'I can't be sure but it looks like he had a major operation at some time. Quite unusual I'd say. It's certainly an identifying feature!'

'You're right there.' Russell shook his head sadly. 'Not sure how much help it will be though. I can't seem to make any progress with this case.' He sighed. 'Thanks anyway John, I'll leave you to get on.' Turning to Weeks, he said: 'Come on constable, let's go and see what Lee has to say for himself.'

The injured PC was in a room farther down the corridor. Russell and Weeks entered the room and were greeted by the sight of the constable in the hospital bed, propped up by several pillows, a bandage circling his face. Russell sat down at the bedside, his DC remained standing beside him. 'Well constable, what have you got to tell us?' The officer looked crestfallen. 'Not very much, Sir,' he mumbled.

'How come you didn't stop the murderer entering the man's room? You did see him go in... didn't you?'

His already glum face crumpled even farther and he answered, his voice hardly above a whisper: 'I was asleep, Sir.'

Russell started. 'What did you say?'

'I was asleep, Sir.'

'Oh for God's sake!' Russell ran his hand through his hair and shook his head. 'I don't believe it! You were supposed to be guarding the man and waiting until he regained consciousness.'

'He *had* been up all night, Sir,' Weeks muttered.

The DI exhaled noisily. 'Hmm. I suppose so. My fault for not sending a relief earlier I suppose.' The constable relaxed slightly. Russell's voice softened. 'You'd better tell me what you do know.'

'Well, something woke me and I looked up to see this huge bloke coming out of the room. I started to say: 'What are you doing here?' but I only got the first couple of words out when I saw him swing his fist; it connected with my jaw and knocked me out cold. Next thing I know I'm lying in bed with my face hurting like hell. Sorry.' He lowered his eyes and a pained look crossed his face.

'A big bloke, you say. Can you describe him?'

'Not really. I'd no sooner opened my eyes than he'd landed me one.'

Russell snorted. 'You must remember something, surely? What was he wearing for instance?' Lee's face was a picture of abject misery. 'Anything...?' the DI asked.

Lee appeared to be thinking hard. Russell waited patiently. Then the PC looked up, a ghost of a smile crossed his face. 'Boots.'

'Sorry?' Russell was puzzled.

'He was wearing brown boots. I saw them as I went down.'

'Ah.'

Lee appeared to think even more intensely. 'But not ordinary boots. They had kind of felt tops and I saw a little buckle on the side of one of them.' Russell looked at Weeks who flipped his notebook open and riffled through it. He stopped turning the pages and looking up smiling.

'"They were kind of brown leather at the bottom but with a sort of woollen bit on the top half, and a little strap and buckle on the side". That's what Spratt said when we questioned him about the big German.'

'Hmm. So it was the Miller brother Ludwig who killed the man then?' Russell raised an eyebrow.

'Seems likely, Sir.'

'That's just what we need. A knife-wielding maniac on the loose.'

'Do you think he's a danger to the public Sir?'

Russell rubbed his chin and thought for a moment. 'No, I don't think so. Well I hope not. I guess the man in the hospital bed was his target and he sloped off as soon as the deed was done.'

'But how did he get here?'

'Good question. The last time we saw him, he was on *Moonshine*, heading out to sea.'

'Then they must have turned round and dropped him ashore somewhere.'

'They must have, constable.' The DI slid back his cuff and looked intently at his watch. 'So it was just after six this morning when we last saw the boat.'

'That's right.'

'And it's almost three pm now.' Russell sighed. 'Nine hours. Plenty of time.' Nobody spoke for a few minutes then he asked: 'What's the nearest place they could have dropped him off.'

'Er, Nottery Quay, Sir.' The two detectives looked at the injured policeman, surprised that he'd spoken.

'How do you know that?'

'It's p-p-part of my beat, Sir,' he stammered.

'I see. So how long would it take someone to get here from the quay…assuming he walked?'

The constable thought then answered: 'About three-quarters of an hour, Sir.'

'Damn!' Russell slapped his hand on his thigh. 'That means he could be back there now. Maybe even on the boat, heading out to sea.'

'But Nottery's tidal, Sir.'

'And?'

'High tide won't be until about six o'clock.'

Russell became animated. 'So he can't be picked up until then?!' he said, excitedly.

'Well a bit before. Say half-four at the earliest.'

'So our man will have to lie low until then?'

'I guess so, Sir.'

'*Well done!*' Russell said, rising from his chair, his original anger at the man's negligence temporarily forgotten. 'Come on, lad,' he said beckoning towards Weeks, as he headed for the door, 'we've got a killer to catch.'

～O～

The two men clattered along the corridor, down the stairs, across the foyer and out through the doors. As soon as they left the shelter of the building, the full force of the rain drove down on them, slanting at 45 degrees.

'Damn and blast it!' Russell said, as he sat heavily in the seat and slammed the car door. The rain hammered down on the metal roof as Weeks pressed the starter and the engine coughed reluctantly into life. As they set off the wipers could barely cope with the downpour, reducing the vision to a blur and rendering the car's progress painfully slow. Russell could barely contain his frustration. 'This bloody weather! He's going to be long gone if we don't get to the Quay soon!'

'Not necessarily, Sir.' Weeks almost had to shout to be heard above the noise of the rain. 'It's been chucking it down for an hour or more so that would have slowed him down too. Plus the boat won't be able to cross the bar to the harbour for at least another hour.'

Russell harrumphed. 'I suppose so,' he said, settling himself back in his seat, and controlling his temper with difficulty. As they drove toward the coast, the rain eased a little and Weeks was able to speed up. There was hardly any traffic on the road and, after five minutes they had entered the outskirts of the town and were within sight of the quay. 'Slow down, lad. We don't want to give him any warning.' Weeks slowed the car to a walking pace. 'Turn in here,' Russell said, indicating a narrow track behind a row of black-weatherboard warehouses. 'I've got an idea.'

On the quayside, near where the car was stopped, stood a curious, hexagonal stone building. This small structure was the harbourmaster's office. With windows on five sides it commanded views, not only of the waterside, and out towards the harbour entrance but nearly the whole of the quay. 'If we make a dash for it while it's still raining, we should be able to get in without being noticed.'

'Good idea, Sir.' The two men left the shelter of the car and, keeping close to the timber walls of the warehouses, made their way to the quayside. They waited briefly as the downpour eased.

Then, as it stepped up a gear, Russel nodded, rain flipping off the brim of his trilby, and they ran across the narrow gap towards the office. Luck was with them as he turned the handle. The door was unlocked and it opened easily. They bustled inside and stood panting. The whole exercise had taken only a matter of seconds so it was unlikely that they had been seen.

The interior was barely ten feet across and contained very little, just a couple of stools and a small table with a map of the harbour and a book of tide tables lying on the surface. On the one wall without a window was an old faded photograph of the quay, with a number of sailing boats tied up alongside and next to it, a pair of binoculars, hanging by a leather strap from a hook.

'Ah, good,' the DI said, lifting them down and placing them on the small table. The two men perched on the stools, water dripping off their sodden clothes. After a while, steam starting to rise in the confined space.

The rain was easing, reducing to a mist, with an occasional quick, heavy squall blowing in off the sea and battering the glass. The thunder had reduced to a distant rumble, as the storm moved along the coast. The two men sat for perhaps half an hour, saying little, intent on keeping watch.

There were two or three false alarms when hardy souls braving the elements scuttled by, head downs and muffled in oilskins. The two detectives initially alerted, quickly realised the damp passers-by were just that and relaxed again. As the air in the room heated up condensation began building on the windows. Weeks stood and reached out, preparing to wipe one of the panes with his sleeve. Russell grasped his arm. 'No, lad,' he said. 'Sit tight; it'll clear in time and we don't want anyone to see us moving about.'

'Sorry, Sir, you're right,' Weeks said, again taking his seat. They sat in silence, Russell's unfocused eyes staring into the distance.

After a further ten minutes the DC cocked his head to one side. 'Listen, Sir.' The DI, roused from his reverie, sat up. They could hear the note of a diesel engine approaching.

'You look for the boat, constable, and I'll keep an eye out back.' The pair sat, watching intently. The windows were still smeared with condensation but were clear enough to see anything going on outside. Russell thought he caught a movement in the shadows between two buildings. Weeks spoke, almost in a whisper. 'There it is!' His boss risked a quick glance seaward and could see the dark shape of a vessel heading towards them. He swivelled his head back again, just in time to see the shadow grow into the form of a large man, bent over, making his way across the front of the warehouses. As the engine note grew louder, the man left the shelter of the buildings and, crouching low, jogged in the direction of the edge of the quay.

'*Now!*' Russell said, flinging open the door. The two detectives burst out of the harbourmaster's office and hurtled towards the big man. The boat was slowing, only yards from the quay wall, and Ludwig was still some distance away. He had been taken unawares and as he turned, Weeks launched himself at the man's legs, knocking him to the ground. A lesser mortal would have lain there, winded, but the German was on his feet almost immediately, easily brushing the constable aside. The bow of the boat was practically touching the stonework of the quay.

Wolfgang was leaning out of the wheelhouse. '*Spring auf!*' he cried, his high-pitched voice almost cracking with effort. Rankin stood on the foredeck, one hand gripping a shroud, as he stretched forward his other hand reaching towards the big German. Ludwig made to leap the remaining few yards but Weeks had hold of one booted ankle and he stumbled. Russell rushed forward and, throwing his whole weight at the man, brought him to the ground again, only feet from the edge of the quay. '*Ludwig! Komm schnell!*' The little man was willing his brother to get on board the boat, Rankin stretching even further forward. But with both the policemen pinning him to the ground Ludwig was unable to make any farther progress. Acting quickly, Weeks tried to snap a pair of handcuffs on the man's wrists. But with an almost inhuman roar he flung the detectives aside and stumbled towards the boat. Just as he was about to leap the short distance he caught his foot in a loop of rope lying on the cobbles. Arms windmilling, he fell headlong into the water with a resounding splash, between the boat and the quay. Almost simultaneously, two black police cars came hurtling round the corner and on to the quayside, bells clanging like demented telephones.

The cars screeched to a halt and half a dozen uniformed constables tumbled out. They rushed to the edge of the quay and four of them clattered down the stone steps to a small wooden jetty. Ludwig was thrashing his arms in an attempt to grab the rope that Rankin was now holding over the side of *Moonshine*. Suddenly the fingers of one hand connected and he grasped it. His other arm came out of the water and he gripped the rope and pulled hard, lifting his body more than a foot out of the water. Almost immediately he splashed back into the water, still holding on to it. There was a strangled yell and Rankin crashed down on top of him, overbalanced by the superhuman pull. They both went under, remaining submerged for several seconds.

When they finally surfaced, stunned, the policemen were able to grab the men and, with great difficulty, haul them on to the jetty. Just managing to pin them down they secured Rankin but struggled to get the handcuffs round the giant's wrists. Instead they tied them with a handy length of rope. Seeing the two remaining PCs on the quay, Wolfgang panicked and slammed the engine into reverse. The propeller churned, sending up a plume of spray and the stern dug into the water. As the blades gripped, the boat gathered momentum and powered backwards. After a dozen yards it slewed round, the engine was put into forward gear and *Moonshine* sped off towards the harbour mouth.

Russell and Weeks had picked themselves up and brushed down their wet and muddy clothes as best they could after their tussle with the German giant, who was now being escorted up the steps to the quay. The ducking in the sea and the blow he had received when Rankin came crashing down seemed to have subdued him. The soldier was in an even worse state and two of the PCs were all but carrying him up the slippery stone staircase. Both men stood on the quayside, water running off their sodden clothes and puddling round their feet. Rankin needed the support of the officers to stand up but Ludwig shrugged off a helping hand and stood sullenly, his head bowed and his bound hands clasped, as if in prayer, before him.

Russell walked up to him and began: 'You are under arrest and….' but got no farther. With a roar that wouldn't have shamed a raging bull, Ludwig lowered his head and charged. Russell had the presence of mind to leap sideways and the bulk of the huge man just brushed his sleeve. The constable standing behind him wasn't so quick, or so lucky, and he was knocked flying and hit the cobbles with a sickening thud. A gasp escaped from between his lips. Then he lay still as the German took to his heels and raced away.

'*Quick*! After him!' the DI yelled to the other policemen. They were standing horrified, rooted to the spot. Galvanised into action by his shout, they began running after the retreating figure who already had a head start. As he turned the corner round the warehouses the leading PC was a good 50 feet behind. 'Arrgh!' Russell groaned. 'For God's sake, don't let him get away.'

Minutes passed while Russell and Weeks, the sodden soldier and the winded PC, sitting dazed on the cobbles, waited on the quayside. Russell slid back the wet cuff of his jacket, looked at his watch and let out a grunt of frustration. Then, around the corner of the warehouses a group of blue uniforms appeared, but without the German. '*What!*' the DI yelled, 'Where's Wolfang?'

'We lost him, Sir,' the leading policeman panted sheepishly.

'But both his hands were tied! He was soaked and dazed!'

'I know, Sir,' his companion continued. 'He ducked down an alley, we followed, but by the time we got to the end there was no sign of him. He's a tough brute.'

'Yes, we know that, but he can't have vanished into thin air…. can he?'

'No, Sir.' The five PCs were standing in a dejected huddle.

'Well, go and look again! Search the warehouses from top to bottom. I want that man found! Go! *Now!*' The constables headed back to the warehouses. Russell turned to Weeks then prodded Rankin in the chest with his finger. 'Come on. Let's get this miserable specimen back to the station. Perhaps we can get some sense out of him now.'

'So let me get this straight. You've lost our prime suspect and this…' he pointed a quivering finger at the khaki-clad figure, slumped in a chair. '…this excuse for a soldier has told you nothing?' Superintendent Stout was standing in the doorway of the interview room, his body rigid with anger, his face puce, his eyes bulging. 'That's *it!*' he hissed between clenched teeth. 'You're off the case, both of you!' He turned on his heel and strode to the door. But, before he left the room, he turned and faced Russell and pointed his finger at him: 'And I don't want to see your face around here! You'd better take some leave!' With that, he marched down the corridor and into his office, slamming the door so hard the solid wall shook.

The detectives had driven back to the police station with Rankin and the shaken PC who, despite assuring them he was okay, had been dispatched to the hospital for a check-up. The soldier had been frog-marched into the interview room and pushed roughly into a chair, his dripping clothes turning the seat and surrounding floor dark with seawater. Weeks and Russell had left him to stew while they found dry clothes for themselves. Ten minutes later, each wearing a borrowed uniform jacket, they returned, gripping steaming mugs of tea. As they re-entered the room Rankin had looked up beseechingly. Then he scowled as he realised there was no tea for him. They questioned him for half an hour but he refused to tell them anything they didn't know or had guessed already. He admitted that he had met the brothers before the war but would say no more than that. He wouldn't explain his subsequent dealings with them, however hard they pushed him. Threats of a long prison sentence if he was convicted of being an accessory to murder had little effect, if anything making him more stubborn in his resolve to say nothing.

That was when the Superintendent had walked into the room and laid into them. After he departed, Russell had called for the custody sergeant to put the man in a cell then he and Weeks retreated to his office. They sat dejected, a single-bar electric fire providing enough heat to cause steam to rise from their damp trousers. The PCs had returned from searching the derelict warehouses but had found no trace of Ludwig. He did indeed appear to have "vanished into thin air". 'Well, lad,' Russell asked wearily. 'What do we do now?'

Weeks shook his head, his curly hair flopping over his face and making him look like a scolded spaniel. 'I don't know, Sir... now we're off the case. I've got plenty of paperwork to keep me busy. What will you do?'

As the super doesn't want me around, there's nothing for it but to go back home... and brood.' Not usually given to melancholy, the DI looked thoroughly miserable and deflated.

Normally, when he got back to his little home after a trying day, when nothing had gone right and he started questioning why he had ever become a policeman, his mood soon lifted. With the coal in the stove crackling, Aggie lying contentedly before its welcoming warmth and something nourishing bubbling on the stove, things would drop into perspective and all would become right in his world. But this evening, nothing could cheer him and his mood became progressively bleaker. The dog sensed this and lay quietly, chin on paws and one liquid brown eye looking up sadly at her master. Russell thought Beethoven might help so he put *Sonata 14, The Moonlight*, on the turntable and gently lowered the needle. He sat back waiting for the music to soothe him, as it always did. But it was only a few minutes into the Adagio when, with a deep sigh, he stood again and lifted the needle. Even Wilhelm Kemff's sublime interpretation wasn't helping. 'Come on Ag, let's walk.' The dog immediately came to life and leapt to her feet.

Shutting the door behind him he set off down the path, the dog bounding along in front. The rain had stopped but the heavy grey sky still glowered oppressively. Russell strode along, shoulders hunched and hands thrust in the pockets of his raincoat. Aggie was delighted to be out, her tail up, waving from side to side, and her head down, sniffing among the plants along the side of the stony track. When they reached the end of the path, they both climbed up the embankment that protected the low-lying land from the sea, went over the ridge at the top and clattered down on to the shingle. A blast of wind gusted off the waves, ruffling the dog's shaggy coat and making the hair on Russell's hatless head swirl round like strands of seaweed. The wind's freshness lifted his mood. He straightened up, breathed the ozone-laden air deep into his lungs and crunched along the beach. The shingle strand stretched away towards the horizon. The tide had barely begun to ebb, the waves falling noisily on the shore, sending up showers of spume and small stones. As Russell walked his shoulders lifted, he withdrew his hands from his pockets and swung his arms in time to his steps. This was more like it. He started whistling *Mr Sandman*.

With his mind clearing he thought about his predicament. At the time he had honestly felt that with the capture of Ludwig and Rankin he was about to make a breakthrough. But with the German's subsequent disappearance and the soldier's unwillingness to speak, his hopes of an early resolution of the case had been quickly dashed. He couldn't blame Stout for his anger and actions, he probably would have done the same in the circumstances, but he knew he would feel cheated if another team was brought in and achieved a result. After all, he had already done a large amount of legwork, with Weeks's help, he acknowledged, and it seemed only fair that they should get some of the glory. But he was getting ahead of himself. There was *no* resolution in sight plus he was on suspension. So what could he do?

The new team that Stout was about to put in place would have all the information he had gathered, plus Weeks's copious notes to sift through, so perhaps they might have better luck than he had. A fresh set of eyes could well spot something that had been missed, but he doubted it. He and his constable had been diligent to a fault. Russell was sure they had been as careful as they possibly could have been; they had just been dogged by bad luck. In addition, they had been dealing with a pair of murderers - yes, he was certain they were guilty - who were not only foreign nationals but seemed to have spent most of their time outside the country. Also, the first two deaths had been bad enough but losing the third man had been a cruel blow. Russell was almost certain that the man stabbed in the hospital bed could have been the key to unlocking the mystery.

By now he had walked a fair distance along the beach, his internal dialogue had refreshed his mind and he was starting to feel more determined to do something that would help to unravel the tangled mess this case had become. But what? He stopped and stared out across the grey sea, the dirty-looking waves rolling relentlessly towards the shore. The smell of ozone from the tumbling water filling his nostrils. That's France over there, not more than a couple of dozen miles distant, he thought. France?... Bruissement?... Maybe he was off the case, but there was nothing to stop him doing a little discreet investigating of his own. With that thought he turned, whistled to the dog, who had been playing catch-me-if-you-can in the shallow surf, and set off back home and to the telephone.

'Operator.' The female voice was brusque. Russell could image her sitting in front of a switchboard, a jack plug in her hand, ready to connect him to...

'Ah, yes,' he said hesitantly as he shuffled through his notes, searching for the number. He hadn't expected to be answered so quickly and the switchboard operator had caught him unawares. 'Sorry - just a moment.' He imagined her drumming polished red nails on the countertop. 'Here we are. I need a number in Boulogne.' He was sure he heard a sigh. Or perhaps it was just interference on the line. He recited the number written on the page in front of him and waited while there was a jumble of clicks and buzzes. Then a series of long unfamiliar ring tones.

' 'ello. Bruissement.'

'Guillaume! You're still in the office.'

'Ah, Sonny! But of course. A policeman's work is never done.' The Frenchman sounded genuinely delighted to hear his voice. ' 'ow can I 'elp you?'

'Well, how long have you got?'

Bruissement chuckled. 'All the time in the world for you *mon ami*. What is the problem?' Russell began by telling him about the German they'd rescued and his subsequent death at the hands of Ludwig. Then he went on to outline the watch he and Weeks had kept in the harbourmaster's office; how they had captured Rankin and the big German, only to lose both him and Wolfgang, who had sped off in the boat. Bruissement had remained virtually silent throughout but when the DI told him how the soldier had refused to talk, he couldn't contain himself. 'Poouf!' he exclaimed. If I could get my hands on him...' His voice tailed off. 'Pardon, please continue.'

'Anyway,' Russell said, 'the upshot is, I'm now off the case.'

'And you would like me to help you?' Russell could imagine the twinkle in his friend's eye.

'I rather think so. I believe I would like to talk to your contact in Berlin.

There was a pause, then: 'I have a better idea than that.'

Russell was intrigued. 'What is that?'

'Why don't you meet him?'

'Really?'

'Why not? You would probably make more sense of the information he can give you if you meet face to face.'

'But isn't it a rather difficult journey? After all, isn't he based in Ludwigsburg?

Bruissement let out his breath sharply. 'Pff! Not so difficult, but maybe long. But does that matter? You are off the case, so your time is your own, *non*?'

Russell thought for a moment. He hadn't been in Europe since 1945, and then under very different circumstances. It would be interesting to travel through the continent and see how it had changed, a decade on. 'Hmm, maybe you're right.'

'*Bon!*' Bruissement said. 'I will construct you an itinerary. You will have no problems travelling through France and into Germany.'

Ludwig lay still, huddled under the ragged tarpaulin that had been flung carelessly over a pile of rotting fish boxes in the corner of the ruined building. Despite the smell, he had remained there for some time. With his thick strong fingers, he'd worked steadily at the knots in the ropes binding his hands, only pausing when a clatter of feet on the warehouse floor signalled the entry of his pursuers, making him lie silent, holding his breath. They came close, and one kicked the pile. Another lifted a corner of the canvas, quickly dropping it at the sight of the boxes and letting out a disgusted '*Pooh*' at the smell, but the German remained undiscovered, the thud of their boots fading as they moved on to the next warehouse. He smiled to himself as the rope slid easily from his wrists. No one could tie knots like Wolfgang could. He waited a further 10 minutes then carefully rolled out from under the tarpaulin. He stood, and reaching out with his arms and tipping back his head, stretched, easing his cramped muscles. He walked cautiously to the entrance, the battered wooden door hanging drunkenly from its hinges, and carefully peered out. The light was fading, the grey overcast sky hastening an early twilight. He moved soundlessly out into the alley between the buildings, stopped to get his bearings, then headed purposefully away from the waterside.

Ludwig had trudged along the road leading from Nottery Quay to Collinghurst for half an an hour. A number of times he'd had to throw himself flat in the weeds and scrub at the roadside, as the headlights from a passing vehicle strafed the road, but he had remained undiscovered. After a few more minutes he saw the rutted track and realised where he was. Turning away from the road, he followed it, the fitful moon, appearing fleetingly from behind dark clouds, showing him the way. He was soon at the chain link-covered gates. The moonlight showed a shiny new padlock holding them closed. Grasping it he rattled it hard and cursed. He let go, the metal clanging against the gate, and cast around the ground at his feet. Reaching down he picked up a large chunk of ballast-filled concrete. He lifted it above his head with both hands and brought it down with all his strength. The concrete connected with the padlock, smashing it loose from the chain round the gates. With a satisfied grunt Ludwig put his shoulder to the gates, which now yielded easily. He stepped through the gap, turned and closed them behind him, then headed off towards the shadowy buildings.

Pushing through the undergrowth behind the kiln Ludwig felt his way into the room that had been concealed. He reached out blindly and found the edge of the table and, to his relief, his hand closed round a matchbox. A shake of the box revealed it still contained matches. He took one out and struck it - the resultant flare showed the room in a state of chaos. He guessed the police had been through it and removed everything of interest but, amazingly, he saw that a pile of crumpled clothes had been left in the corner. Just before the match burnt his fingers he spied a stub of candle which he lit with a second match. As the flame spread up the wick it cast a friendly light into the room. Quickly, he shrugged off his still-wet clothes and gratefully pulled on a dry set, not bothered by their grubby state. Once dressed, he found an unopened tin of sardines and, peeling back the lid with the key, greedily ate them with his fingers. The food temporarily satisfied his hunger and the dry clothes comforted his skin. He stood and considered his predicament – and his options.

Saturday

Citroën DS – a front-engine, front-wheel-drive executive car with aerodynamic and futuristic styling and innovative technology, designed by Flaminio Bertoni and Andre Lefebre and launched in 1955.

EARLY THE following morning Russell pulled shirts, underwear and pyjamas out of the opened drawers in his compact bedroom. It had been formed from one of the compartments of the Victorian carriage and there was just enough room for his bed, a slim wardrobe and a small chest of drawers. An overnight case lay open on the bed and he put the clothes in along with his shaving kit, hairbrush and Brylcreem. Weeks had dropped by first thing to pick up Aggie and to bring his boss up to date with the investigation.

'Amazingly,' the DC said, a grin spreading across his boyish face, 'Stout has put me back on the case. I think he realised that it would be quicker for me to brief the new chaps than for them to work it out for themselves.'

'Who are the "new chaps"?' Russell asked.

'Believe it or not, he's put Parker and Barrow on it.'

'*What*?' Russell looked incredulous. 'Bonnie and Clyde? Those two old timers? Blimey, they should have been pensioned off years ago.' His eyebrows were raised to his hairline and his large jaw hung open.

'He feels the case'll be in safe hands,' Weeks said, in an attempt to placate the DI.

'Oh for goodness sake! If they were only a fraction as dynamic as their namesakes, I could understand it but those two...' he shook his head sadly, '...They give real meaning to the word plod.' Weeks looked down and remained silent. 'So what have they come up with so far?' Russell demanded.

'Well,' Weeks began, 'they've ordered a watch on all ports in the county in case Ludwig tries to skip the country.'

Russell exhaled noisily. 'That's no bloody good. If he does try to get away, it'll be at dead of night on a deserted beach, not on some ferry to the continent. What else have the dynamic duo done?'

'Oh, they're organising a thorough search of the derelict warehouses.'

'Well that's a waste of time. The German will be long gone.' Russell furrowed his brow and thought for a moment. 'I'll tell you what *I'd* do if I was him...'

'Weeks looked up. 'What, Sir?'

'I'd get as far away from the coast as possible for the time being - until the hoo-ha dies down at least.' He paused. 'Do you know what I think he might have done?' Weeks cocked an eyebrow. 'Did that little hidey-hole at the brickworks get cleared out?'

'I don't think so. Just the important things: the paperwork and so on, the things we found in the bag.'

'So all the stuff the brothers left behind is still there.'

'Yes,' the DC said slowly. 'I guess it is. No one's got round to clearing it out thoroughly.'

'That's where you'll find him then.' Russell clapped his hands together. 'You'd better tell them to look there. Subtly of course.

Make them think it's their idea. Now let me finish packing, then you can drop me at the station on your way back to break the news to them - gently. I assume they'll be at work today?'

'Oh yes. The Super has cancelled all leave for the foreseeable future and rubber stamped overtime for anyone who wants it. At least until the case is solved.'

A little while later Weeks stopped the car outside the railway station in Collinghurst and Russell climbed out, carrying his case. 'Now you stay there and be a good girl for Johnny,' he said to Aggie - she was sitting on the back seat and looking intently at her master. The DC beamed. It wasn't often that his boss used his Christian name.

'She'll be fine with me, Sir. We'll have fun together.' He turned and ruffled the dog's soft ears. 'And I'll make sure to keep you up to date with what's happening.'

'Thanks, lad. I'll let you know as soon as I'm back.' He turned and went through the entrance to the station. With a toot on the horn, Weeks drove off.

DI Parker and DC Barrow had taken up temporary residence in Russell's office. Parker had a lugubrious face, a drooping pepper-and-salt moustache, tinged with nicotine yellow, and bloodhound eyes. His dark suit was crumpled and the front was pock-marked with white flecks of cigarette ash. He sat back in Russell's chair with his feet on the desk, his scuffed brown brogues crossed one over the other. His constable, sitting on the opposite side of the desk, was quite different in appearance: he had a narrow, weasel face, clean shaven but with red spots where the razor had nicked his skin. His suit was double-breasted, grey and shiny and, despite his slight build, was stretched tight across his meagre frame. It might have looked elegant if it wasn't a couple of sizes too small.

Much mirth had been caused by the fact that the two men's surnames were the same as the notorious American outlaws and robbers, Bonnie and Clyde, especially as their namesakes had achieved some sort of glamour, despite their crimes, whereas the two policemen were the total opposite, uninspired and unexciting. They had been sitting in silence for some time when there was a knock at the door. 'Come,' Parker barked importantly. The door opened and Weeks stepped into the room. In comparison to the other two officers he was normally full of life and enthusiasm but, warned by Russell, now he was deferential and quiet. 'Well?' the DI asked. 'Any news?'

Weeks kept his gaze lowered, his hands clasped in front of him. 'Not as such, Sir. But I've been thinking about Ludwig.'

Barrow turned to look at the other constable, not bothering to hide the contempt he felt for him. 'Us too,' he sneered. His voice was a nasal whine, affected with a slight lisp.

'And?' Parker demanded.

'Umm,' Weeks stammered. 'Just a thought, but I wondered if he might try to get some dry clothes – or food.'

'And who do you think is going to give him those things?' Parker sniffed, reached into his pocket and brought out a battered pack of Capstan Full Strength. Weeks waited while he tapped out a cigarette, placed it beneath his drooping moustache and lit the end with a Swan Vesta. The DI took a deep drag, blew smoke out of his nostrils and coughed noisily.

'I don't think anyone is going to *give* them to him but I wondered if he might have left some somewhere...' Weeks let his voice trail off. There was silence for a while then Barrow turned his back on him and spoke to his boss. You don't s'pose he'll have gone back to the brickworks, do you, Sir?' he whined.

Parker frowned, the cigarette gripped between his thumb and forefinger. Then he swung his feet off the desk and leant forward. 'D'you know, you might have something there, constable.' And turning to Weeks: 'Why didn't you think of that?' Weeks just shrugged, smiling inwardly. The DI took another long drag on his cigarette, coughed again then rose. 'Come on Barrow. Let's see if we can catch him red handed.' As he moved from behind the desk he looked at Weeks and said: 'Hmm, I suppose you'd better come too. And you can drive.'

The three of them walked out of the police station and piled into the Wolseley that was standing outside. Weeks got into the driving seat with Parker next to him. Barrow was just getting into the back set when he let out a yelp: '*What the…?!*'

The DI looked round to see Aggie staring innocently back at him. 'That's Russell's bloody mutt, isn't it?' he spat. 'What the hell are you doing with it?'

'Sorry, Sir, I'm looking after it for DI Russell. He's gone away for a few days and I haven't had time to drop the dog at home.'

'Well just make sure it doesn't get in the way.' Barrow sat as far away from the terrier as he could.

It didn't take much time to get to the turning off the main road and along the track to the brickworks. They bumped down the rutted path, Parker cursing as he was jolted about, until they drew up in front of the gates. Weeks, leaving the engine running, climbed out and walked up to the gates. He saw the chain hanging loose and turned and called back: 'The padlock's been broken, Sir.'

'For God's sake, open the gates and let's get down there. We need to catch the bugger.' Weeks pushed the gates wide, jogged back to the car, climbed in and, shutting the door, drove down to the buildings.

Ludwig was curled up fast asleep on one of the straw mattresses in the little room, his expression serene and his breathing steady, when his acute hearing picked up the rattle of the gates and he immediately snapped into wakefulness. Rising swiftly, he grabbed the bag he had prepared the night before, swung the door open, left the room and pushed his way through the undergrowth. Moving more quickly than a man only just awake had any right to, he made his way along the length of the warehouse behind the kiln and disappeared into the scrubby trees beyond, just as the Wolseley skidded to a halt in front of his hideout. Barrow was the first out of the car, the little terrier hot on his heels. He pushed through the bushes but after a few seconds he came dashing out again. 'He's gone!' he yelled, his voice well into the upper register.

Parker was just emerging from the car, looking even more crumpled. '*What*?'

'Legged it, Sir. No sign of him.'

'Let me see!' the DI snapped, pushing past his constable, almost tripping over Aggie as she came bounding through the undergrowth. He stumbled and just stopped himself from falling. 'Bloody dog!' he said, aiming a kick at the terrier, who easily side-stepped, avoiding his foot. 'Grrr!' Parker mumbled, and disappeared into the hideout. Weeks was close behind, eager to see inside. 'Well he's been here,' Parker said. He reached down and put the palm of his hand flat on the straw-filled sack. 'Warm. He can't have left long ago.' He turned, almost colliding with Weeks, who moved quickly to one side but still received a scowl from the other man. They had emerged into the weak sunlight before Parker spoke again. 'Come on, spread out - let's catch the bugger.'

Ludwig crouched motionless behind a multi-stemmed elder tree, the ragged canopy and his drab clothes rendering him virtually invisible. He watched as the dishevelled figure of Parker came blundering along the side of the building towards him. The German readied himself to leap into action but before the policeman was within 20 feet of the hiding place, he veered to the side and followed the rear wall of the warehouse. Lumbering round the back, he turned the farther corner and disappeared out of sight. Ludwig took his chance and broke cover. Crouching low and keeping close to the wall, he headed back towards the front of the complex. Peering cautiously round the kiln, he could see no sign of the other policemen.

The Wolseley stood, doors wide open, and when he approached the driver's side he noticed the key, still in the ignition. He instantly threw his bag into the car, swung his bulk into the driver's seat and started the engine which immediately roared into life. Slamming the door, he put the car into reverse, swung the wheel hard over and, with showers of gravel and dirt thrown up by the spinning tyres, turned the vehicle to face the way it had come. He banged the gear into forward, dropped the clutch and rammed his foot hard on to the accelerator. The car shot forward, the force causing the two nearside doors to slam shut, and bumped, at speed, towards the entrance, a great plume of dust rising from the rough track. Weeks and Barrow came running out from the far side of the buildings, shouting, but it was too late, the German had got away. They were soon joined by a panting Parker. He bent forward, his hands resting on his thighs, just above the knee, struggling for breath. After a few moments, when he could breathe again, he let out a long stream of invective, initially directed towards the disappearing German but latterly towards Weeks. 'Why the *hell* did you let him get away?!' How the *bloody hell* did he start the car so easily?!' He paused and stood upright. His face darkened and he said slowly: '*Nooo…*' The word came out as a low growl. 'You left the keys in the ignition – didn't you?'

Weeks had never looked more crestfallen. 'Well,' he began quietly, 'we got out in such a hurry…' The DI's eyes began to bulge and, if he'd been a cartoon character, steam would have issued from his ears and nostrils. As it was, he looked fit to explode. 'Sorry, Sir.' the DC said miserably.

A low groan, starting from deep in Parker's stomach, worked its way up to his throat and came out as: '*SORRY*? I'll give you bloody *SORRY*!' Now get up to the road and flag down a car, any car. We need to get back to the station, pronto. And hurry, I'm right behind you!' Weeks turned on his heel and fled up the track, almost disappearing into the cloud of dust thrown up by the Wolseley.

Russell's train journey to Dover was uneventful. He was able to sit in a seat by the window and watch the Kent countryside slide by. Hop gardens, the bines twining ever upwards, were interspersed with apple orchards, the blossom fading as fruit buds formed. Distinctive oast houses, their conical kilns topped with sparkling white wooden cowls, and peg-tiled farmhouses nestled in the soft folds of the gentle landscape. 'Perfect composition for a Rowland Hilder watercolour,' he thought.

The carriage Russell sat in was old and worn, the velour fabric on the seats threadbare and faded. It beat out a regular rhythm as it rattled over the joins in the rails, swaying drunkenly on uneven stretches of track. There had been talk of extending the electrification across the Southern network of railways but, for now, the trains were still steam hauled, witnessed by the smut-specked glass and the curls of smoke drifting lazily past the window. Although relaxed the DI felt a little apprehensive about the journey he was undertaking even though his friend, Bruissement, had assured him he had made all the arrangements and it would run smoothly. Part way through the journey he got up to go to the lavatory. When he returned through the swaying carriage he noticed a newspaper that someone had left behind. As he still had a while before his arrival he picked it up. It was one of the more sensational tabloids but he took it with him so he could have a flick through its pages when he got back to his seat. The paper had been folded over across the back page but when he opened it out the banner headline gave him a shock.

MURDER VICTIM NUMBER THREE

The story went on to outline what the reporter had managed to glean - which wasn't a lot - but it didn't paint the police in a very good light. At least his dismissal wasn't mentioned. He shrugged and sighed, glad to be getting away from it all - for a while at least.

By mid-morning he was boarding the ferry to France. Unlike the Cote d'Azur, he had travelled on a few days before, it was a much older and battle- weary vessel. It had obviously been used as a troop ship during the war, judging by its battered and dog-eared appearance, and Russell was glad when the French coast came into sight. Standing by the rail as the ship slowly nosed into its berth, he easily identified the smiling face of his friend, standing behind the barrier on the quayside. He waved and received a cheery acknowledgement. 'Welcome back to France.' Bruissement's voice came drifting over the closing gap between ship and shore. Russell made his way down the gangplank with the other disembarking passengers. As he neared the quay the Frenchman pushed his way past the barrier and, striding towards him, opened his arms and clasped him to his ample frame in a warm Gallic embrace. Russell, taken by surprise, responded with typical English reserve but was secretly pleased with the reception. 'It's good to see you, Sonny,' Bruissement beamed. 'Come with me, I have a surprise for you.' Grasping his friend's elbow he led him through the customs hall, waved on by the uniformed officials. When they exited on to the street he threw his arm wide and nodded towards a shiny new car standing at the kerb. '*Voila*! What do you think?'

Russell stood transfixed. The car was like nothing he'd seen before. It sat low, its lines more reminiscent of a futuristic space craft than a humble motor car. He couldn't help showing his enthusiasm. '*Wow*! Is it a Citroën?'

'*Mais oui*. It is the new DS, just launched. I 'ave this one on trial for a day or two. Come on, I'm taking you for a spin.' He held the passenger door open, while taking Russell's case and ushering him into the car. After shutting the door Bruissement walked round to the other side and settled into the driver's seat. He turned the key in the ignition and the engine purred into life. Russell, settling back into the soft leather upholstery, was mildly surprised when the whole car started rising.

'*What*?' he exclaimed.

Bruissement chuckled. 'It 'as hydraulic self-levelling suspension. You wait. It is like riding on a magic carpet!' He pushed the column-mounted gear lever forward and the car moved smoothly away, travelling over the cobbled street as though it was smooth Tarmac.

Russell was bemused. 'Where are we going? I thought I had a train to catch?' The Frenchman let out a laugh that started somewhere deep inside him and came out as a throaty roar. 'Gauloises,' Russell thought, but didn't say anything.

Through the laughter Bruissement said: 'Don't worry, you 'ave plenty of time. Just sit back and enjoy the ride.'

Russell relaxed. 'Fair enough, but where are we going?'

'Ah. We are going to a little village called Wissant. There is a restaurant there that is a favourite of mine called Le Vivier. The speciality of the 'ouse is seafood.' He held up his hand before Russell could speak. 'Don't worry *mon ami*, the chef knows you are coming and is making something very special for you.'

The car all but floated over the rough roads through the town and they were soon out in the countryside. They passed through Wimereux, which showed signs of rebuilding after operation Wellhit in WW2. Then the villages of Ambleteuse, Audresselles and Audinghen before arriving twenty minutes later in the village square of Wissant. To one side was the squat bulk of the 15th-century church of Saint Nicholas, next to it the WW1 memorial. Nearby was the half-timbered Hotel Normandy and on the other side of the road, a low stone building, with a tractor and substantial wooden fishing boat on a trailer standing outside. 'That is a *flobart*, a fishing boat particular to this region,' Bruissement explained, as he got out of the car. 'The tractor takes the boat down to the beach and launches it into the sea. They catch some wonderful fish that are served fresh here in Le Vivier!' Russell, getting out of the car to stand beside him, smiled. 'Ah, I am sorry my friend, you don't eat fish. I 'ope you don't mind if I do?'

'Of course not,' Russell replied. 'Just as long as I don't have to.' His eyes twinkled.

'No, no. I said there would be something special for you.' The Frenchman was as good as his word. Once seated at a table in the cosy restaurant Russell was presented with a plate of slim asparagus spears, topped with a perfectly poached egg. He was a little baffled by the scattering of dark crumbs on the dish. 'A-ha!' said the Frenchman. 'That is the surprise. Do you know what it is?' Russell shook his head. 'Truffles!' Bruissement announced triumphantly. 'The patron was out early in the woods and brought them back, just for you. Taste,' he said, gesturing with his knife.

Russell lifted a forkful of the egg and truffle to his mouth, chewed, then swallowed. 'Mmm. Slightly earthy, a little like mushrooms,' he said reflectively.

'*Exactement*!' Bruissement declared. '*Bon appetit*!' The two men ate in companionable silence. Russell with his delicious truffles and asparagus and the Frenchman with a huge platter piled high with seafood, which he demolished manfully, the discarded shells piling up on his side-plate. They drank from the glasses of Sancerre that the waiter had poured, the bottle cooling in an ice bucket. When their plates were wiped clean with chunks of crusty bread, they were cleared away and replaced with heaped bowls of strawberries. The empty wine bottle and glasses were taken away and replaced with golden Beaumes de Venise. Russell, unused to drinking wine at lunchtime, was feeling quite light-headed. When they had finished, Bruissement clapped him on the shoulder and said: 'Come on, *mon ami*, let us get some air. We will take a stroll to *la plage*.'

'But what about the train?' Russell asked, rising from his seat.

'Ah, plenty of time. Come on.' It took only a few minutes to walk the short distance from the square to the beach and soon they were looking out across the flat sand. 'What do you think?' the Frenchman asked.

Russell was astonished. 'It looks just like the beach at Shell Bay!'

'Well that is just over there,' Bruissement said, pointing out to sea. 'Maybe 40 kilometres. On a clear day you can see the coast of England. Today, it is a little misty, *non*?' They stayed, for a few more minutes, taking in the view, then Bruissement said: 'Okay, now we must go, or you may miss your train.'

A little later they were back in Boulogne. Bruissement was standing on the platform of the Boulogne-ville station, Russell, leaning out through the open carriage window. 'Don't forget to ring me when you arrive.' A deep, throaty chuff-chuff came from the Chapelon Pacific locomotive at the head of the train and it began moving out of the station. Russell repeated his thanks for the splendid lunch and car trip, waved then leant back into the carriage and closed the window.

Weeks stood by the roadside anxiously scanning both ways for any sign of traffic. DC Barrow was soon standing beside him, shortly joined by his wheezing boss. 'Where the bloody hell are the cars?' he demanded, between gasps for breath. They stood, a sorry group, for a few more minutes until the sound of an engine caused them to stare along the road. Then, of all things, a police car came into view, travelling at speed and slewing into the brickworks entrance, narrowly missing the three men. The nearside wing and bumper of the car were crumpled. The uniformed passenger wound down the window and leant out: before he could speak Parker gestured towards the damaged car and snarled, 'What the bloody hell happened to you? Beaumont, isn't it?'

The constable in the car was visibly shaken. 'We were out on patrol and just coming round that nasty bend up the road when this madman in a Wolseley came tearing round on the wrong side. Joe, Constable Bruce that is, only just managed to swerve out of the way before we had a head-on. The blighter just caught our wing. We were about to turn round here and give chase.'

'That's our bloody car!' Parker shouted, his face turning puce and his hands clenching into fists. He wrenched the car door open. 'Out!' he said, grabbing Beaumont by the sleeve and pulling hard. The constable tumbled from his seat, the DI slumped in and snapped: 'Get in the back, quick!' The PC and the two detectives piled into the rear of the car, Weeks grabbing the dog, then slamming the door shut as Bruce, driving, swung round in a tight arc, scattering stones and dust, and drove back up the road.

'What do you mean, Sir, your car?' Beaumont ventured timidly.

'It's that bloody German. The bugger stole it.' Parker thought for a moment. 'That's why he was on the wrong side of the road. Forgot he was in England. He turned to Bruce: 'Can't you make this crate go any faster?'

'I've got my foot flat on the floor, Sir, but there are five of us in here…'

The DI groaned. 'Oh, for God's sake, there's always something.' They had travelled a couple of miles and were just rounding a bend in an area of woodland when the constable slammed his foot on the brake and wrenched the steering wheel over. 'What the..!' The passengers were thrown to one side and Parker ended up almost on top of the driver. The car, its tyres screaming, slewed sideways and stopped, just short of the Wolseley, its bonnet buried in the front of an ex-army Bedford QL lorry.

The driver of the lorry was standing in the road, looking at the damage, his flat cap pushed back while he scratched the front of his head. On seeing the policeman clambering out of the car he said: 'Bastard came out of nowhere, on my side of the road.'

The door of the Wolseley hung open, the car empty. Steam rose lazily from beneath the bonnet. Parker, marching up to the man, stood inches from his face and bellowed: 'Where is he?'

The man, apparently suffering from shock, didn't answer quickly enough and the DI held his arm and shook it. 'Well? Well?'

The lorry driver then seemed to notice him and looking sideways and gesturing vaguely with his free arm said: 'Ran off… into woods…that way.'

'Wasn't he hurt?'

'Surprised he weren't killed, the speed he hit the front of me truck.' The man looked again at the damage. 'What am I going to tell my guvnor?' He held his hands up to the sides of his face. He looked a sorry sight, his shoulders hunched under a leather jerkin, his threadbare corduroys bagging round his heavy boots.

'Never mind that. Which way exactly did he go?'

While this exchange was taking place Weeks had walked over to the edge of the woods. He turned and spoke. 'This way I think, Sir. The undergrowth has been flattened.'

'Well get after him…' Parker spat. '…AND you three!' he said, gesturing at the other policemen.

Ludwig ran panting through the trees, his left arm across his chest, cradling his other, bloodied, arm. He suspected it was broken, but for now, the adrenaline of the chase was keeping the pain at bay. His drab clothes were torn and streaked with blood. He had a weeping wound where his head had connected with the windscreen on impact and blood was carving red runnels down his dirt-caked face. Regardless of his injuries he stumbled on, not knowing where he was going but determined to put distance between himself and any pursuit.

The woods were quite dense, with a canopy of mature deciduous trees which inclued oaks, chestnut and birch, dotted with tall pines. Underneath was a tangle of saplings, scrubby holly and elder complicated by snaking lengths of briar. The German stumbled and fell several times, his legs wrong-footed by the muddle of roots and brambles. Once he landed on his injured arm, which caused him to gasp in pain, although he managed to suppress an outright cry, fearful that his pursuers would hear him. Pushing himself to his knees, with his good arm, he took a few seconds to listen. A crashing of footsteps told him that they were hot on his trail, and not that far behind. Rising to his feet, he ran blindly on.

The policemen followed the trail of crushed undergrowth and bruised foliage, Weeks leading, Aggie at his heels, with Barrow and the constables close behind and a struggling Parker bringing up the rear, alternately puffing and shouting imprecations. Suddenly Weeks pointed ahead and shouted: 'There he is!'

Following the line of the detective's arm, Barrow seemed to gain second wind and surged forward, passing the other DC and gaining on their quarry. The German fell again, heavily this time, causing him to stay down for longer. Just as he got awkwardly to his knees, Barrow was upon him, crying: 'Got you, you bastard!' With an animal roar Ludwig tried to throw him off, but the pain in his arm had kicked in and weakened him and the DC was just able to keep him on the ground. In a few seconds he was joined by the other three policemen. Between them, they forced handcuffs round the man's thick wrists and gradually his struggles ceased. Aggie danced round, barking excitedly until a wheezing Parker caught up and aimed a kick at the dog, who easily dodged out the way, but quietened.

Russell sat back in his seat, watching the flat landscape of northern France pass by the window. The arable farmland was dotted with poplars, with groups of willow indicating streams and ponds. He thought the railway here seemed in better condition than the one on which he had travelled to Dover. The seats felt more comfortable and the ride smoother. That was his perception, anyway, or perhaps it was because he was travelling in a different country and feeling just a little excited. Bruissement had chosen a fast train for his journey to Paris and, after a brief pause in Etaples, it passed swiftly through several small stations, only stopping when they reached Amiens.

Russell knew the whole area had been devastated during the First World War and heavily bombed again in 1944. While the train waited in the station he had time to examine the crisp white lines of the new station buildings, designed by Auguste Perret and, like much of the town, constructed in concrete. To his eye, this was as modern as the Citroën DS, his friend had so proudly shown him. The unforgiving utilitarian material should have been cold and hard but somehow the sweeping lines of the platform canopies were refined and elegant. Before long a blast on the engine's whistle and a jerk of the couplings, announced they were on their way again.

In just over two hours after leaving Boulogne, the train was pulling into the Gare du Nord. As Russell alighted from the train, he couldn't help but look upwards at the soaring roof. The station had been built in the mid-19th century in the Beaux-Arts style and its grandeur rivalled any of the London termini. Outside he found a cab and showed the driver a page in his notebook with the name of a hotel that his friend had given him. The driver nodded briefly and pointed over his shoulder with his thumb. Russell climbed into the back of the cab and after a few minutes it slowed to a stop and he was getting out on to the pavement outside Passage Jouffrey, just south of Montmartre. He leant into the car's window but the driver spoke so quickly he was unable to understand how much he was asking for. Taking his notebook out he got him to write down the figure, which he did, with a grunt. Russell counted out the coins which the driver took with a nod, then set off for his next fare.

With the constables supporting him on either side, and Barrow and Weeks close behind, Ludwig stumbled back through the wood towards the road. DI Parker walked on ahead, a grin spreading across his face as he anticipated the praise he was sure would be heaped on him for capturing the elusive German. When they reached the road another police car had arrived at the accident and the lorry driver, still dazed, was being questioned by two constables. Parker strode between the policemen and spoke. 'Right, I want this man taken back to the station…' he gestured towards Ludwig, 'and locked in a cell.'

Weeks, more concerned about the German's broken arm than the wrath of the DI, spoke up: 'Don't you think he should go to hospital first, Sir?'

Parker turned and scowled. He grunted. 'Hmm, I suppose so.'

Turning back to the constables he said: 'Yes, the hospital then. And don't let him out of your sight. Once he's patched up, *then* throw him in the cell.' He turned and got into the passenger seat of the damaged Wolseley, gesturing for the two detectives to get in the back. PC Bruce joined them, climbing into the driver's seat but before he could drive off the DI held his hand and called to the other policeman: 'Remember, once he's fixed up, bring him back to the station. And don't let him get away again!'

'Well done! I wish I'd put you on the case from the beginning.' Parker and Barrow sat facing Stout in his office. Each was holding a glass tumbler with a generous measure of the Superintendent's Laphroaig single malt. Weeks stood quietly behind, barely tolerated and definitely not invited to the party. 'Is he in the cells yet?' Stout asked.

'Within the next half hour, Sir,' Parker said. 'Turns out it was only a fracture - his arm wasn't as badly broken as at first thought. We got a call from one of the constables a short time ago saying he'd been strapped up and they were discharging him.'

'Good. When he gets here I want you to interview him straight away; don't give him the chance to relax.'

Barrow coughed and looked a little embarrassed. 'Um, I don't think he speaks English.'

Stout put his hands to his head. 'Oh for heaven's sake! Is there nothing simple in this case?'

Then a voice came from the back of the room. 'I believe that Lewis, the forensics man, speaks German, Sir.'

'Weeks?' the Superintendent said, furrowing his brow, 'I thought you were off the case?'

'Er no, Sir. You said I could help DI Parker and DC Barrow and I, er, seem to have become involved again.'

'Are you all right with this Parker?'

The DI sighed. 'I suppose so. As long as he doesn't get in the way.'

'Fair enough.' And looking towards Weeks: 'Just don't cock up again.' The DC nodded. Stout went on: 'So what's this about Lewis?'

'Apparently he speaks fluent German. He spent some time in a prisoner of war camp where he picked it up.'

'Right. Go and find him and tell him to be ready when the German arrives.'

'Sir.' Weeks turned and left the room. He closed the door behind him, leant against it and let out a long breath. Shaking his head he set off down the corridor in search of Lewis.

Sunday

Aerial tramway or cable car - *a type of lift using one or
two stationary ropes for support while a third
moving rope provides propulsion.*

THE HOTEL booked by Bruissement was very comfortable and
Russell had slept surprisingly well. The previous evening, with
nothing better to do, he had strolled around the streets of the 9th
arrondissement, soaking up the Parisian atmosphere and finding
his way to Montmartre. Although not a religious man, he could
admire the beauty and grandeur of the Basilica of Sacré-Coeur.
There was an English translation outside the church and he read
that construction was started in the latter part of the 19th century
in the wake of the Franco-Prussian war and it was built as a
symbol of the struggles between the Catholic old guard and the
secular republican ideals. Surprisingly it had not been consecrated
until the end of the First World War. But what he found more
interesting was that it was built of travertine stone quarried at
Seine-et-Marne. The material exuded calcite when wet so, when it
rained, the church was literally washed clean and thus remained
sparkling white.

After an early breakfast he had time, before catching his train
to Germany, to stock up on some provisions for the journey as he

knew that in France non-meat eaters were virtually unknown, and probably frowned upon. A baguette, some cheese, apples and tomatoes as well as a couple of delicious smelling pastries would sustain him. It was a bright, sunny day, and, with the knowledge that he had several hours ahead seated in a railway carriage, he walked the mile or so to the Gare de l'Est. Once in the station he made his way to the ticket office and, using his pigeon French, negotiated the purchase of a ticket to Stuttgart. He was directed to the correct platform where the train was already waiting. He found a seat and settled down in anticipation of the journey.

In the Channel, out of sight of land, Wolfgang sat disconsolately on the helmsman's seat in the wheelhouse, as *Moonshine* bobbed up and down on the oily surface of the sea. It was one of those days when it seemed that just below the rolling waves there was a giant monster in restless mood, tossing and turning, trying to get comfortable.

For as long as Wolfgang could remember, he had been in control of his and Ludwig's lives but now he had no idea of his brother's whereabouts or any clue as how to contact him. His last sight of him was a glimpse of him being pinned down on the jetty at Nottery Quay. Wolfgang was so intent on getting away from the police he had momentarily forgotten his brother's plight. When he was a few hundred yards from the quay he had realised the jeopardy he had left him in and momentarily considered heading straight back. But the thought of them both being in police custody had stayed his hand and he pressed on out to sea. Better one brother free than both incarcerated. Now however, he felt lost. Ludwig had always been there. Wolfgang might have the brains, but without the physical strength of his brother he felt powerless. He had to do something… something positive. But what could he do? He needed to think clearly. He stepped out of the wheelhouse and on to the deck. Walking carefully forrard, holding on with one hand to steady himself against the bucking of the simmering sea, he made his way to the short mast on the foredeck. He gripped it tightly and he stared towards the distant horizon. The day was warm but a fresh breeze helped clear his mind.

Now, if the police had managed to hold on to Ludwig, which, knowing his strength, was by no means certain, he would presumably be in a police station, probably in a cell. They would try to make him talk, give them information about the Nazi scum they had disposed of, but he knew his brother would hold out. It would take more than some weak English policemen to get him to give up their secrets, of that he was certain. But if - and it was a big if - they did manage to get anything out of him, it could jeopardise their plans. They still hadn't finished what they had sworn to do, all those years ago and Wolfgang wasn't prepared to give up until the task was complete. There was only one thing for it. He would have to try, somehow, to rescue Ludwig. With that resolve he made his way back into the wheelhouse, started the engine, pushed the throttle forward and turned the bow towards the English coast.

'What did he say?' Parker growled. He and the man from forensics were sitting on one side of a battered table, its surface ringed with stains from tea mugs and burns from cigarette ends. A cuffed and sullen Ludwig sat opposite them. Barrow leant against the wall to one side. The German had grunted a reply to a question that Lewis had translated for the DI.

'Sorry, I didn't catch it, Sir.'

'Well ask him again. Why did he kill those men?'

'Yes, Sir.' Lewis turned towards the German. '*Warum haben Sie diese Männer getötet?*'

Ludwig lifted his head slowly and looked directly at Parker. '*Ich weiß nicht, was Du meinst.*'

Parker held his gaze but spoke to Lewis. 'What did he say this time?'

'He said he doesn't know what we are talking about.'

The DI let out a groan of frustration and slumped back in his chair. 'Of course he bloody does!'

This had been going on for more than an hour. If the German bothered to answer the questions Parker put to him through Lewis, it was with a non-committal or negative reply. Suddenly he stared straight at the inspector and said, in perfect English: 'I would like a cup of coffee.'

Parker sat upright, with a startled look on his face. 'You speak English!'

'*Nein,*' Ludwig said quietly, and dropped his gaze to his hands, linked together on the desk.

'Oh for Christ's sake, get him a coffee! And one for me, too.' Barrow straightened up and left the room.

~o~

Ludwig pushed the cup away, a look of distaste on his face. '*Das schmeckt furchtbar. Ich habe keine Lust es zu trinken.*'

Parker leant quickly forward. 'What was that?'

'Er, he doesn't like the coffee, Sir,' Lewis said quietly.

The DI sat backed and exhaled noisily. 'He can please himself then. Ask him again, why he killed those men.' Lewis translated but there was no answer from the German. He just shrugged and shook his head. 'Oh for Christ's sake!' Parker snapped. 'We're getting nowhere fast. He pushed back his chair and stood up abruptly. 'Right, that's it for now. Put him back in the cell.'

The coast of England was in sight and Wolfgang was now more certain in his resolve. *Moonshine* was steadily heading shoreward, the bow cleaving the sea, a crisp curl of white foam either side, softening as it slipped along the hull, joining the creamy wake astern. Once sure of his bearings, he headed towards the conspicuous landmark of the Martello tower on the shore at Shell Bay. He kept the engine at a quarter throttle, driving the boat into the shallows, until the bow nosed into the soft sand, a few yards from the beach. Satisfied, he switched off the engine and made his way along the now still deck. He stood scanning the shore for movement. After a few minutes he was satisfied the beach was empty and, unlashing a short wooden ladder, he lowered it over the side, hooked it on the gunwale and climbed down into the shallow water. Taking a line and tying it to a convenient stump, he secured the boat so it would not float away on the incoming tide. The day trippers had gone home but he hoped that the ferryman would still be plying his trade, and not yet sinking a pint.

Wolfgang made his way past the Martello tower, his built-up boot dragging in the dry sand, causing him to limp more than usual. He found the effort tiring and was glad when he reached the wooden jetty. He rang the bell then sat down on the boards to wait, closing his eyes and breathing hard after the effort of trudging along the beach. Within a few minutes he heard the splash of oars and looked up to see Spratt's blue boat approaching. The ferryman glanced briefly over his shoulder, checking he was on course for the jetty, but without noticing who was waiting. This suited Wolfgang as he preferred to maintain the element of surprise. And surprise Jack he did.

The boat bumped against the timber work, Jack shipped his oars and turned to throw a line over a post. As Wolfgang got unsteadily to his feet, the ferryman saw who had called him and his jaw dropped. 'What the bloody 'ell...?'

The German grinned. 'Hello, Jack. Are you not pleased to see me?'

All Spratt could do was splutter. 'But, but...'

'I need your help, Jack.' He paused while the ferryman stared, open-mouthed. 'Do not worry, I will make it worth your while.'

Jack regained his wits, and tried to push the boat off. 'You'll be lucky,' he spat, 'after last time!'

Wolfgang grabbed the line looped round the post with his left hand and pulled it tight. 'Not so fast.' The boat jerked to a stop.

'I'm not 'elping you,' Jack growled.

'I think you are.' Wolfgang was sure of his ground now.

'Why should I?' Spratt tried to free the rope but Wolfgang held on tightly.

With his free hand he reached into his jacket pocket and withdrew a handful of notes. 'Will this help?'

Spratt's avaricious nature overcame his desire to get away and he relaxed his grip on the rope. ''Ow much?'

'Shall we say ten pounds?'

'20!'

'What about 12?'

'15!'

Wolfgang appeared to think for a moment, then smiled. 'You drive a hard bargain, *Mr* Spratt. Very well, 15 pounds. Now this is what I want you to do. I wish to know where my brother is.'

'But I don't know. 'Ow would I?'

'I *know* you don't,' Wolfgang said patiently, 'but I want you to find out.'

'But 'ow?'

'First of all, you go into that public house at Compass Point…'

'The Shipwrights Arms?'

'Yes, that is what it is called. And when you go in there, make some *discreet* enquiries. I'm sure that old sailor…'

'Captain Salt?'

'Yes, that is him. I'm sure he has, how you say, the ear of the police. I want to know if they have Ludwig in their police station.'

'But what if 'e don't know?'

'I think that is unlikely, but if it *is* so, we will have to think of something else. However, from what I have heard, he will.'

Jack slumped back on the thwart in the boat. 'So if I find out where 'e is, an' I'm not makin' any promises, you'll give me the cash?'

Wolfgang smiled a thin smile. 'Oh you will.' He held out a white five pound note. 'This is by way of a deposit.' Spratt snatched the note. 'You will get the rest when I have the information. Meet me here, at the same time tomorrow. Now go. And tell no one of this meeting.' The ferryman stuffed the fiver into his pocket, slotted the oars back into the rowlocks, nodded towards the little German and pulled strongly across the estuary. Wolfgang, the smile replaced by a frown, made his way dejectedly back across the beach. The enormity of the task ahead hit him again and he was not sure he could make it happen.

While he had been talking to Spratt the tide had risen and now *Moonshine* was afloat, tugging at her mooring. He untied the rope, waded through the water and laboriously climbed the ladder. Once on board, he hauled it up and stowed it on the deck. Back in the wheelhouse he started the engine and turned the bow out towards the channel.

~o~

Wolfgang thought he had been careful in ensuring the coast was clear before his meeting with the ferryman but, unknown to him, they had been observed. Two tousle-headed boy scouts had been innocently setting up camp when they heard *Moonshine* approach the shore. Curious, they had dropped to the ground and wriggled to the edge of the dunes. They remained hidden behind clumps of marram grass while Wolfgang had made his laboured way to the jetty, near to where they were hiding. The onshore breeze had allowed them to hear some of what had passed between the two men.

As the boat grew smaller, they looked at each other, astonished. 'Blimey! What was all that about?' Sandy, the blonde one, said.

'Whatever it was, it didn't sound right,' Christopher, his dark-haired pal, replied. 'What should we do?' He sat back on his heels, a troubled look on his face.

'Isn't your mum's brother a policeman or something?' his companion asked.

'Uncle Sonny? Yes, he's a detective inspector,' Christopher replied, with pride in his voice.

'Well let's tell him then.'

That's a good idea.' he replied brightly. Then he furrowed his brow. 'Blast, we can't.'

'Why not? Sandy asked.

'Mum said he's gone abroad for a few days. His constable, Weeks, is looking after Aggie.'

'Well let's tell him then.'

Christopher looked thoughtful. 'I suppose we could,' he said slowly.

'Do you know where he lives?' his friend asked eagerly.

'Yes. Not far from Uncle Sonny's railway carriage, although he's got a proper house - well sort of - more of a shack really. What's the time?'

Sandy looked at his wristwatch. 'Quarter past five.'

'I suppose he'll be finishing work soon. How long do you reckon it'll take us to get there?'

'Half an hour if we cut across the dunes.'

'What are we waiting for then?' Christopher got to his feet. 'Come on, let's get going.'

The two boys knew the dunes well and made good progress, reaching the stony track in 25 minutes. They passed Russell's railway-carriage home and several other eccentric buildings, continuing along the track until Christopher stopped in front of a small, neat dwelling. Its single story was timber framed with flat white panels, probably asbestos sheet. The roof was clad in faded red tiles, laid in a diamond pattern. The garden, like the others, had no soil, just shingle, and was dotted with Red Valerian and Euphorbia. A Tamarisk hung over the fence along the front, a muddle of untidy branches. Mexican fleabane grew in profusion along the path to the front door. There was no sign of life and just as the boys were wondering if they had made a fruitless journey, a plume of dust and the sound of an engine announced that a car was coming along the track. The vehicle slowed to a halt in front of the house and as soon as the driver opened the door, Aggie jumped out and bounded over to the boys, leaping up at them, her tail wagging furiously. She was followed by Weeks who gave them a cheerful grin. 'Hello lads. What are you doing here?' he asked.

'So he won't talk either?' Superintendent Stout was beginning to wonder if he had made a mistake after all. Bringing in the two detectives sitting across the desk in his office was starting to look like an error of judgment.

Parker looked even more crumpled and crestfallen than usual. 'Afraid not, Sir. Either he refuses to answer my questions or says he doesn't know anything.'

'What about the squaddie, Rankin?'

'He's still in the cells, Sir.'

'Well get him out and have another go at him. Really lean on him this time.'

~O~

'I told that other detective... Russell... I know nothing about them two Germans. How long are you going to keep me here?'

Parker got up and walked slowly round to the other side of the battered table, leant down close to the soldier and whispered directly into his ear. 'We'll keep you as long as we need to.' Then he stood up and shouted: 'SO START BLOODY TALKING!' walked back to his chair and sat down. He pulled a cigarette from the packet on the table, put it between his lips and lit it. Rankin was visibly shaken by the outburst but kept his mouth tight shut. Parker blew out a plume of smoke then spoke, more quietly this time.

'Let's try again. We know you drove the lorry that Wolfgang and Ludwig used to dump the body in the water at Compass Point. We also know you drove it to Shell Bay to meet them on the *Moonshine*, and I dare say you were at the building site as well as at the brickworks.' He raised his eyebrows and cocked his head to one side but Rankin remained silent, his arms folded protectively across his chest. 'Don't worry, we'll be able to prove this before too long.

'The fact that you were seen on Moonshine with the brothers at Shell Bay is pretty damning but when you fell overboard at Nottery Quay and we fished you out of the drink it is fairly conclusive that you are tied up with them, don't you think?' Rankin sat silently, looking down at his hands. Parker banged his fist so hard on the table, the empty tea mugs leapt in the air and a pen clattered to the floor. 'WELL?'

Rankin looked up at the detective. 'S'pose so,' he mumbled.

They sat in silence for a minute or so then the DI tried another tack. 'How did you meet?'

Rankin looked perplexed. 'What? Oh, how did we meet? Well....' He leant back in his chair, put his hands in his lap and frowned. He had obviously decided to start talking. 'It was in Germany. At the end of the war. I was out there fighting for me king and country...' Parker tutted but the soldier went on: 'I stayed on after the hostilities was over. I was involved in...' he paused, '... let's say, in a little buying and selling.'

'You mean the black market.'

'You could call it that. Anyway, things was going well...'

Barrow piped up for the first time. 'You were making a killing.'

'I wouldn't say that, but I was doing okay. Then something happened.'

Parker cocked an eyebrow and stubbed out his cigarette. 'Go on.'

'I weren't the only one involved in... the black market.' he said quietly. 'There were a couple of local fellas. For some reason they thought I were moving in on their territory, undercutting them and pinching their customers...' He was visibly warming to the task of explaining his presence now. 'I weren't of course, but that's not how they saw it. They started to get nasty.'

'How do you mean, nasty?'

'At first, just threats: 'Keep away from *our* customers, or else!' That sort of thing. To begin with I didn't take it seriously. Carried on as normal. Then things changed.'

'Why, what happened?'

Rankin shuffled in his seat and, when he was more comfortable, he continued. 'I had this young chap working with me. German he was. He ran errands and delivered goods, that sort of thing. He was pretty reliable so I was surprised when he didn't turn up for work. I left it a couple of days then made some enquiries, discreet like. No one had seen him. I were getting a bit worried so went round to his apartment. He was there all right. He only opened the door a crack. Didn't want to let me in. Finally, after talking for a while I persuaded him.'

When he did open the door I couldn't believe me eyes. He was a mess. He'd been roughed up good and proper. Cuts all over his face, a black eye. By the way he winced when he moved, a broken rib or two. He didn't want to tell me what happened at first. Finally he broke down in tears and sobbed. Turned out it were these other fellas giving me a warning.

'I was furious and wanted to get straight after them. But this young chap pleaded with me not to. They'd told him if I tried anything, they'd break his legs - and mine. By the time they'd finished with our faces, we'd never win a beauty contest. This took me aback a bit, I can tell you.'

'So what did you do?' Parker knew this wasn't the whole truth, but let him carry on.

'I needed time to think. I didn't want to leave him but he said he'd be all right. But, he didn't want anything to do with my business any more. I told him I understood. I gave him some money to help him out. He wouldn't take it at first but I insisted. It was the least I could do. Then I went to a bar I used regular, ordered a beer and sat at a table in the corner.

'I was on my second bottle when these two Germans came up to me. One was little. The other, a giant of a man.'

'And you hadn't seen them before?'

'What? I, er, no, I hadn't.'

Parker pushed the ashtray aside and opened a file that was on the table. He turned a couple of pages. 'Let me see. According to your army records...' A look of alarm crossed Rankin's face. The detective went on: '...According to your records, you spent some time in Germany *before* the war, with a German family. Now that family wouldn't happen to be called Miller, by any chance, would it?' Parker exchanged a smug grin with his constable. 'Well? I'm waiting.'

Rankin sighed noisily. 'I suppose you'll find out sooner or later. So yes, I did spend time with them in '39. But once the war started, we lost touch. Different sides, see. By the way, they were called Müller then.' Parker made a note on his pad. 'Anyway, you can imagine how surprised I was to see them. 'Specially after six years. They seemed quite pleased too...' He smiled at the memory. 'We sat down and had a good catch up. Reminiscing about the great times we'd had before the war. Well, me and Wolfgang did, Ludwig didn't say much. Never does.'

'Yes, we know.' Another look was exchanged between the two policemen. 'Go on.'

'Then Wolfgang asked, all innocent like, what I'd been doing since the end of the war. I told him the same as you, a bit of buying and selling. He smiled. "And now you are in a bit of trouble," he said. 'What do you mean?' I asked. Wolfgang smiled again. "Word gets around." So I told them what had happened. "Don't worry," he said, "we'll soon sort it out for you." Then he looked at his brother, "Won't we, Ludwig?" Ludwig grinned and said nothing but nodded his head. Then Wolfgang drained his glass and stood up. "Come on brother," he said, "we've got work to do." He looked at me and smiled that funny lopsided smile of his and said: "We'll be in touch." Then they left.

Russell settled back in his seat. The suburbs of eastern Paris soon gave way to open countryside. The train was surprisingly comfortable and he sat back and enjoyed the journey. When he arrived at Vitry le François he had to change trains. He found the platform for his connection to his next destination, Metz, and was soon on his way again, dozing happily. He hadn't thought that he needed so much sleep but perhaps it was because he was relaxed after the tension and drama of the past few days. A couple of hours later the train pulled into Metz; he stood up, stretched luxuriously and made his way on to the platform. He had to wait a little longer this time but just as he was beginning to get anxious, the train pulled in and he was on his way again.

On this stretch of the journey Russell got out his picnic. At home this action would have been greeted with surprise if not hostility but, here in France, no one raised an eyebrow. In fact he saw at least three other people in the carriage doing the same thing. His next stop was Strasbourg, where the customs officials came aboard the train. The man who examined his papers looked at Russell and smiled, but refrained from asking what an English detective was doing on a train bound for Germany. He returned them and moved silently on, leaving Russell sitting in his seat, smiling too. The formalities were soon over, the officials left the train and, with a mournful blast from the locomotive's whistle they were on their way again.

Sandy and Christopher were sitting side by side on a piece of driftwood in Weeks's front garden. He had found a bottle of lemonade, which still had some fizz, and each of the boys clutched a chunky glass full of the bubbly liquid. 'Right lads, now you've got a drink and you're sitting comfortably, you'd better tell me what you've seen.'

'Well, Sir...'

Weeks grinned. 'I think you can call me Johnny if you like.'

Sandy grinned back. 'Thank you, Sir, er, Johnny. Well, we were just setting up camp in the dunes when we heard a boat approaching the beach.'

'We were surprised,' Christopher went on, 'because we picked that spot as no one goes there, once the trippers have gone home. Anyway, we heard this engine and when we looked we could see a boat coming in to the shore.'

'Don't worry, Johnny, We made sure we couldn't be seen,' Sandy added.

'So what happened next?'

'This little man put a ladder over the side of the boat and climbed down. We saw him wade through the shallow water then walk along the beach. Thing is, he seemed to find it difficult.'

'How do you mean?'

The boys looked at each other. Sandy continued: 'We weren't close enough to see clearly but he seemed to have something wrong with his leg.' Weeks tilted his head to one side and raised a quizzical eyebrow. 'I dunno, Johnny, he could walk on it but it seemed to drag in the sand.'

Weeks nodded. 'I think he may have had a built-up boot.'

'Oh yes! That must have been it!' Christopher enthused.

'Go on.'

'Well, he came right past us, climbed on the jetty, rang the bell then sat down. It wasn't long before that ferryman, Jack Spratt, came across the estuary in his boat.'

Sandy was eager to carry on. 'When he saw the little man he tried to go back but he held on to the rope so he couldn't. Anyway, they had a conversation and some money was handed over.'

'Did you hear what they said?'

The boys exchanged a glance. Christopher took a gulp of his drink. 'Not all of it – just bits.'

'What can you remember?'

Furrowing his brow Sandy said: 'I think the little man wanted Jack to find something out for him.'

'Any idea what?'

'We couldn't hear very clearly but I think it was something about his brother?'

Christopher butted in: 'Yes I remember, he wanted to know if his brother was in the police station!'

Weeks leant forward. 'Are you sure?'

'Yes!' said Sandy eagerly, 'that's why he gave him the money!'

'Well done. Can you recall any other details?

'Umm. Oh yes. He told Spratt to ask that captain at Compass Point, You know, the one who owns the place, and the railway.'

'Captain Salt?'

'That's him!'

'Was that it then?'

Sandy looked at Christopher. 'Can you think of anything else?'

His friend shook his head slowly. 'I don't think so.' He paused, then spoke again. 'Oh yes, he told the ferryman to meet him there tomorrow.'

'Do you know when?'

Another pause. 'I'm not sure, it was difficult to hear everything. Maybe the same time? Sorry.'

'Don't worry. You've been really helpful.' Weeks looked up. He could see the sun getting lower in the sky. 'Now, can I give you a lift back to your camp?'

Christopher tipped up his glass and drained the last drops of lemonade. 'No that's all right, Johnny,' he said rising, 'we'll cut across the dunes and I reckon we'd be back before you in the car.'

'Fair enough,' Weeks said, grinning at the boys. 'You might have to come into the station to repeat all that. I'll let you know.'

'Ok, Johnny,' Sandy said. 'Glad we could help. Thanks for the drink.' With that the two boys trotted out of the garden and back along the track, waving over their shoulders as they went, Weeks holding Aggie's collar to stop her racing after them.

~o~

DI Parker had paused the interview and asked for tea to be brought in. It was getting late, plus it was Sunday, and everyone was feeling jaded. However, he was determined to get more out of the squaddie before the day was done, hence the refreshment. Mugs of thick brown liquid were placed on the table, along with a chipped bowl of sugar and stained teaspoon. Rankin helped himself to three heaped spoonfuls and stirred them into his tea.

'Right, you were telling us what happened when you hooked up with the Miller, sorry, *Müller* brothers again,' Parker growled.

Rankin took a swig of his tea, put the mug down in front of him, cupped his hands round it and cleared his throat. 'Well, I didn't know what they were going to do. But I felt much happier having them around.'

'Why was that?'

''I knew what they, well Ludwig especially, was capable of.'

'How do you mean? Had you seen him in action before?'

The soldier took another drink of his tea. 'Yes,' he said, his voice almost inaudible.

'Pardon?'

'Yes, I had - ' slightly louder.

'When was that?'

Rankin sighed. 'Well, you've worked out that I knew them before the war. So I might as well tell you.

'I met them in the mountains, near Innsbruck. It was summertime. I'd gone to do some climbing there. I was out one day and didn't realise how long it would take to get back down from the mountain. It was getting dark and I was a long way from the village where I had me digs. I lost me way and was stumbling down when I came across a log cabin, quite high up. There was lights in the windows and smoke coming out of the chimney. I were desperate so I banged on the door. It were opened almost immediately. I got quite a fright.'

'Why was that?'

'It were Ludwig, and he filled the doorway. I'd never seen anyone so huge before. At first I thought I'd made a big mistake. Then he stepped aside to reveal his brother. He saw I was in a fix, and invited me in. There were another man there who turned out to be a third brother, Franz. We spent a very nice evening. They fed me and gave me plenty to drink and asked me to stay the night.' He smiled at the recollection. 'When they found out I spoke reasonable

German they was delighted. They said the cabin belonged to their family and asked me to stay for as long as I liked.'

Next morning Ludwig went down to the village. Turned out it weren't so far away. Collected me things. Paid me bill at the guesthouse where I'd been staying. Wolfgang, Franz and me had breakfast. When their brother returned, the four of us set off to explore the mountains.'

Parker looked perplexed. 'Wait a minute. We've had no mention of a third brother.'

Barrow leant across and flicked through the papers in the file on the table. 'Here, Sir,' he said, holding up the photograph that had been found in the secret hideout at the brickworks.

'Oh, yes,' Parker said slowly. 'I wonder what happened to him?' He looked up at the squaddie, just too late to see the pain that passed across his face. 'Well, carry on.'

Rankin took a deep breath. 'I had a wonderful time. Some of the best days of me life, I must say. Just walking, climbing and talking. Some of the steeper climbs were too much for Wolfgang. But he was happy to sit and wait. Quietly smoking, or just watching, while I climbed with his brothers.'

'How long did you stay with them?'

'About three weeks in all.'

The DI consulted the notes he had been making. 'You mentioned you'd seen Ludwig "in action" before.' He looked quizzically at Rankin.

'Yes. Let me think.' The soldier considered for a few moments. 'We'd been out climbing as usual. For a change, we'd walked down to a little town called Mutter. Then went up on the Muttereralmbahn.'

Parker snorted. 'What's that when it's at home?'

'It's a cable car that takes you higher up the mountain.'

'Mmm, I see. Carry on.'

'Well, everyone was cheerful as we went up. Even Ludwig said a few words. That were quite unusual. We reached the top and got out. I remember the air was real clean and fresh. I felt at ease and happy. As usual, Wolfgang was content to stay there while me and his brothers climbed higher. He said he would enjoy looking at the scenery. Maybe have a hot chocolate at the café there. Told us not to rush, but take our time.

'We set off up a path. It were quite narrow and winding so every now and again we had to stand back, pressed against the rock or balanced on the edge, to let those coming down get past. After a while we got to a really narrow bit. There were a rock face on one side and a steep drop on the other. Ludwig was leading, me next, Franz bringing up the rear. I could see a group of four young blokes coming down. They was laughing and joking. We stood to the side of the path.'

Getting by the big German meant they had to slow down and creep by him. Getting past me was a bit easier. It should have been the same with Franz. But, with the mood they was in, jokey like, they thought it were funny to bump into him. Made him lose his balance and fall backwards. I grabbed him. Just managed to stop him from tumbling down the steep slope. Instead of saying sorry, the youths thought it was really funny and went on their way, laughing. In a flash, Ludwig ran past us and grabbed two of them by their collars. He actually picked them off the ground. Dangled them over the edge of the sheer drop. He was so mad. He yelled: '*Sie sollen sich entschuldigen!*"

'What does that mean?' Parker wanted to know.

'Oh, it means: '"You will apologise!".'

'I see. What happened then?'

'The other two turned white. They began to say sorry and to

plead with Ludwig. He were still dangling them by their collars. I was sure he was going to let them go over the edge. But after what seemed an age, but was probably only a few seconds, Franz shouted: *'Nein Ludwig! Mach das nicht!'* and reluctantly he brought them back above the path where he dropped them in a heap. Before they could get up he landed a massive kick to the side of one. Trod hard on the hand of the other. Both yelled out in pain. They quickly realised there could be more of the same to come. They got to their feet, and without turning round, stumbled down the path. I were shaking. I was sure he would have dropped them over the edge if Franz hadn't spoken. That's when I knew what Ludwig was capable of.'

Russell's train drew into Stuttgart station. It had been a long, if uneventful journey and he hoped Bruissement's contact would be there to meet him. He wasn't disappointed as, walking along the platform towards the exit, a smiling figure came towards him with a hand extended. 'DI Russell?'

He took the proffered hand and received a firm handshake. 'That's right. Call me Sonny.'

'Great. My name's Greg Judd. Guillaume told me about you.' Greg was not much more than five feet tall and as thin as a rake. He had short dark hair, neatly parted to one side and a large pair of dark-rimmed glasses that magnified his eyes. His smile was infectious. 'Right, come on then.' His accent was East Coast American and refined. 'Give me your case,' he said, taking Russell's luggage, 'and follow me.' With that, he set off at a cracking pace along the platform.

He led the way out to a maroon Opel Kapitän parked by the kerb, put the suitcase in the boot and opened the passenger door for Russell. Climbing into the driver's seat he looked at his watch and said: 'It's half after six. Do you want to check in to your hotel and freshen up or shall we go straight to the office and have a look at some papers?'

'That sounds fine. It would be good to do something after sitting in trains for so long.'

In less than half an hour, during which time they made pleasant conversation, learning a little about each other, they reached the quiet market town of Ludwigsburg. Turning off the High Street, Judd stopped the car outside an unassuming townhouse, the headquarters of the organisation known in short as the Z-commission - the full title, a more unwieldy 'Central Office of the State Justice Administrations for the Investigation of National Socialist Crimes'. Leading Russell up the steps to the front door, he put a key in the lock, opened the door and ushered him inside. 'There's often someone working late,' he said, 'but I guess everyone's packed up and gone home tonight.' He led the way up a wide staircase to a large landing and opened the door to one of the rooms leading off it. The room had a desk and two walls lined with shelves, piled high with files. The floor was also littered with more folders, some of the stacks teetering precariously. The American moved a pile of papers off a chair and said: 'Please sit, Sonny. Sorry about the mess. I never seem to get to the end of the files before another lot are dumped on me.' He sat on the chair at the other side of the desk.

'Sounds like a tough job.'

'Well it is and it isn't. I generally enjoy the work. There's nothing more satisfying than tracking down one of the SS men, finding out where he's hidden himself and starting the process of bringing him to trial. But it gets frustrating when you reach a dead end, usually when you're this close to getting your man.' He held out his hand with his thumb and forefinger a fraction of an inch apart. 'Then you've got to start all over again.'

'What's your success rate? I mean, how often *do* you get your man?'

Greg furrowed his brow and thought for a moment. 'Difficult to say.' He shuffled some papers in front of him. 'Not as often as I'd like, but then many of the Nazi officers covered their tracks well. However, I've had some success with tracking down your dead Germans.'

'Really?' Russell leant forward.

'That's right. Your two mystery men…' He shuffled the papers some more until he found what he was looking for. 'Ah yes, our friend Bruissement passed on the details of…' he paused and turned a couple of pages, '…of Rudolf Bausewein and Kaspar Bockelmann. Bausewein was an Obersturmführer and Bockelmann an Untersturmführer, both fairly low-ranking officers. I was able to delve into our archive and discover what they were involved in. It would probably be instructive if I gave you a bit of background.'

Russell nodded. 'Go on.'

The American turned a few more pages in the file and took one out. 'Well, in July 1933 the German government instituted what was grandly called 'The Law for the Prevention of Progeny with Hereditary Diseases'.'

Russell shuddered. 'That doesn't sound all that pleasant.'

'It sure wasn't. This law called for the sterilisation of all persons who suffered from diseases considered hereditary. It included mental illness, learning difficulties, physical deformity, epilepsy, blindness, deafness and severe alcoholism.'

'They certainly meant to cover all bases.'

'They sure did. With the law's passage the Third Reich stepped up its propaganda against the disabled. It regularly labelled them "life unworthy of life" and highlighted their burden on society.'

'It's quite unbelievable how coldly calculating they could be.'

'That's not the worst of it.'

'How so?' Russell asked.

'Well you probably know about the euthanasia programme?'

'I know a little about it.'

'Did you know it extended to the systematic killing of the institutionalised mentally ill and physically disabled?'

'No, I wasn't aware of that.'

'Well, I'm afraid to say it was rife. It was supposedly a secret operation, coded named T-four.'

'T-four? What does that stand for?'

'Oh, that's simple. It referred to the address of the co-ordinating office in Berlin - Tiergartenstrasse four. Anyway, it seems that tracking down and dealing with these unfortunate souls was the main preoccupation of your two Germans. Obviously, they didn't work alone and I've found two other Nazi officers who worked closely with them.'

Russell thought for a moment. 'Are there descriptions of the men?'

Greg flicked through the file. 'Yes here we are. Max Krull and Achim Pfeffer. Krull was another Untersturmführer but wait, Pfeffer had the more senior rank of Hauptsturmführer.'

'Hmm. That's interesting. What did they look like then?'

'Hauptsturmführer Pfeffer, one point six five metres tall.' He chuckled. 'That's about five foot four, not much more than me.' Still grinning, he went on. 'Weight, 90 kilos.' He whistled. 'Wow, he was a tubby chap, a good 200 pounds, that's more than 14 stone

- obviously liked his food - must have looked like a barrel. Bet they had fun finding uniforms to fit him! Let me see, blonde hair, no distinguishing features.'

'What about the other one - Krull was it?'

'That's right Untersturmführer Max Krull. He weighed 100 kilos. That's about 16 stone, but he was one point nine metres, that's well over six feet.' He peered at the sheet in front of him. 'But what about this: he had a very distinguishing feature.' Russell cocked his head to one side. 'A scar running from navel to throat.'

Russell sat up straight in his chair. 'Say that again?'

'Why, is it important?'

'It could be.'

Judd peered down. 'Let me just check I'm translating this correctly.' He studied the page for a few moments. 'Yes, a distinctive scar, starting just above his umbilicus or navel and finishing just below his laryngeal prominence. I guess that's his Adam's apple.'

'Well I'll be jiggered!' Russell sat back heavily.

It was Greg's turn to look quizzically. 'Does that mean something to you?'

'It certainly does. You know there was a third victim, killed by the brothers?'

'Er, the one who was made to walk the plank, then stabbed in hospital?'

'That's the one. Crooks, the pathologist, showed me the man's chest and, it had just such a scar. Plus he was a big man. What colour hair does it say he had?'

The American looked again. 'Let me see. *Rote haare.*'

Russell smiled. 'Let me guess - red hair?'

'Correct.'

'That's our man then.'

Judd leant back in his chair and stroked his chin. 'So, three of the four SS officers we know were involved with T-four are now dead, and, somehow, your two Miller brothers are probably responsible. The thing is, why?'

Russell stroked his chin. 'Hmm, that's exactly what I want to know, too.'

Weeks was facing a dilemma. He knew he should pass on to DI Parker what the boys had told him but, knowing the inspector, he wasn't sure it would be taken seriously. Alternatively, he could turn up at the rendezvous on his own, but that could be potentially dangerous. He wished he could speak to DI Russell about it. He would know what to do. The trouble was, he was several hundred miles away. So, as he didn't know exactly where, he would have to make the decision on his own. Weighing up the alternatives he decided the sensible thing would be to tell Parker, and hope he *would* be taken seriously. With this in mind, he got in the car and drove to the police station. When he arrived the duty constable told him that they were in the interview room. He knocked and put his head round the door. Parker looked up and scowled. 'Yes? What do you want?'

'Can I have a word, Sir – please?'

He stood in the corridor outside the interview room with Parker and Barrow. 'So you want me to believe the word of two *boys*. I repeat, two *boys* who allegedly, saw two men, having a conversation about trying to find someone?'

'But Sir, it must have been Wolfgang. They saw him struggling across the beach,' Weeks said imploringly. He'd been trying to persuade the DI for 10 minutes to take what Sandy and Christopher had told him as the truth but he had remained unconvinced.

Parker sighed and shook his head sadly. 'He was probably struggling because the sand was soft and deep. I know I would have.' He gave Barrow a knowing look.

Weeks tried one more time. 'Don't you think we should at least stake out the beach tomorrow evening?'

'Listen constable. I've got three murders to solve. I've got two men in custody, who are, undoubtedly, heavily involved with these murders. And these two men are on the verge of spilling the beans, and therefore helping me to wrap up the case.' Weeks made to protest but Parker held up a warning finger. 'So I haven't the time, or for that matter, the inclination, to go on some wild goose chase.' Weeks looked deflated.

'But,' the DI went on, 'if you want to "stake out" the beach on your own, you have my blessing.' He looked pointedly at his wristwatch. 'Right, if there's nothing else, I've got a suspect to interview. Come on Barrow.' With that he turned on his heel and went back into the room.

Monday

The Waffen-SS – created as the armed wing of the Nazi Party's Schutzstaffel, (SS: 'Protective Squadron').

IT WAS a bright Monday morning, the Shipwrights Arms had been open for business since 11 am but the only occupants were the landlord Alf, polishing glasses as usual, and Jack, nursing his first pint. 'You're quiet this morning,' the landlord said. 'Something bothering you?'

Jack shook his head. 'Nah, bit of a heavy night, that's all.' Alf went back to his polishing. The truth was that Spratt's meeting with Wolfgang had unsettled him more than he liked to admit. He knew he'd done quite well out of the Germans financially, plus there was a promise of more to come, but he was wondering if it had been a mistake to get involved in the first place.

Since he'd first met them, and found the boat for them, there had been three dead bodies and he'd been subjected to a barrage of questions by the police, not to mention the ducking and near drowning he had received, when he threw himself overboard from *Moonshine*. He liked his quiet life, ferrying tourists to and from Shell Bay and drinking in the pub and, as long as Mrs Spratt didn't give him too much grief, it was nigh on perfect. But since the Miller brothers had appeared on the scene, all this had gone to pot and any amount of money didn't make up for the stress he'd been put under.

He was just ruminating on this when the door opened and Captain Salt breezed in. 'Morning Alf,' he said, walking towards the bar. 'I'll have a tot of me usual, and one for this fine gentleman.' He clapped the ferryman on his shoulder and sat down on the stool next to him. 'You look glum Jack. What's up?'

'That's what I said too,' Alf added.

'Oh you know Skip, pressure of work an' all that.'

Salt chuckled. 'Pressure of work, Jack? You're the last person in the world to have any pressure. Unless it's from your delightful wife Joan.' His eyes twinkled as he smiled through his beard.

'No, she's all right. The lads 'ave been keeping her stall topped up wiv fresh fish an' them tourists 'ave been buyin' plenty of 'er cockles an' whelks, so I've 'ad no grief from that quarter lately.'

'Well, what is it? Come on, spill the beans.'

Jack took a deep draft from his pint then put the glass carefully back down on the bar. He considered for a few moments and spoke. 'I know it shouldn't bother me, but I've bin thinkin' about that big German.'

Salt cocked a bushy eyebrow. 'Really?' He took a sip from his glass.

'Yeah,' Spratt went on, 'I knows 'ow I shouldn't but I feels a bit sorry for 'im; the duckin' 'e got at Nottery, then I 'ear 'e had a bang in a car before bein' 'cuffed and hauled off by the law.'

'I shouldn't feel too sorry for him, Jack,' Salt said surprised, 'he's quite possibly been responsible for the death of three men.'

'Yeah I know, but he seems such a gentle giant. It's 'is brother who's the mastermind.'

'Really?'

Spratt realised he may have said too much and backtracked. 'Well, 'e was the one who was supposed to 'ave done all the talkin' weren't 'e?'

Salt nodded thoughtfully. 'I suppose so.'

'Anyway,' Jack went on more confidently, 'What 'appened to 'im after 'e got nabbed?'

'They hauled him off to the police station in Collinghurst I believe.'

'Oh, so is 'e banged up in the cells?' Jack asked as casually as he could.

'For the time being.'

' 'Ow's that then?'

'Well…' Salt looked round conspiratorially and lowered his voice. 'I've heard that Detective Inspector Parker is about to make a breakthrough.'

'Really?'

'Look, keep this under your hat. He expects to charge him with murder.'

Spratt was alarmed. 'What? When?'

'Within the next 24 hours.'

'What'll 'appen to 'im then?'

'Presumably he'll be taken to court and formally charged.'

'I see.'

The Captain realised he'd probably said too much. 'Jack, if you breathe a word of this…'

'Don't you worry, Skip,' Spratt tapped the side of his nose with his forefinger and winked. 'Mum's the word.'

Greg had taken Russell to a restaurant in the town after they had finished examining the file on the Germans in his office. He'd told the American that he was a vegetarian. 'No problem. They do a great *Rösti* with *Spinat* und *Spiegelei*.' Russell's initial misgivings turned to delight when he was given a kind of fried potato cake, served with spinach and a fried egg. It was delicious. After a comfortable night in a nearby *Gasthaus*, Russell returned to the office in the morning and was shown up to Greg's room. The American's hair, so neat the night before, looked distinctly rumpled and the lenses of his glasses magnified the bags under his eyes. However, he stood up from his seat, smiling a welcome.

'Hi, Sonny. I think I've got something that might interest you.'

'Hello, Greg, have you been here all night?'

Judd chuckled. 'Not quite. I came for an hour or two after you went off to your bed and I was here again early this morning. Take a seat and I'll tell you what I've found.' They sat and Judd continued. 'Our friend Bruissement sent me other paperwork in addition to the details of the SS officers.'

'Oh yes?'

'Yeah, it's a heap of information about your two German brothers who've been creating so much havoc. You know them as Wolfgang and Ludwig Miller. That sent me off on completely the wrong tack at first. I spent a long time, going round in circles, trying to track them down using that surname. Then I had a brainwave. I thought, what if they'd changed their name? It happened a lot with people who were escaping their past - for whatever reason. But what might it have been before they changed it?' He looked up, his eyes sparkling.

'I started by trying variations of Miller. Things like Mailer, Miler, Maller, Mellor, Mallet without any success. I even tried translations like Hirse, which means Millet in English - still no luck. I guess I must have been half asleep - not surprising, considering I was in the office before six this morning - because the truth was staring me in the face. And ... it was much simpler. Müller! Obvious really, as it's a direct translation of Miller. I felt pretty stupid, as you can imagine.'

'I'm not surprised you missed it. I'm sure I would have done if I'd had only a few hours' sleep. Anyway, did that help in your search?'

'It sure did. In no time I found reference to Ludwig Müller, Soldat. The lowliest rank in the German army, the Wehrmacht.'

Russell smiled. 'That makes sense. He might be built like - I don't know - like the side of a house, but he appears pretty low in intelligence.'

'Not the brightest then, but cunning.' Russell nodded. 'Frustratingly, I found no reference to Wolfgang Müller, however hard I looked.'

'Do you mean in the military records?'

'Yeah, that's all I had to go on.'

'I guess that's not surprising, as he appears to have a disability. Something wrong with one of his legs - polio perhaps?'

'Ah, that would explain it. He would probably be excused military service because of that.'

Russell slumped in his chair and sat in silence for a few moments. He suddenly sat up, saying brightly: 'Hang on, I think there was another brother! We found a photograph in their hide-out at the brickworks of Ludwig and Wolfgang with another young man. On the back were their names and he was called...let me think...um...I've got it - Franz!'

Judd echoed the DI's enthusiasm. 'Right! That's given me something to go on. Let me see.' He started going through the typed pages, littered across his desk. After several minutes he held up a page. '*Eureka*! Obergefreiter Franz Müller!'

'What does Obergefreiter mean?'

Judd frowned and thought deeply. 'Ah, I think you'd call him a senior lance-corporal, therefore of a higher rank than his brother.' He continued reading the page in front of him. When he reached the bottom he turned it over. 'Oh!' he exclaimed.

'Mmm?'

'Strange. It says he's deceased. That's a surprise. I wonder what happened?

'No idea,' Russell said. 'The photograph is the only indication of another brother.'

$$\sim\!\!o\!\!\sim$$

Parker and Barrow returned to the interview room after talking to Weeks on Sunday evening. They sat briefly, before the DI said: 'We're all a bit jaded. I think we'd better pack up for tonight and continue tomorrow.'

The following morning they reconvened and Rankin was led in by a uniformed PC. The room had the rancid smell of stale cigarettes and sweat. Parker was in feisty mood, anticipating that the scent of fear would be added to the odours. 'Right, where did we get to?'

Barrow consulted his notes. 'Rankin had been telling us how he'd met the Müller brothers before the war and how he'd realised what Ludwig was capable of, Sir.'

'Yes, well, that's all very interesting but we need to know more about what happened when you met them *after* the war.' He looked pointedly at the soldier. 'You said they told you they'd sort out your problem. Then they'd be in touch. Let's take it from there, shall we?'

Rankin took a deep breath, placed his hands on the table and linked his fingers. 'I didn't hear anything from them for a while. I kept a low profile. Didn't meet up with any of my contacts. I basically mooched around. Also I didn't see the two fellas who'd threatened me either. Then, after about three days, I was sitting in the bar, nursing a beer, when it went dark. I thought a bulb had gone. Then I turned and saw that it was Ludwig standing over me. He'd crept up, without making a sound. I remember feeling glad it wasn't me he was after. Wolfgang was just behind him. He walked round and stood at the table. 'You won't have any more trouble from those two,' he said, and smiled at me. It weren't a warm smile. 'Now, we'll leave you in peace but remember, *Du bist mir etwas schuldig.*

Parker leant forward and said: 'Don't be clever - what the hell does that mean?'

The soldier appeared lost in thought. After a moment he looked the policeman. 'What?'

'You said something in German.'

'Oh - sorry. Hmm, it means '"You owe me one".'

'I see. So what happened next?'

'Nothing.'

'Nothing?'

'Well, not straight off.' Rankin licked his lips and shuffled in his chair. 'I decided not to try to shift any more stuff for the time being. Just keep me head down. A few days later I was sitting in a cafe, having a coffee. I picked up a paper that someone had left on the table. I opened it and a news item caught me eye. The headline said that two bodies had been washed up on the bank of the river. That was all. Then I realised that someone had torn off the bottom of the page.'

'What did you do then?'

'I left the café immediately and went round the corner to a *Zeitungsladen* - newsagents that is – and bought a copy of the paper. I sat down on a bench and turned to the article - carried on reading.'

'What did it say?'

'Well that was the strange thing. I feared the worst, but it just said that it was thought they'd fallen overboard from a boat. The police didn't think there were anything suspicious. It were just an unfortunate accident. I read further down and there were a description of the men. I couldn't believe it. The descriptions fitted the two fellas who'd threatened me. I was so tied up in reading, I didn't notice that someone had sat on the bench next to me. Then I felt a hand on my arm and looked up.'

'And?'

'It were Wolfgang. He leant over, pointed at the paper and said: 'You won't be getting any further trouble from them.' Then he stood up and smiled, tapped the side of his nose and said: 'Don't forget...' He turned and walked away without saying another thing. I tell you, I was so rattled, I left Germany a few days later. Came back to Blighty and joined up again.'

'So you didn't see him anymore?'

'No, that was the last I clapped eyes on him until he came back into my life a couple of months ago.'

'Well, why don't you tell us about that then?' Parker lit a cigarette and eased himself back into his chair. Turning to Barrow he said: 'I think tea is in order, don't you constable?'

'Okay, Sir,' Barrow said, rising from his seat and heading off to the canteen.

'Now we've established the names of the four SS men involved in searching out the mentally ill and physically disabled, can we discover anything farther about them?' Russell asked.

Judd got up and went to one of the racks on the wall. He took down a dog-eared file and, after placing it on top of the pile already on his desk, opened it and started looking through the papers. 'This may help us to find out where the SS men went after the war. The files are not exhaustive and there are a lot of gaps, but this is where we'll find it, if it's been recorded. Just give me a few minutes.' He paused. 'Oh, would you like some coffee?'

'That would be nice.'

'Hang on, I'll see if anyone's in yet.' He moved some folders aside and uncovered the telephone. He picked up the handset and dialed a number. After a moment: 'Hello? Karena? Any chance of coffee?' He smiled at Russell. 'For two, please. Bless you, you're an angel.' He put the receiver down and continued going through the papers.

Russell stood up and walked idly around the room. He started looking at the files on the racks, but with his limited grasp of German he could make little sense of the lettering on the spines. His wandering was interrupted by a knock on the door. Opening it he was surprised to see a pretty blonde girl holding a tray with two steaming cups and a plate of biscuits. He took the tray. 'Thank you… *fräulein*.'

'*Bitte schön*, Herr Russell,' she said, backing out of the room. Russell was sure that she was blushing.

'Quite a cracker, eh?' Judd said. 'Efficient, too. She compiled much of this.' He tapped the file. 'Anyway, I think we're getting somewhere. It seems neither Bausewein nor Brockelmann left Germany. They were the first two victims, weren't they?'

Russell took a sip from his cup. 'Yes, that's right. Coffee's very good by the way.'

Judd smiled then looked down at the sheet in front of him again. 'Bausewein got a job in a large department store, ironically working in soft furnishings. He seems to have done well and became a senior manager. Brockelmann went into the motor trade, selling Mercedes. And Krull,' - he turned over a couple of sheets - 'he resurfaced in France. Paris actually.'

'Can I ask a question?' Russell asked, looking puzzled.

'Sure. Fire away.'

'If you know so much about them, how come they haven't been brought to trial before now?'

Judd gave an ironic laugh. 'If only. We can go so far but, the trouble is, most of them have done a good job of covering up what they did when they were in uniform. So it is nigh on impossible to get enough evidence to convict them.'

'That must be frustrating.'

'You bet! We try but often they've integrated so well into their new lives that we just can't winkle them out.' He looked back at the pages and frowned. 'These details are about as up to date as we can get, but let me see if I can find out any more. Enjoy your coffee and give me a few minutes.' He picked up the phone and dialed. When the person at the other end of the line answered Judd spoke in fluent German.

About the only thing Russell could understand was the name Rudolf Bausewein. After a short time the American replaced the receiver. He ran his finger down the sheet and picked up the phone and dialed again. This time Russell recognised the name Kaspar Brockelmann. In a third phone conversation Max Krull's name came up. When the handset went down for the last time Greg leant back and rested his hands in his lap and frowned.

'What?' Russell asked.

'Well, it seems all three of them left their jobs suddenly, with no explanation.'

'Let me guess. In the past few weeks?'

'Yup. Bausewein and Brockelmann three weeks ago and Krull within the last week.

'That ties in with the murders. The first two turned up dead a couple of weeks ago and we rescued Krull last Friday. The Müller brothers must have picked them up, transported them across Germany and into France then taken them over to England to finish them off. It seems very elaborate. It makes you wonder why they went to so much trouble.'

'Yes it does, doesn't it?'

Russell thought for a moment. 'Greg, you've tracked down three of the Nazis, what about the fourth? Pfeffer, wasn't it?'

'Ah,' Judd said, and turned back to the file.

Rankin was in full flow now. 'It was such a surprise. I had a few days' leave. I was sitting in a greasy spoon in Collinghurst, having a mug of tea and a bacon buttie - reading the sport in the paper. Someone said: "Okay if I sit here?" I didn't look up, just said "Fine by me." I was sat there quiet like, for a while longer. Then he spoke again. "Anything interesting in the paper?" I looked up. Couldn't believe me eyes. It were Wolfgang! "Surprised to see me?" he said. You bet I was. He was the last person I expected to see.'

'I would've thought you'd be pleased to see him. After all, you were good friends – once,' Barrow said.

'Well we had been friends, before the war. But when we had that trouble on the mountain…' Rankin's voice tailed off.

'So what happened next?' Parker lit another cigarette, inhaled deeply, tilted his head and blew a plume of smoke towards the ceiling.

'I think we chatted for a while. Don't really remember what we talked about. Then he sat quietly for a bit before speaking again.'

Parker blew out more smoke then asked: 'What did he say?'

Rankin sighed. 'He said: "Remember that favour I did for you?" I nodded. "Well, it's time for you to pay me back." My heart sank.'

'Why was that?'

'Cause I was pretty sure whatever he wanted me to do, it wouldn't be straightforward.'

The DI stubbed his cigarette out and let the silence hang in the air for a few moments. 'So what was it?' he asked.

'He wanted me to supply him with a vehicle.'

'Why did he think you'd be able to do that?'

'He'd been checking up on me. He'd found out that I worked in bomb disposal and had access to a lorry. I told him it wouldn't be possible. The security was too tight at the barracks. He reminded me that I owed him and did I remember about those two fellas that drowned? I said I did. And he said it would be a shame if the police re-opened the case. I was sweating. Couldn't see how I could get out of it.'

'So you agreed?'

'I had no choice.'

'Right. Tell us what happened.'

The soldier wriggled in his chair and hung his head. 'The first time I took the Bedford…' he mumbled.

'Speak up!' growled Parker.

Rankin lifted his head and looked directly at the DI. 'The first time I took the lorry, I had to meet them at Nottery Quay. I turned up in the dark. Had to wait a while. Then I hear this boat coming in. Couldn't see it at first – 'cause it had no lights. The engine was cut before it reached where I was standing and it bumped gently against the quay. Someone chucked a rope and I tied it to a bollard. Ludwig jumped ashore. Then helped Wolfgang over. He checked the rope and retied it. Then we had a chat.'

'What about?'

'Wolfgang asked if I know where the old brickworks was. I said I thought so. Then he said did I have a tarpaulin? I said yes and he told me to lay it out in the back of the truck and wait.'

'What happened then?'

'I dropped the tailgate and put the tarpaulin in and waited. In a few moments Ludwig came up to the lorry carrying something over his shoulder. He heaved it into the back of the lorry.'

'What was it?'

'It was pitch black so I couldn't see, but then I heard a groan. And I realised.'

Parker raised an eyebrow. 'What?'

'It was a man. And he didn't sound too healthy. That shook me. Anyway, Ludwig went back to the boat. A few minutes later he come back with another body. Well, I say body, but he was alive. I could hear him moaning. Ludwig dumped him in the lorry then punched him hard. The moaning stopped.'

Barrow had turned pale. 'Any more bodies?' he asked.

'Not this time. Wolfgang came over and told me to drive to the brickworks. And to drive careful. Then he went back to the boat. I went off with Ludwig. When we arrived, he got out. I could see in the headlights that he had a pair of bolt cutters. He sliced through the chain and pushed the gates open. He got back in the cab and we drove down the track. He told me to wait and then got out again. I was glad as I didn't want anything to do with whatever he was up to. After a while he got back in and told me to drive to Nottery again.'

'Why was that?'

'We had to pick up Wolfgang. He was waiting on the quay with a bag. He told me to stop off at that new housing estate on the way. When we got there, Ludwig climbed out and went into one of the houses. After a few minutes he returned with a roll of something - carpet I guessed. Then I drove them both back and said was that it? I thought I'd got off lightly. Then Wolfgang said: "We want you back here in two days' time". Me heart sank. He came up right close to me and said: "And don't tell anyone. Understand?" I told him I wouldn't and set off for the barracks.'

~o~

Judd put the receiver down, his eyes sparkling. 'Found him!'

'Pfeffer?'

'That's right, Hauptsturmführer Achim Pfeffer, only he's not called that any longer.' The American had been on the phone for some time, making several calls. 'It seems he's changed his name to Micha Salz. Quite clever really,' he smiled.

Russell smiled back. 'Let me guess - the surname translates as salt. Salt and pepper.' He furrowed his brow, thinking. 'Micha? - *of course*, an anagram. Have you found out where he is?'

'I have indeed. He's tucked himself away in a little French town called…' - Judd looked down at the pad he'd been writing on - '… Saint-Valery-sur-Somme. Do you know it?'

Russell nodded. 'I've heard of it. I think it's in Picardie, down the coast from Boulogne.'

'Apparently he runs a *boulangerie* there.'

'He obviously likes the quiet life. Oh, I assume he's not deceased?'

'Not as far as I know.'

'So the Müller brothers haven't got to him yet?'

'It would seem not.'

'So…' Parker had paused the interview in order that they could all have a break and he could have a stretch. After ten minutes he had returned to his chair, pulled it away from the table, its legs scraping noisily across the floor. He sat and took another cigarette from the pack on the table and lit up. 'So. You had to go back two days later?'

'That's right,' Rankin said. 'I weren't happy about it. Couldn't see how I could get out of it though. So I went. I drove up to the gates of the old brickworks. Thought at first they was padlocked, but when I rattled the chain it fell open. They met me at the bottom of the track. Ludwig put some sort of a bundle in the back of the lorry.'

'What was it?'

'It was too dark to see. I didn't want to think about it anyway.'

'What then?'

'Wolfgang told me to drive to Compass Point.'

Barrow interrupted excitedly: 'That's where the first body was dumped!'

'Thank you, constable, we know that. Carry on Rankin. What happened when you got there?'

'I just drove the Bedford down to the quay and Wolfgang told me to kill the engine. He and Ludwig climbed down, took the bundle out of the back and rolled it into the water.'

'Did you know what was in the bundle then?'

'It was pretty obvious really although they hadn't told me. I saw that it didn't appear to be weighted. I said: "Won't it be found?" Wolfgang said that was the idea. I didn't understand at the time.'

'So did you drive them back to the brickworks?'

'I did. We didn't talk on the way back. I hoped that I'd paid my debt. I thought I had. But then we arrived.'

'And?' Parker cocked his head to one side, leant forward and rested his forearms on the table.

'Ludwig climbed out of the cab and I thought I'd got away with it. Then Wolfgang turned and said: "You did well tonight." I breathed a sigh of relief. But it weren't to be - as he spoke again: "But I'm afraid you still owe me." I asked him what he wanted. "I want you back, with the lorry, on Sunday evening. And don't be late." Then he smiled that strange smile of his and joined his brother.'

'So,' the DI said, leaning back, 'They were holed up in the brickworks for, let me see, four days, and no one knew?'

'I guess so.'

'But Russell and the forensics team went all over the site and didn't find hide nor hair of them.'

Barrow sat up eagerly. 'Yes, Sir, but they didn't find that secret hiding place until later in the week.'

'Hmm. Quite right, constable.'

Barrow was still excited. 'And it was Inspector Russell's dog that found it.'

'Bloody dog,' Parker mumbled. Then to Rankin: 'So did you go back on the Sunday?'

'Of course I did. I'd seen what Ludwig was capable of. I wasn't about to let them down.'

'What happened this time?' He leant back in his chair, hands thrust in his jacket pockets.

'They still had the tarpaulin. They bundled something wrapped in it into the back of the truck.'

'Where did you go?'

'Back to that new housing estate. They took the bundle into the house - then I knew it was a man.'

'How come?'

'By the noise he was making. I'll never forget it. Sounded like an animal in pain.' He put his hands over his face and exhaled noisily. 'It were horrible,' he whispered.

The DI let it pass. 'Then what?'

'After about half an hour they came out again. Wolfgang asked me to back the truck up to the door. Ludwig had the bundle over his shoulder. But there weren't no more noise coming from it.'

'Where did you go?'

'We drove a few miles up the road to another building site...'

'And put the body in the cement mixer!'

'Yes, thank you, Barrow. I was rather hoping this man,' - he pointed at the soldier - 'would tell us what happened.'

'But I didn't know. Not 'til I read about it in the paper. I stayed in the lorry all the time.'

'So presumably, after they got back in the cab, you took them to the brickworks again?'

'No, I drove them to Compass Point. They went back to the boat. I really thought that was the end of it. But no, I *still* hadn't paid off me bleedin' debt.'

'No?'

'No, they wanted me one more time. I was to meet them early on Friday morning at Shell Bay.'

Parker turned over some pages in the file and held up a sheet. 'Ah yes, the mysterious scrap of paper that Jack Spratt found. One of the few things Russell did deduce. *With the help of a Frenchman,* of course. And I quote from the translation: "High tide, Friday, 05.35. Shell Bay, petrified forest". A lot of good it did him though.' He snorted.

~o~

'Okay, so we have to assume that the Müller brothers have been picking off these former Nazis, one by one, for some reason. Now what could that be?' Russell had his hands clasped behind his head, chin jutting.

'Revenge?' the American offered.

'But for what?'

'That I can't tell you, but whatever the reason is, it must be pretty serious. Three deaths, and all suffered particularly nasty ends.'

'Yes, that's right. Keelhauling, flogging, then walking the plank. All very strange.'

'Maybe, but each distinctive and definite.'

'Let's think,' Russell said. 'What could...' he turned round the page on the table so he could read it. '...What could Pfeffer, Bausewein, Bockelmann and Krull have done to the Müllers that was so bad, so profound, that they would feel the need to wreak such bizarre revenge on them?'

'Well...' Judd said slowly. 'As you know, a lot of the fiercest fighting, towards the end of the war, took place on the Eastern front.'

'With the Russians?'

'That's right. It was there that the Waffen-SS committed some of the worst atrocities against their fellow countrymen.'

'How so?'

'Well, knowing that the tide of war had turned against Germany, many of them had been making plans for their eventual escape for some time. However, Hitler was determined that the German army should continue battling the Russians to the end. The regular soldiers - the Wermacht - were forced to carry on fighting, whether they wanted to or not, and irrespective of whether they believed there was any point in continuing. And it was the SS who insisted they went on with the battle. There are numerous instances of enlisted soldiers being summarily executed for supposedly refusing to fight. I'm pretty sure it was often just an excuse to make examples of them so the others were scared into continuing, even when they knew there was no hope.'

'Pretty brutal.'

'Oh yes. The Nazis were nothing if not brutal, right up to the end. The poor rank and file were left to carry the can, so to speak, while they just melted away.'

'So, do you think something so appalling happened to brother Franz that three SS men needed to be executed?

'It's possible. After all, the file says that he is deceased; perhaps Ludwig and Wolfgang were so devastated that they vowed to avenge his death.'

'Maybe.' Russell was thoughtful for a while. Then he said: 'However, tracking down three men and torturing and murdering them, for the death of one, just doesn't seem right. There's got to be more to it than that.'

Judd ran his hands through his hair. 'Yes, I agree with you. Let me see if I can do a bit more digging.' He pulled back his sleeve and looked at his watch. 'Goodness! It's five after one already. You must be hungry. Time for lunch, I think. We can carry on later.'

'Excellent idea,' Russell agreed.

Parker continued with the interview. 'So, you were there early and what happened?'

'I waited for a while. It were still dark. The sun hadn't risen. I parked the Bedford by the Martello Tower. I got out and stood on the sand. I heard the engine of the boat first. Then I could just make out a shadowy shape as it came up to the beach. The engine stopped. There were a splash and Ludwig appeared out of the murk. He looked grimly at me, grabbed me arm and said: '*Bleib wo Du bist* - Stay there.' I did what I was told and waited.

'Then what?'

'I heard the ferry bell ring. After a while there was the sound of a boat being rowed across the water. Next, Ludwig shouted: '*Komm hier!*'

'Presume that means 'Come here'?'

'That's right. So I found my way to the jetty. Lying on the walkway was a man, out cold. I recognised him as Spratt, the ferryman. Ludwig said: '*Hilf mir ihn zu tragen*'. Oh, that means 'Help me carry him'. Between us, we lugged him through the shallow water and got him on the *Moonshine*. We climbed up after. Wolfgang said he wanted me to go back to the brickworks. Wanted me to clear out their '*Schlupfwinkel*'.'

'You what?'

'Sorry, 'hiding place'. I thought they'd come to take me away. Told him no, I'd already stolen the lorry *and* gone AWOL. It got a bit heated. Ludwig grabbed me by the throat. I couldn't breathe. Thought I was a goner. Luckily Wolfgang told him to let me go. Then I noticed some poor bugger, trussed up in the fish hold. I was just asking about him when we saw your lot turn up.'

Parker turned to his companion and snorted. 'That was Russell's abortive attempt to solve the case.' Barrow beamed at him. Parker smiled at the constable and turned back to the soldier.

'So what occurred then?'

'Can't remember exactly. It all happened so quick. I think Wolfgang started the engine and moved the boat away from the shore. Spratt chucked himself overboard, Wolfgang said: '*Scheisse*!' then, '*lass ihn*' - 'leave him'. He took the boat round in a big arc. Ludwig tied a short plank over the bow. When we got near the beach – in sight of the rozzers – he forced the poor sod who'd been in the fish hold to walk the plank. He soon fell in the water and Wolfgang roared off.'

'Where did you go?'

'Nowhere really.'

'What do you mean, nowhere?' the DI growled.

'Just out to sea. Out of sight of land. It were 'orrible. I'm not a good sailor at the best of times. Wolfgang cut the engine. We just sat there, bobbing up and down.' He shuddered at the thought of it. 'I was sick as a dog. Couldn't keep anything down. Wolfgang was all right. Been on boats most of his life. Ludwig looked a bit green but he didn't throw up. I could hear them talking, quiet like, but couldn't catch what they were saying. Then Wolfgang started the engine and we headed back.'

'What, to Shell Bay?'

'No. Although I didn't know at first. They were very secretive. Told me nothing. Then as we approached the shore I recognised where we were.'

'Where was it?'

'Nottery Quay. I asked what was happening. Wolfgang shut me up. He drove the boat right up to the stone steps. Ludwig tucked a knife in his waistband and jumped ashore. Wolfgang said he'd be back between four and five. Then we turned and headed out again.'

~O~

Russell and Judd returned from lunch and resumed their seats in the office at the Z-commission. The American riffled through the papers on the desk. He pulled out a sheet and pushed his glasses up on the bridge of his nose with his forefinger. 'I wonder if the key to the whole riddle lies with Hauptsturmführer Pfeffer?'

Russell was relaxed in Judd's company. He felt he had an ally; someone who was in tune with his ideas. 'What makes you say that?'

'We-ell. He was the most senior of the four, he's the only one left alive and he hid himself the farthest away.'

'But why rule out the others? Bausewein, Bockelmann and Krull. Shouldn't we be finding out more about them?'

'Hey! I'm not ruling them out! The trouble is, all we know about them is here. He tapped the file in front of him. 'I'm sure, with a bit of digging, we could probably turn up more info. But ... it would take some time. And, my suspicion is, we don't have much of that, do we?'

'I suppose not. If we don't get to the bottom of what this is all about pretty soon, we could have another death on our hands.'

'True.' Judd leant back, mirroring Russell's pose. They sat in silence for a few minutes. Then he spoke. 'Let's look at this from another direction.'

'O - kay,' Russell said slowly. 'What are you thinking?'

'I was wondering, what's happening in the police station back in the UK?'

Russell barked out a laugh. 'What? With Bonnie and Clyde in charge!'

'Who?' Judd joined in the laughter.

'Detective Inspector Parker and Detective Constable Barrow. Don't you know?'

'What?' Judd was still grinning.

'Those are the surnames of the notorious couple who, supposedly, killed nine police officers as well as several civilians during the Great Depression in the 30s.'

'Sure, I know about them; I was just amused that the names of two upstanding members of the British constabulary would be associated with such so-called legends.'

Chortling, Russell replied: 'I'd hardly call them upstanding. In fact I'm surprised they're standing at all. I'd have thought they should have been pensioned off years ago.'

'Anyway, joking aside,' Judd said eventually, 'let's get back to my original question: *What's* happening back in the UK?'

Russell sat up in his chair, put his hands flat on the edge of the desk and spoke earnestly. 'Well, with any luck, my constable, Weeks, might have some influence on proceedings. But even without that, I hope Parker and Barrow will at least follow procedure and *may* just get a result. I'm hoping they'll have recaptured Ludwig, as I told Weeks where they might find him. Though I doubt, if they do, that he'll give much away. I'd pin my hopes on Rankin.'

'The squaddie?'

'The same. I know that he was in Germany before the war and met them then, so I'm surmising that he met them again after '45, but as to the circumstances, who knows?'

'If your constable *is* working with, er, Bonnie and Clyde, maybe he'd know. Why don't you give him a call?'

'What, ring him from here?'

Judd chuckled. 'It's not so difficult. Give me the number and I'll see if I can get through.' Russell found it and turned his notebook so the American could read it. He picked up the phone and after a moment said: '*Kannst Du mir eine Nummer in England anrufen, Karena?*'

There was a pause. He smiled. '*Schön'Dank, das ist lieb von Dir. Die Nummer lautet..*' and he recited the number the Englishman had shown him. Judd put the receiver down and looked up. 'Karena is going to try the number then come back when she gets through.'

After a few minutes the phone rang and he picked up the handset. '*Ja? Danke Karena.*' He passed it over to Russell who held it to his ear.

There was some static on the line, a few crackles then, 'Sir? Are you there?' Weeks's voice came through loud and clear.

'Hello, lad. How's it going?'

'Not bad, Sir. Well, a bit of a mixed bag to be honest.'

'Okay, I'm all ears.'

'Well, Bonnie and Clyde, sorry, DI Parker and DC Barrow have been interviewing Rankin all morning.'

'What have they found out?'

'Rather a lot, as it happens, so I'll have to edit it.'

'That's fine, lad. Just give me the essence.'

'As you know he met Wolfgang and Ludwig before the war. Oh, by the way…' Excitement entered his voice. '… Their surname is actually Müller!'

'Sorry to steal your thunder,' - Russell winked at Judd - 'but we already know.'

'Oh. Ah well. As I was saying, he met them before the war. They did some climbing together in the mountains near Innsbruck.'

'Can I interrupt you?'

'Of course.'

'Have you been sitting in on the interviews?'

'At first, yes. Then DI Parker told me to get on with something else. Luckily, I have a reasonable relationship with Barrow - us constables stick together - and he's kept me informed.'

'I see - please carry on.'

'Apparently, when they were climbing, Ludwig showed his true colours and almost dumped a couple of blokes over the side of the mountain.'

'Goodness!'

'It was only Wolfgang telling him *"No!"* that stopped him dropping them. Anyway, they didn't meet up again until after the war when Rankin was running a black market operation.'

'Really?'

'Yes. He'd started having trouble with a couple of blokes who accused him of trespassing on their patch. Apparently they beat up one of his men as a threat. The Müller brothers turned up, out of the blue, saying they would sort it out. A few days later, two bodies turned up in the river. Apparently the police weren't suspicious - they assumed the men had fallen overboard from a fishing boat. However, Wolfgang made it obvious that he and Ludwig were responsible and said that Rankin *"owed them"*. That's why he had to help them when they came here.'

'That makes sense.' Russell glanced up to see Judd putting an imaginary mug to his lips. He nodded, and gave him the thumbs up and carried on. 'Did he see them again in Germany?' The American went off to get their drinks.

'No, apparently the experience rattled him so much that he came back to England and joined up.'

'So when did they meet again?'

'Wolfgang approached him in a café in Collinghurst and said he'd come to collect his debt.'

'Ah. So that's why he became involved with them.'

'Yes, he felt he had to as the Germans had a hold over him.'

Judd returned with the coffee. Russell nodded his thanks and continued talking to Weeks. 'Was Rankin involved with the murders?' He took a sip from his cup.

'Apparently not. They just got him to drive the lorry, shifting the men about, both alive and dead.'

'And he definitely didn't participate in more than that?'

'So he says.'

Russell sighed, 'I'm inclined to believe that. You've done well, lad.'

'Sir...' Weeks spoke hesitantly.

'Yes?'

'There's something else.'

'What's that?'

'I had a visit from your nephew yesterday'

'Christopher? He's a good lad. What did he want?'

'He was camping at Shell Bay with his friend Sandy and they saw something which they thought was important.' Weeks then went on to outline what they had told him.

'Oh my, that is significant. I presume you told Parker?'

'I tried to, but he wasn't interested. Said he couldn't take the words of two *boys* seriously.'

'But they're scouts, for heaven's sake! Plus Christopher's one of the most observant boys I've met.'

'That's what I told him, but he wouldn't have it. He said: "I've got three murders to solve so I haven't got the time, or the inclination, to go on a wild goose chase".'

'Idiot.'

'He did say if I wanted to stake out the beach myself I would "*have his blessing*".'

'Mmm. Not sure that's a good idea. Could be dangerous,' Russell suggested cautiously.

'Do you think I ought not to go then, Sir?'

'Prudence suggests you shouldn't go on your own but...' - he paused for a moment, thinking - '...if you don't, you could miss something vital. I just wish I was there with you.'

'Me too, Sir – me too.'

'Is there any chance of you getting anyone to go with you?'

'I doubt it. Parker made it quite clear that he didn't think it was worth the bother.'

'I suppose if you just observed from a distance and stayed clear you would be okay.'

'That's what I was hoping you'd say.'

'Well do it, but just be *careful*. We don't want more any nasty incidents.'

'Thank you, Sir. I'll watch myself.'

'And do let me know how you get on – if anything happens. You can get me here for the rest of day.' He read the number off the telephone, then said goodbye and hung up.

~o~

Parker was pretty sure that he knew the rest of Rankin's story but he wanted to hear it from the man himself. The soldier looked worn out. The interview had taken all morning and part of the afternoon. After his initial reluctance he had been all too willing to tell his side of the matter. He had probably given them enough to charge Ludwig with the murders but hard evidence was thin on the ground. Parker decided they would have another go at the big German when they had finished with Rankin.

'So after you dropped Ludwig off at the quay you headed out into the channel again?'

'Yes. We didn't go out so far this time. Just a couple of miles. Then we motored slowly, just in sight of land. After an hour or so, he turned the boat and we went back.'

'How was Wolfgang - on his own?'

'He was much friendlier. I think that was why he kept the boat moving this time. He knew I wasn't a good sailor. We talked about the great fun we'd had – when we first met. Time passed quickly. It wasn't long before we headed back to Nottery. You know the rest.' With this last, short sentence, Rankin slumped in his seat and wearily dropped his chin on his chest.

Parker looked at his watch. 'Right, that's you done for. We'll have to think what we're going to charge you with. Constable?'

'Yes, Sir?'

'Take him back to the cells and bring the German up.' Barrow rose from his seat and beckoned to the soldier. Rankin stood up slowly. He looked thoroughly defeated. Just as they were leaving, the DI spoke again: 'Oh, and get a couple of constables to go with you when you get Müller. I don't want him doing a disappearing act again.'

After the three policemen had brought Ludwig in he sat heavily in the chair and stared at Parker, scowling. Parker stared back. 'Right, now we know you speak English. Are you going to answer our questions?'

The German slowly folded his arms across his broad chest and said: '*Nein*,' almost in a whisper.

'Oh, for God's sake! Get whatisname down here!' Parker's frustration was palpable. Barrow looked at his boss, uncomprehendingly. 'You know, the bloody fingerprint wallah.'

'Lewis?'

'Yes, that's him. Go and find him - pronto!' Barrow left the room quickly. After a few minutes there was a light tap on the door. Parker: 'Come!'

The door opened and a constable popped his head round. 'What is it?' Parker said irritably.

'Sorry to bother you, Sir. I've got PC Lee here.'

'So?'

'He was the policeman who he...' he nodded towards the German, '...socked on the jaw.'

'So?'

'We'll he's still off sick but he's come in as he thought you might like him to identify the prisoner.' He nodded at Ludwig again.

'I suppose so,' Parker said grudgingly. The PC's head disappeared and was replaced by Lee's bandaged face. Parker stared at him. 'Well?' He indicated Ludwig with his thumb.

'Yes, Sir, that's him.' The injured officer's voice was muffled, his words indistinct.

'Right, thanks.' Lee was just about to leave when Barrow appeared, followed by Lewis. 'About time. Come on, you've got some translating to do.' The DI's mood was fast deteriorating.

Lewis turned to the constable. 'Hang on, Lee.' Then turning back to Parker he said: 'I've got something that you might find useful.' He held out a small metal object.

'What is it?'

'I believe it's a buckle off a boot.' Ludwig shifted in his seat.

Parker took the buckle. 'What boot?'

Lewis looked pointedly at the German, on the other side of the table. 'His. Isn't that right Lee?'

Lee just nodded.

'Thanks, constable, you can go now.' Turning to Barrow: 'Have a look at his boots constable.' Barrow walked round to the other side of the table and crouched down. Ludwig remained immobile.

'There's one missing, Sir!'

'Is this it?' the DI handed him the buckle.

Barrow stood up and walked round behind the German's chair and crouched down on the other side. He held it up to the boot. 'It matches!' He stood up and gave it back to Parker.

Parker turned to Lewis. 'Where did you find it?'

'*I* didn't. It was one of the cleaners at the hospital.'

'Where?'

'It was wedged in the frame of a hospital bed – the one where the last German was murdered.'

Parker sat up. His day had just improved considerably. 'Wonderful,' he said slowly and put the buckle on the table. He turned to Lewis. 'Come and sit here.' He patted the chair vacated by Barrow. Lewis sat. 'Ask Müller if he's going to answer our questions.'

'*Wollen Sie jetzt unsere Fragen beantworten*?' Ludwig continued to stare, in silence.

Barrow, leaning against the wall, spoke. 'Here we go again.'

The DI turned to him, 'Thank you, constable.'

'Why don't we try a different approach?' Lewis asked.

Parker sighed. 'What do you suggest?'

'Why don't we ask why they brought the men to England?'

'Go on then, give it a try.'

'*Warum haben Sie die Männer nach England gebracht?*'

Ludwig spoke. '*Was?*'

'*Die M*änner. *Warum sind sie hier gebracht?*'

'*Wir wollten ein Exempel statuieren.*'

Parker butted in. 'What did he say.'

'He said they wanted to set an example.'

'An example? Who to?' He flicked his fingers - as if at an imaginary fly. 'Ask him.'

Lewis turned to the German. '*Ein Exempel an wem?*'

'*Am dreckigen Naziausschuß!*' he spat.

'I think I understood that.' Parker chuckled. 'Ask him which Nazi scum in particular.'

'*Am dreckigen Naziausschuß*?' asked Lewis.

Ludwig sat, glowering. He remained silent for a while then he growled: '*Der Ausschuß der meinen Bruder ermordet hat.*'

'What? Something about his brother?'

'Yes, he says the ones who killed his brother.'

'Well!' Parker leant back and breathed out noisily. 'So *that's* what all this is about.

Weeks left the police station early and drove towards Compass Point. He turned off along the stony track and parked his car outside his cottage, deciding he'd be less conspicuous if he made his way across the dunes on foot. Aggie was delighted as she was able to scamper about, following scents and hoping to surprise rabbits. As he neared the beach, he could see a thin ribbon of smoke curling towards the sky. Making his way towards it, a small tent came into sight, pitched in a hollow. The terrier, running on ahead, had already announced his presence and the boys were making a fuss of her.

'Hello, Johnny!' they chorused cheerfully. 'Great to see you. What are you doing here?'

Weeks sat down beside them, on a groundsheet spread out on the sand. 'I'm following up your lead.'

They looked incredulously at him and Christopher spoke. '*Really*? On your own?'

'We thought you'd have half the Collinghurst police force with you,' Sandy added.

'Afraid not, boys.' Weeks shook his head glumly.

'But why not?'

'Let's say DI Parker and DC Barrow didn't think it important enough to send anyone else.'

Sandy snorted. 'Ha! Bonnie and Clyde? Wouldn't know a baddie if he came up and bit them!'

Weeks smiled. 'Now, now. That's no way to talk about officers of the law.'

'Well,' said Christopher, looking heavenward and tutting, 'we know what we saw and we thought it looked pretty serious and needed investigating.'

'I agree, and so does your Uncle Sonny.'

'Ooh! Have you spoken to him? Where is he?'

'He's in Germany, in a place called Ludwigsburg. I talked to him. He said he thought I should come and observe what happens.'

'Can we observe, too?' Sandy asked excitedly, kneeling up on the groundsheet.

'I don't see why not. As long as we're careful and only watch from a distance.' He looked at his watch. 'Half four... I doubt anything will happen for an hour or so. Any chance of a cuppa while we wait?'

The boys busied themselves with the fire and a billycan of water, preparing a battered teapot and tin mugs. Weeks saw now that they went about their tasks quietly and efficiently. It reminded him of the happy times he had had as a sea scout, before the fun was cut short by the war. If only Parker could have seen them he might have realised they could be trusted. Unfortunately, he was on his own, but if he heeded Russell's advice to be cautious nothing should go awry, he reasoned.

Before long, the water in the billycan was bubbling merrily. Christopher carefully lifted it off the fire with a cloth and poured the boiling water over the tea leaves in the pot. Soon they were sipping the brew and munching on biscuits from their supplies.

'Hey, Johnny - look,' Sandy said, pointing. Weeks looked up to see tendrils of vapour floating in off the sea. In a matter of minutes visibility was greatly reduced as the sea mist thickened.

'At least we won't be spotted,' Christopher said

'True.' Weeks looked at his watch again. 'Time we took up our positions.'

They doused the fire with sand then made their way cautiously to the marram grass on the edge of the beach. Sure enough, after a while an engine could be heard approaching, although there was no sign of the craft.

'Quiet now,' the policeman whispered, unnecessarily as the boys were holding their breath and peering excitedly into the mist. 'And hold on to Aggie. We don't want her giving the game away.' Christopher gripped the dog's collar tightly.

The boat's engine was suddenly cut and there was a splash. Then they heard someone shuffling slowly along the beach. The footsteps came close enough for them to see the shadowy outline of Wolfgang's slight form. They crouched lower, unseen by the German making his laboured way along to the jetty. As the sound faded, Weeks knew that that the ferryman would have little to tell him so made a rash decision.

'Boys,' he whispered, 'I'm going to take a look at the boat while there's no one aboard. You stay here.'

Christopher was about to protest. Instead he said: 'Okay, Johnny – but take care.' With that Weeks stood up and crept off into the mist. They stared hard but could see nothing. Then they heard talking.

'So what have you found out about my brother?' The voice was high and reedy but quite clear.

'Not much.'

'That's Jack Spratt, the ferryman,' Sandy whispered. 'I recognise his voice.'

'Who's the other one?'

'Don't know, must be the German. Shh. Let's listen.'

'What then?' asked Wolfgang.

''E's bein' 'eld at Collinghurst,' Jack replied, his voice gravelly.

'And?' The German sounded agitated.

'I spoke to Salt…'

'The Navy type who goes in the Shipwrights Arms?'

'Owns it, actually.'

'I am not interested in what he owns.' Wolfgang's voice was shrill. 'Just get on with it!'

Jack growled. 'All right. Keep yer 'air on. It seems that the copper on the case - Parker I think…'

'Is he the one who has been nosing around? The one who bungled the capture of my brother?'

'Nah, that's Russell -'e's off the case - this is a new bloke. Don't think 'e's very good.'

'He cannot be any worse. So tell me about Ludwig.'

'As I said,' Spratt replied slowly, ''e's bein' 'eld at Collinghurst. And Parker reckons that 'e'll 'ave 'im charged with murder within the next 24 hours.'

'*Scheisse*!'

'Oh, an' that was yesterday evenin'.'

'*Gott im Himmel*! *Was kann ich wissen*?'

'Whassat?'

Wolfgang spoke slowly. 'What can I do now? I need help to finish what we started.'

'What do you mean?'

'We have one more problem to eliminate.

'Eh?'

The German was weary. His shoulders slumped. He was obviuosly struggling to cope without his brother. 'How can I go back to France and finish the job by myself?'

Spratt was intrigued. 'So what's this thing you've gotta finish?'

'Mmm?' Wolfgang seemed in a daze. 'This thing? It is nothing *you* can help with.'

The ferryman shrugged. 'Ah well, in that case, I'll be on me way. Where's me money?'

'What?'

'The dosh. You promised me the other ten quid if I found out where your brother was.'

'Go to hell!' Wolfgang hissed.

'You bastard!' Jack's voice was raised. 'You promised me that money!'

'I will promise you more than that!'

Jack sounded startled. 'All right, all right! You can put the gun away, I'm going.' There was a splash as his oar went in the water then, shortly afterwards, the boys heard the German coming back.

They waited a few more minutes but Weeks still hadn't returned 'What should we do?' Sandy whispered anxiously.

'I don't know. He told us to stay put. Let's just wait a little longer,' Christopher replied, frowning. The sound of the boat's engine suddenly bursting into life made them both jump as if they had been shot.

Christopher's grip loosened on the terrier's collar and she shot forward, down the beach. The boys got to their feet and raced after her. Soon they were at the water's edge. The mist was even thicker and they could barely see a few yards ahead. The sound of the engine fading and some white water swirling at their feet were the only indications that the boat had ever been there.

'Johnny must be on board. What do we do *now*? He might be killed!' Sandy was near to tears.

'Hang on. Let me think.' Christopher was concentrating hard. 'I think we should go to Collinghurst and tell Bonnie and Clyde what's happened.'

'But it'll take us *hours* to walk there,' Sandy protested.

'Wait a minute. What's the time?'

Sandy looked at his watch. 'Nearly 5.30. Why?'

'Have you got any money?'

'A little. Why?'

'We could get the last train that goes from Compass Point to Collinghurst. It gets to Snargate Halt at 10 to six. If we hurry we can just make it.'

'But what about the mist?'

'C'mon – quick. Back to the camp. We'll get the map and a compass. Shouldn't be too difficult to find our way to the station.'

$$\sim\!O\!\sim$$

Russell and the American sat across the desk from each other, the coffee pot and cups empty in front of them. 'What do we do now, Sonny?'

Russell drew in a large breath then let it out slowly. 'As you say, there's probably not much mileage in delving into the pasts of the three dead Waffen-SS men.'

'Well, I'm sure we could find out more, but as we agreed, time could be running out. Especially for Achim Pfeffer. Or as he is now - Micha Salz.' Judd sat back, a grim look on his face.

'So how do we find out more about him?'

'I doubt if there's much more we can discover here, in Germany.'

'So where can we look?'

Greg sat up. 'I think it's time for a chat with our friend Bruissement in Boulogne. I'll give him a call.'

'Guillaume, how are you?' Judd smiled as he spoke.

'*Ah! Mon ami Am*êricain. Tres bien! And you?' the Frenchman's voice was loud enough for Russell to hear what he was saying quite clearly.

'Good thanks. Listen Guillaume, I've got Sonny Russell here…'

'Ah, *bon soirée* my English friend!' the Frenchman bellowed jovially.

'…and we need some help.'

Judd outlined what he and Russell had discussed over the previous 24 hours. Bruissement listened quietly at the other end of the line until he had finished. 'So 'ow can I 'elp you?'

'We need to know about someone in Saint-Valery-sur-Somme.'

'Interesting. What do you wish to know?

'Apparently, there's a German there who runs a *boulangerie*. During the war he worked with the three dead SS men, and like many of his "comrades" went to ground. But - in France.'

'That is unusual but not unknown.'

'He was originally called Achim Pfeffer but changed his name to Micha Salz.'

'I know him! Well, I know his shop!'

'Do you?'

'Yes, I have bought bread several times from there. It is *très bien*! I had no idea he was German.' He paused. The line crackled. "If I remember *correctement*, he speaks French *parfait*.'

'Good, that might make it easier.'

'But my friend, *you* speak perfect German. *That* would make it easier.' It was not hard to imagine the Frenchman sitting in his office in rue Perrochel, his blue eyes twinkling.

Judd was perplexed. 'What are you suggesting?'

Simple. Come here and we will go to Saint Valery together!'

The American looked startled. 'What?'

'You and Sonny Russell jump on a train. As soon as you can. I will meet you at *la gare*. We will 'ave a discussion then go down there and see 'ow the land lies.'

When Weeks left the boys, he had dashed across the sand, splashed quickly through the shallows and scrambled up the ladder that Wolfgang had put over the bow of *Moonshine*. Once on board he made his way straight to the wheelhouse and stepped over the threshold. He glanced around. There was a chart table with little on it but navigational paraphernalia: an unrolled chart, a pencil, a pair of nautical dividers. A compass in gimbals was bolted to the bulkhead. Binoculars hung from one hook and a yellow oilskin and sou-wester from another. He backed out and made his way down the companionway to the cabin.

There were two bunks, one with an unrolled sleeping bag on it, on the other a couple of sailcloth bags. He started rummaging through them, finding nothing but crumpled clothes. Forrard there was a galley. He opened drawers and found only cutlery and cooking implements; lockers held pans and food, tinned and in packets. He turned and looked around. There were more lockers below the bunks.

Weeks knelt and opened the first one. It contained just a bundle of ropes. He was about to close the door, and move on, when he stopped. He pulled the ropes out. He saw knots. Dozens of them. All different. All beautifully tied. He even recognised some: reef knot, bowline, sheepshank and... one unusual but very familiar to him now, a double constrictor knot.

'My, my,' he said quietly to himself. 'This neatly ties the brothers to the murders.' He smiled at the joke he had just made. Still smiling he started putting the ropes back in the locker when he was startled to hear the boat's engine turn over. His expression turned to one of disbelief and he felt panic rise in his chest. He stood, rooted to the spot, wondering what on earth he should do. The engine revs rose and the boat started moving, initially in reverse as the bow was pulled out of the soft sand. Then, as the craft slewed round, the young policeman lost his footing and was thrown sideways. He cracked his head on the bulkhead with a horrible thud and blacked out.

Ludwig sat impassively in his seat in the interview room. He leant back, arms folded tightly across his barrel chest, legs outstretched, one booted ankle crossed over the other.

Parker frowned. 'There's something been bothering me. He leant forward and put his elbows on the table, cupping his chin in his hands. 'Do you know what it is?' The German remained tight lipped. The detective continued. 'What I want to know, is what happened to the knife. Any idea, Herr Müller?' Still no response. Turning to the side: 'Lewis, ask him where the knife is.'

Lewis took a deep breath. 'Ludwig.' The German looked at him, unblinking. '*Wo ist das Messer*?' The German gave a shrug and looked down.

'Try again,' Parker growled. 'Ask him where he's hidden the knife.'

'*Wo haben Sie das Messer versteckt*?'

Ludwig looked up. '*Wo Sie es nicht finden können.*'

Lewis translated before Parker could speak. 'He said where we can't find it.'

The DI snorted. 'Yet again we're getting nowhere.'

'Could I have a word … outside? asked Lewis.

'Hmm. I suppose so. I could do with a stretch.' He got up with an effort. 'Come on then.' Lewis followed him through the door, closing it behind him. In the corridor Parker rested against the wall and lit a cigarette. 'What is it?' he asked wearily.

'I've been wondering about that knife for a while. Crooks, the pathologist, says all three men were probably killed with the same knife. A thin blade. He found traces of fish scales in the first victim's wound so surmised it might be a fish-filleting knife.'

'Yes, we know that.' Parker blew out a plume of smoke. 'What's your point?'

Lewis pressed on. 'The knife could have come from the boat *Moonshine*. If we could find it, there may be some fingerprints. Also we could get Ted Spencer to identify it.'

Parker dropped the part-smoked cigarette on the floor and ground it savagely with his heel. 'Who the hell is Ted Spencer?'

'Um, he was the previous owner of the boat.'

'Oh, I see.' Parker wasn't going to let Lewis know he hadn't read all the notes. 'So what do you suggest?'

'Well, Ludwig obviously had the knife when he went to the hospital but didn't have it on him when he was arrested after he crashed the police car - did he?'

'No,' the detective agreed grudgingly. 'He was clean. No knife.'

Well I don't think he'll just have dumped it.'

'Now come on. He'd get rid of it as soon as he could surely?'

'No, hear me out, Sir. I think after using it three times he may well have become attached to it, so to speak. So I don't think he'd just discard it.'

'So where do you suggest he's hidden it?' Parker said, humouring him.

'Listen, I don't want to sound critical of your methods, but the secret hideout at the brickworks was never properly cleared out, was it?'

'True,' Parker reluctantly conceded. 'So are you suggesting we turn it upside down?'

'Might be an idea – I'm happy to help,' Lewis added.

'Dead right. You're coming along for sure.'

～o～

Parker, Barrow, Lewis and PC Beaumont climbed out of the car at the bottom of the track outside the brickworks. The brushwood and branches had been cleared away and the door to the Germans' hiding place was now quite obvious.

Parker pushed the door open and peered inside. 'Cor blimey! It's a bit cramped. You two…' - he motioned to Barrow and Beaumont - 'There's not room for all of us in there so you have a mosey around and see if anything's been missed. Me and Lewis are going to turn this place inside out.'

Working systematically, they examined the mouldering cans and packets on the makeshift table. They pushed it to one side and searched through the debris of paper and rags that had been concealed underneath. They found nothing. Pulling the straw-filled sacks aside and piling one on the other, Lewis knelt on the grubby floor and, with the aid of a powerful torch, searched around the area where the walls met the floor. With the beam from another torch Parker searched the shelving. He found shards of clay tiles and old cigarette packets, broken brick-making tools and empty bottles, but no knife.

'This is hopeless,' the DI grumbled, breathing heavily from the exertion, his initial enthusiasm replaced by his default sour nature. 'I don't know why I bloody well listened to you.'

'I'm sorry, Sir,' Lewis said, 'I was sure he'd hidden it here.'

The physical effort had obviously been too much for the unfit DI and he flopped down heavily on to the makeshift mattresses. No sooner had his broad posterior compressed the straw than he yelped and arched his back. 'Ow! What the bloody hell was that?! Something sharp stuck in my arse!' He scrambled back to his feet as quickly as he could and rubbed his backside.

Just as he was about to protest farther, Constable Beaumont came running up to the doorway, closely followed by Barrow. 'Sir!' he said panting, 'Look what we've found!' He held out a small canvas bag. 'It was in the bushes, behind that big shed. The German must have dropped it when we were looking for him.'

'Yes,' Parker growled, 'and when he nicked our car. Give it to me.' He took the bag and loosened the strings at the neck. Turning it upside down he shook it. Some dry, but grubby clothing fell out, followed by a couple of tins, a plain packet and a box of matches. As the box hit the ground, the tray slid out, scattering matches across the soil. Parker shook the bag hard but there was nothing farther inside. 'Bloody hell!' he barked. 'I thought we were in luck for a moment.'

While this had been going on, Lewis had slit the uppermost mattress with his penknife and was feeling around inside. He gave a triumphant shout: 'Sir! Look at this!' Carefully he withdrew his hand, scattering straw and chaff. As he brought it out the others could see he was holding a slim-bladed knife by the tip.

'Well I'll be buggered. So *that's* what spiked me.' Then, reluctantly: 'You were right, after all. Let's get this back to the station and you can dust it for prints.' Lewis carefully wrapped the knife in his handkerchief, the men climbed back into the car and headed off to Collinghurst.

The DI was the first through the door of the police station. He was just about to go to his office when the desk sergeant called out to him. 'Inspector Parker ... There are two boys waiting to see you.'

'You what?'

'Two nice lads. Said it was very important. I put them in the interview room.'

'Couldn't you've talked to them?'

'They said they'd only talk to you.'

'For God's sake, I've got enough on my plate without bothering about daft boys.'

'I think perhaps you should see them, Sir. They were very insistent.'

'All right,' he said grumpily, 'But they'd better not be wasting my time.'

The other officers had caught up with him. He sent Lewis off to process the knife. To Barrow he said: 'You come with me,' and marched ahead of him into the room where the Christopher and Sandy were waiting.

~o~

The two young friends were sitting side by side at the table, trying not to show their nerves.

'Right, you two. This had better be good. I'm in the middle of a murder investigation.' The DI slumped down opposite them. Barrow sat next to his boss. Parker lit a cigarette, threw the packet down on the table and blew smoke towards the boys.

Christopher coughed, swallowed, then spoke. His voice was firm, as was his resolve. 'Sir, we have important information for you.'

'Yes, yes. Spit it out!'

Undeterred by the policeman's tetchiness he carried on. 'Well, Sir. We were on the beach…'

Parker leant forward and glowered. 'You're the brats that Weeks told me about, aren't you?'

Christopher was determined to carry on. He swallowed and spoke firmly. 'Yes, we are.' And then quietly: 'You didn't believe us then.'

'What makes you think I'll believe you now?' Parker took a long drag on his cigarette then rested it on the ashtray.

Sandy spoke for the first time. 'Because we know what happened to Johnny - I mean Constable Weeks – and he's in great danger.'

Parker's jaw actually dropped and it was a few seconds before he spoke. 'What did you say?'

Now that the boys knew they had his attention they were more confident. Sandy went on: 'We think he's been captured by that other German.'

'The one with the funny leg,' Christopher added.

'Right,' the DI sat back and folded his arms. 'You'd better tell me everything. Start from the beginning.' Something distracted him and before they could answer he bent down and peered under the table. Looking back at him were a pair of soft brown eyes. 'What's that bloody dog doing in here?' he bawled.

'Sorry, Sir. Constable Weeks was looking after Aggie when he disappeared. We had to bring her with us.'

Parker grunted, shaking his head in disbelief. 'Well just make sure you keep the damn thing quiet. Now, spill the beans.'

Taking it in turns, the boys outlined what they had witnessed on the beach. At first the DI was sceptical, especially when they said there had been a thick sea mist, but their clarity and recollection persuaded him they were telling the truth.

'So you're sure he mentioned France?' he asked. The boys nodded. 'It's a blinking big country. I wonder where?' he asked the room in general.

'It could be Boulogne,' Barrow volunteered.

'Really? That's where that French detective is based.'

'Bruissement.'

'That's him.'

'Perhaps he can help?'

'Maybe. Only one way to find out – we'll have to get him on the blower. Meanwhile,' he looked towards Barrow, 'perhaps you could take these young gentlemen home?'

'But…' Sandy's protestation was cut short by a swift kick from Christopher. He closed his mouth and glowered at his friend.

Barrow began to rise from his seat. 'Come on then, lads.'

Just after they'd left the room, Lewis entered.

'Well?'

'It's a match,' Lewis smiled. 'They're definitely the German's dabs.'

'Brilliant. Good news at last.'

Lewis held up his hand. 'Just to make sure, I'm going to take the knife over to Crooks the pathologist to get a match with the wounds on the victims.'

'Fair enough.' Parker looked at his watch. 'It's getting on a bit. Will he still be there?'

'Yes. I've already telephoned the mortuary and caught him before he left. He's going to wait for me.'

'Good. In that case we'll let Herr Müller stew overnight.'

The boys were settled on the back seat of the police car, the terrier sitting between them. Barrow turned and grinned at them. 'Well done, lads. It's not often that the boss is impressed, but he certainly was with the info you had.' The boys grinned back. 'Right, where to? What's your address?'

'Umm,' Christopher began. 'Could you possibly take us to Shell Bay?'

Barrow raised an eyebrow. 'Why do you want to go back there?'

'We're camping in the dunes and all our stuff is there.'

'Fair enough. Sit tight - it's going to be a bumpy ride.'

'What do you think about Guillaume's suggestion?' Judd asked. They were sitting in the American's office discussing what to do next.

'I've got a gut feeling that time, as you suggested, is running out. Is there any way we can get across to France more quickly?' He looked earnestly at Judd. 'My trip here on the train was very enjoyable but I wasn't in a hurry then.'

Judd sighed. 'Yes, you're right.' He sat back and scratched his head. 'I wish there was an overnight train that could get us there quicker... Unfortunately, I don't think there is.'

The two men sat in silence for a while, each with his own thoughts. Then Judd spoke. 'There *may* be a way,' he said slowly.

'Oh yes?'

'We might be able to fly. Do you know if there's an airfield near Boulogne?'

Russell scratched his head. 'No, I don't think there is.' He paused. 'Hang on, there's an airfield at Le Touquet. I've flown there from Lydd airport in Kent.'

'Is it anywhere near Boulogne?'

'Better than that, it's even closer to Saint Valery!'

'Right. Let me see what I can do.' Judd opened his address book and found a number. He picked up the telephone and dialled. After a few moments he spoke rapidly in German. The only words that Russell vaguely recognised were '*Flughafen*' and '*Stuttgart*'. After several minutes, during which the American became increasingly animated, he put the receiver down and smiled. 'Success!'

'Really?'

'Yup. A friend of mine - he's a pilot – has got access to a Piper Clipper.'

'I think I know it. It's a neat little four-seater, isn't it?'

'Right. It's based at Flughafen Stuttgart-Echterdingen.' He smiled. 'That's Stuttgart airport to you.'

'That's what I thought.'

'And he's prepared to fly us to Le Touquet.' His eyes twinkled behind his glasses. 'It's gonna be an early start I'm afraid.'

'How early?'

'Sun-up. That's about 5 am. That okay with you?'

'Of course, if it gets us there quickly. The sooner we get hold of Herr Salz, the happier I'll feel.'

~O~

Wolfgang stood grim-faced in the wheelhouse on *Moonshine*. The news that his brother was being held at Collinghurst, and was going to be charged with murder, frustrated him beyond endurance. Not only did he now realise that he was unable to do anything about his imprisonment but he would have to finish the task they started together, alone. He was out of the shipping lane so slipped a loop of rope over the spoke of the wheel. This would hold the vessel's course while he went below to make himself a mug of hot coffee.

Weeks woke to find he was lying on the cabin floor with his hands tied tightly together. He looked down. He recognised a double constrictor knot. His head was thumping in time to the beat of the boat's engine and he felt sick. He closed his eyes against the pain. When he opened them again the form of Wolfgang, standing over him, swam into view.

'So what do you think you are doing on my boat,' he asked, smiling grimly.

'What?' The DC shook his head slowly, trying to lessen the pain. The boat, with the engine ticking over, was rocking uncomfortably.

'This was not a wise move.' The German's voice took on a sinister tone. 'Now I have to decide what to do with you.' The boat gave a lurch and so did Weeks's stomach. He retched and brought up his last meal, just missing Wolfgang's feet. '*Ach*! *Widerlich*!'

'Sorry,' Weeks slurred, and was immediately sick again. Wolfgang tutted in disgust and walked out of the cabin and up the companionway steps, moving easily, in tune with the motion of the boat.

Tuesday

Kidnapping - *the unlawful taking away of a person against their will. This may be done for the furtherance of a crime.*

DI PARKER and DC Barrow were sitting in the office at the police station. Parker had his feet up on the desk, a cigarette gripped between his thumb and forefinger. A curl of smoke rose lazily from the glowing tip. He was feeling smug. Lewis had come in earlier with the news that the knife they had found was a perfect match for the wounds inflicted on the three victims. So, with the fingerprints, there was now no need to show it to the previous owner of *Moonshine* - whatever his name was. His gloating was dashed by the unannounced entry into the room of Superintendent Stout. Both detectives got smartly to their feet, Parker quickly standing on the cigarette end that he dropped on the floor.

'Right …' The Super, sitting down on the spare chair, gestured for the others to return to their seats. '… We've got enough evidence to convict Müller of murders. It's a shame we can't get his brother, too. Any news from France?'

'I'm afraid not, Sir,' Parker said, his voice deferential. 'Our contact …' He looked down at the paper in front of him. '… Bruissement …' he enunciated carefully, '…had left his office when we tried to contact him yesterday evening.'

'Have you tried him today?'

'Yes, but he hasn't turned up yet.'

Stout groaned in frustration.' Isn't there anyone else who can help over there?'

The DI looked decidedly uncomfortable. 'It doesn't seem so, Sir. Nobody else seems to speak English …'

'… And you don't speak French?'

Parker looked down. 'No, Sir.'

'Oh, for heaven's sake!' Parker squirmed in his seat. Stout continued. 'And I suppose you don't know what's happened to Constable Weeks?'

'Afraid not, Sir.'

'So … although we've got the main suspect in custody, we're missing his brother - who seems to be the mastermind behind this sorry affair - as well as a detective constable.'

'Yes, Sir.'

He banged his fist on the table. 'It's not good enough!'

Barrow coughed nervously. 'We have got the soldier, Rankin, Sir.'

'Maybe, but he was only the driver ... wasn't he?' Barrow nodded. 'Right, well keep trying until you get hold of the French detective or you two will be on the next ferry to Boulogne. And it won't be a pleasure trip!' the superintendent thundered. He stood up abruptly and left the room.

Parker waited a few moments after the door had closed before he spoke. 'I hate the sea. You won't get me on a bloody ferry - not if I have anything to do with it.' He grunted and picked up the telephone handset and dialled the switchboard. 'Get me that number in Boulogne again.' There was a pause. 'Of course the same one!' He slammed the receiver down and turned to Barrow. 'Idiot.' The DC knew better than to respond and they sat in silence until the phone rang. 'Yes? This is Parker. Ah, Bruissement.'

'Yes, it is I. What is it you wish to speak me about?' The Frenchman's voice was cool.

'Er, we understand that one of our officers has been kidnapped and is on his way to France.'

'Pardon?!'

The DI enunciated slowly, 'I - said, one - of - our - officers …'

Bruissement interrupted. 'Yes, I comprehended what you said, I was just surprised. Who has been kidnapped?'

'Weeks.'

The Frenchman gasped. 'DI Russell's number two?'

'Correct.'

'What happened?'

'He was foolish enough to be caught nosing around *Moonshine*, which belongs to the Müller brothers, and Wolfgang's got him.'

'And 'e is 'eaded for France?'

'So it seems.'

'Why France?' Bruissement asked.

'We don't know. I thought you might be able to help.' Parker's words hung in the air for some moments. The line crackled.

Then Bruissement spoke. 'I will tell you what I know. We think Wolfgang Müller has a reason to 'ead for Saint Valery.'

'And where is that?'

'It is just down the coast from Boulogne.'

'But why there … may I ask?'

' 'E is after number four.'

'Number four?' Parker was puzzled.

'I 'ope you are sitting in comfort – it is a long story.'

'Very comfortable thank you. Go ahead.' The Frenchman went on to explain.

Apart from lighting a cigarette, the DI sat quietly and listened. Bruissement explained in detail what Russell had told him. When he came to the end the DI spoke.

'So Russell and this American …'

'Judd.'

' … Judd. They are flying back from Germany.'

'Ah *oui*. They will be arriving later this morning.'

'And you are going to meet them at Le Touquet.'

'*Exactement*!'

'You do realise Russell is off the case?' Parker growled.

'Yes, I am aware of that.' There was sadness in Bruissement's voice.

'So he shouldn't be involved,' Parker said.

After a pause the Frenchman said: 'Are you planning to come over then, Inspector?'

'Ah … well,' he stammered. 'I'm not sure I can be spared from my duties here.'

'Well, perhaps you should 'ave a leetle word with your Superintendent?'

'Are you suggesting what I think you're suggesting?'

'That DI Russell should be reinstated? *Mai oui* – but of course.'

'Hmm. I'm not sure he'll agree.'

'Then it is up to you to persuade him, *non*?' Amusement crept into Bruissement's voice. 'Unless, of course you would like to catch the ferry over to Boulogne?'

'I'll have to see what I can do,' Parker muttered.

'Meanwhile, I 'ave alerted *la Garde côtière* here and I suggest you inform your English coastguard.'

~O~

Moonshine moved easily through the waves. The wind was light, no more than force two, only occasionally rising to a gentle three. The mist acted like oil on troubled waters, rendering the surface of the sea smooth, the tops of the waves barely breaking. Wolfgang perched on the helmsman's seat, holding the wheel lightly, making automatic adjustments. The mist had been patchy as he crossed the Channel but once he was a few miles off the French coast it had become thicker, so he motored slowly north for several hours before turning and motoring back. This was how he had spent most of the night, grabbing a few minutes' sleep here and there.

When day broke the mist was still thick. It was a couple of hours before high tide so he decided it was time to risk entering the Channel. He was sure that both the English and French coastguards would be looking for him but the covering mist had been on his side. However, he needed to conceal the boat so that when the murk lifted it wouldn't easily be spotted.

But … there was still the problem of what to do with the policeman - the task ahead was going to be difficult enough without such an unwelcome encumbrance. If only Ludwig was with him - he missed his brother's bulk and muscle, let alone his moral support. Suddenly he had an inspiration - the policeman was young and fit, despite his *mal de mer*. With a little persuasion he could be a replacement for Ludwig, albeit a less powerful and menacing one. And Wolfgang had just the right persuasion… His brother had preferred a knife, but he knew that his own Luger pistol would come in useful sometime. He slipped the loop of rope over the spoke of the wheel and went below.

Weeks had managed to get himself upright, his back against the bulkhead. He looked decidedly unwell. His skin was pale and pasty, his eyes rheumy. He looked blearily at Wolfgang. 'Where are we going?'

'We are off the coast of France, in the Baie de la Somme. We will soon be making landfall.'

'Are you going to tell me where?'

Of course. Why not? We are going to Saint-Valery-sur-Somme.'

Weeks arched his back, struggling to make himself more comfortable. 'Why there?'

Wolfgang paused and thought for a moment. 'I will untie your hands if you promise not to do anything stupid - this should help to remind you.' He took the Luger out of his pocket, pointed it at Weeks, then laid it on the bunk. He crouched down and worked skilfully at the knots until the ropes came free. Weeks rubbed his wrists gratefully.

'You now have a choice. You can agree to help me or …'

Weeks looked warily at the little German. 'Or what?'

Wolfgang touched the pistol and gave a cold smile. 'I doubt even you could swim with a bullet in your leg … or somewhere more painful.'

Weeks shuddered and closed his eyes wearily. 'What do you want me to do?'

Wolfgang's smile widened, but held no warmth. 'That is better,' he said quietly.' Standing he moved towards the galley. He turned and said: 'You look terrible. I had better feed you up if you are to be of any use to me.'

They had taken off from Stuttgart airport in the Piper Clipper at just after 5am. With a cruising speed of around 100 knots it would have been possible to make the trip in a little over four hours. But the pilot was concerned that the fuel might not last the journey so they touched down near Reims. Russell was glad of the chance to stretch his legs and grab a coffee although anxious to be on his way again, once the refuelling was done.

Just before ten am they were circling over Le Touquet. Russell could clearly see the terminal building, with the words 'Gateway to the Continent' in large letters on the roof. He could also see the unmistakeable form of Bruissement standing by a black Citroën traction Avant.

The pilot brought the Piper down expertly in a classic three-point landing on the Tarmac strip and taxied up to the terminal. When the aircraft had rolled to a stop, Judd climbed out of his seat and held the door open for Russell. Bruissement came over from his car and folded him in a warm embrace. Slightly embarrassed he stood back while the Frenchman did the same with Judd. Then flinging his arms wide he said: 'Ah, *mes amis*, it is good to see you both! You must be hungry and thirsty. I know I am. And Sonny … I 'ave some good news … and some bad news for you. Follow me and I will tell all.' Bruissement winked and led them into the airport café.

They found a table overlooking the airstrip and soon the waiter had brought warm croissants, *pain au chocolat, pain au raison* and steaming *bols* of coffee. 'First the good news: your Superintendent Stout has had you *réintégrére!*'

'Re-instated?' Judd asked. 'Why, that's marvellous.'

'What? But how? I don't understand.' Russell paused, the croissant he was about to bite into hovering just short of his mouth.

Bruissement chuckled. 'I 'ad a talk with your Inspector Parker…' Russell raised an eyebrow. '… I told 'im you were *en route* to Le Touquet and suggested that 'e 'ad a talk with Stout.'

'How on earth did you get him to agree to that?'

The Frenchman's chuckle turned into a laugh. 'A little bird suggested to me that your DI Parker does not like to travel by boat.

'E soon realised that it would be better if you were the man on the ground. I think the thought of crossing the channel made 'im - 'ow you say - a leetle green round the gills.'

'And the Super agreed?'

'*Apparement*. So now you are on business official.'

Russell put down the remains of the croissant and let out a long breath. 'Well. That *is* a surprise.' After a few moments he sat up and spoke again. 'You said there was bad news, too.'

'Ah ... I am afraid there is a little complication.'

'And that is?' Russell returned to his croissant and took a sip of coffee.

A concerned look crossed the Frenchman's face. 'It is your right 'and man ...'

'Weeks?'

'Yes. I am afraid he has been *kidnappé*.'

'*What*?' Russell jumped to his feet, scattering crumbs and spilling coffee in his agitation.

Bruissement held his hands up, palms outwards. 'Please to be calm, Sonny. Sit down and I will tell all.' While mopping up the spilt coffee with a napkin the Frenchman explained what Parker had told him about Wolfgang and how the scouts, Christopher and Sandy, had persuaded him to take it seriously.

Russell shook his head. 'This really complicates matters.'

'Maybe. But perhaps we will be able to turn the situation to our advantage.'

'I don't see how.'

Judd spoke for the first time. 'Listen. It sounds like the situation is difficult enough as it is. Why don't we sit back and decide the best way to deal with it, Hmm?'

'You are right, *mon ami américain*. Let us work out *un plan d'attaque*.'

~o~

Wolfgang steered *Moonshine* carefully between the muddy banks of the estuary. He allowed the tide to carry the vessel, keeping the engine at low revs, just enough to retain steerage. The mist meant that visibility was greatly reduced and he didn't want to risk running aground. There were a couple of heart-stopping moments when the keel touched the bottom but the tide easily lifted the boat up and forward. He knew it would be imprudent to land at the quay as although, as far as he was aware, no one knew where he was headed, the police may have been alerted. So he looked out for a creek where he could conceal the boat.

After a few more minutes, a channel opened up to starboard. Putting the helm down the German nosed the craft into the narrow opening, reed-topped mud banks closing in on both sides. Twisting and turning they had travelled only a short distance along the channel before a decrepit looking jetty came into view. He let the boat drift up to it and bump the timber. Apart from a little shudder, the structure stayed firm, so he guessed it would be strong enough for the purpose of mooring, plus the banks and reeds would help to conceal *Moonshine*. He stepped out of the wheelhouse and threw a loop of rope over a post on the jetty.

'You come up here,' he called to Weeks

The tousled head of the young policeman appeared from below. 'Yes?' he said warily. He'd managed to eat most of the food that Wolfgang had prepared and the colour was returning slowly to his cheeks. 'What do you want?'

Wolfgang had walked to the bow and thrown another rope over a stump of timber. 'You may start by securing that.'

Weeks nodded and swung his leg over the gunwale. He stood unsteadily on the jetty, his balance shaky after all the hours at sea. He made his way to the rope and did his best to secure it. The German obviously did not approve of his efforts as he scowled and tutted. Weeks shrugged, thrust his hands into his trouser pockets and hung his head.

'Oh, I suppose it will do. Now get back here and help me get the dinghy over the side. But remember, I have a pistol and I will use it if necessary. We are going into the town. You will do exactly what I say and you will not get hurt. If you disobey...' His words hung in the air.

Wolfgang untied the neat knots that held the small wooden craft secure and the two men manhandled it over the side of *Moonshine* and into the water. 'Right, you get in first. You are going to row me to the quay.' The policeman climbed down into the dinghy and settled himself on the central thwart. Wolfgang handed down the oars then clambered down, his withered leg making the descent clumsy and a canvas satchel slung over his shoulder causing additional hindrance. Weeks automatically put out a hand to steady him but the German thrust it aside.

'I can manage!' he snapped angrily. Weeks shrugged and slotted the oars in the rowlocks while Wolfgang pushed the dinghy away from the bigger boat. 'Now row!'

The younger man had learnt to handle a boat when he was in the sea scouts and he pulled strongly. Wolfgang sat in the stern, telling him when to alter course. With the tide in their favour it only took ten minutes to reach the quay where they moored by a flight of stone steps. The German looped the painter round a ring set in the dripping stone wall and deftly tied it off.

'Right. Get out of the boat, slowly climb the steps and wait at the top for me. And no tricks. You know what I have in my pocket.' Weeks did as he was bid and with an effort Wolfgang joined him on the quay. Then pointing to the right he said: 'This way.'

They set off and were soon walking along Rue de la Ferté. They received no curious glances from the few people they passed, despite their odd appearance - Weeks in his rumpled clothing and the German with his awkward gait. Halfway along the narrow street, Wolfgang stopped in front of a *boulangerie*. 'Now, remember what I said. I have the gun in my pocket. Do exactly what I say. Understand?'

Weeks nodded. 'Yes, I understand,' he said resignedly.

The bell above the door jangled cheerfully as the two stepped inside. There were no other customers and the rotund *boulanger* had his back to them. He was stretching up to a shelf attempting to get a tin that was only just within his reach. At the sound of the bell he started to turn, smiling a welcome. But immediately his cheerful expression was swiftly replaced by a look of horror, the tin slipping from his grasp and clattering to the floor. Beads of sweat broke out on his forehead and he put out a hand to steady himself, clutching the edge of the counter.

Wolfgang, pointing the Luger, smiled icily. 'I see you remember me, Herr Pfeffer.'

'S-Salz,' the man stammered. 'My name is Salz – Micha Salz.' The sweat was running down his fat face now and he was shaking uncontrollably. He pointed towards the front of the shop. 'You can see my n-n-ame above the window.'

The small German chuckled mirthlessly. 'I don't care what you call yourself now. I will always know you as Hauptsturmführer Achim Pfeffer. Now, you will write a note saying the shop is closed.'

'What?' the *boulanger* said, almost in a whisper.

'You heard,' Wolfgang hissed. 'Say you are ill.' He threw back his head and let out a high-pitched laugh. 'You certainly will be!' With trembling hands Salz found paper and pencil and scribbled a few words. When he had finished he looked up. Still pointing the pistol at the baker Wolfgang turned his head slightly towards Weeks. 'Take the paper and put it on the door.' The policeman moved forward and picked up the note. He walked to the door and wedged it under the edge of the frame. As he was turning back Wolfgang said: 'And pull down the blind.' Then to Salz: 'Take off your apron. We are going to your house.'

'B-but...'

Wolfgang waved the pistol. 'You will do what I say – *now!*'

~O~

Judd: 'So what's your idea, Guillaume?' The three men were still in the airport café, now on their second coffees.

The Frenchman put down his cup and pursed his lips. 'As I said on the telephone, I think we should go down to Saint Valery, but ...' he held his finger to his lips and spoke in a whisper, '... but tread carefully.'

Russell had been thinking hard but had failed to come up with any ideas. 'What do you suggest we do?'

'This is what I think.' Bruissement sat back, put his hands on the table and linked his fingers. 'We should drive down. It will take us no more than 40 minutes, maybe 50. We will park the car *discrètement*. I will show you where the Boulangerie Salz is, then we will drive past and park the motor car. Sonny, you and I will wait at a safe distance while you' - he gestured towards Judd - 'will go into the *dépôt de pain* and engage M. Salz in conversation.'

'*Hmmm*. What will I say?' the American wondered.

'Oh, I don't know. Perhaps something about 'ow good his bread is. 'Ow it 'as been recommended by a friend. Perhaps, 'ow there is nothing like it in Germany. Just try to steer the conversation so you can establish *un rapport* with 'im. Somehow you 'ave to gain 'is trust. Maybe begin to talk German with 'im. I am sure 'e will be delighted to meet a fellow countryman.' Bruissement winked. 'Then, 'e will open up to you.'

'Oh, I don't know how convincing I will be …'

Bruissement spread his arms expansively and beamed. '*Trust me, mon ami américain*. It will be fine. You will see.' He clicked his fingers for the bill. 'Now we must get going.'

The journey, as Bruissement had predicted, took just over 40 minutes. Once in the town he drove the Citröen slowly along Quai Blavet, which skirted the estuary and moored fishing boats, then turned into Rue de la Ferté. As they motored along the narrow street he pointed to the right.

'There it is.' Russell and Judd looked and could see a discreet shop with the legend *Boulangerie Salz* above the window. The Frenchman drove on for another hundred yards or so and parked on the Quai Pérée.

Turning to Judd he said: 'Right. Sonny and I will wait here while you go and reconnoitre.' The American grimaced, but opened the door, got out and walked back the way they had just come.

'So what do we do next?' Russell asked.

'We wait to see what Greg has found out.'

They settled in their seats and looked out across the quay. The mist that had been hanging over the sea was starting to lift a little and the shapes of the marshes were beginning to show more clearly. To their right, at the end of the railway track, a small Corpet-Louvet locomotive stood on the turntable, the steam from its chimney swirling and blending with wisps of mist. But they had been settled for only a few minutes when the car door was wrenched open and Judd tumbled into his seat. 'He's not there!'

'*What?*' the other two said in unison.

'There was a handwritten note on the door. '*Fermée. Pour cause de maladie*'.

'He is sick? How strange,' Bruissement said. '*Mon Dieu*! What can we do now?' He slumped back in his seat and snorted.

'Perhaps we can find his house?' Russell suggested.

The Frenchman sat up. 'But of course! Come, let us interrogate his neighbours. He climbed swiftly out of the car, plucked the keys from the dashboard, slammed the door shut and strode back towards the *boulangerie*. The other two men struggled to keep up with him. Salz's immediate neighbour was a *fleurist*. Bruissement went into the shop while the others waited, but he was quickly outside again, shaking his head. '*Non*. They 'ave not seen 'im.' On the other side was a *confiserie*, its window filled with brightly coloured sweets and candies. Again, the *propriétaire* had not seen the *boulanger*. Next was a *bureau de tabac*. The *patron* was outside, arranging copies of *Le Figaro* in a wire rack. Bruissement asked if he had seen Salz.

'Why yes!' he said. 'He came past. Not half an hour ago.'

'Was he on his own?'

'No, he was with two other gentlemen.' Bruissement and Judd exchanged a glance.

'Did he say anything?'

'Yes, he said he was feeling unwell and these friends of his were helping him home.'

'Can you describe the friends?'

The man thought for a moment then spoke again. 'Well, it was strange, as the one who seemed to be in charge was a little man. As they walked away I noticed that he was limping badly.'

'And the other?'

'He was younger. Had a mop of dark curly hair. Looked unhappy.'

'Can you tell me where M. Saltz lives?'

'Rue de Puits Salé. It is no more than 10 minutes from here.'

'Which house?' When there was no immediate reply Bruissement said: 'We are the police. We need to contact him urgently, *mon ami!*'

The *patron* looked flustered. 'Umm. I can't remember what it's called but it's a big white house. Oh, and it has a brick barn attached on one side.'

'Which way do we go?'

'That way.' The man pointed up the street. 'Keep going along Quai de Romere, into Rue de la Port de Nevers and it's on your left. The house is about 100 metres farther on. You can't miss it.'

Bruissement nodded. 'Thank you, *monsieur. Tres bon.*' He then set off at a cracking pace which belied his sedentary appearance.

Russell almost had to trot to keep up. 'What did he say?' he asked as the conversation had taken place exclusively in French. As they hurried, Bruissement explained, with additions from Judd, who was just about keeping up. In fewer than the ten minutes they had been advised they had rushed through a stone archway and were turning into Rue de Puits Salé.

As his eyes grew accustomed to the gloom Weeks could see that the barn was used as a store. Boxes and barrels were stacked neatly, lengths of timber leant against the wall and bulging sacks were piled up in the corner. Wolfgang had made Salz sit on an old stool, in the middle of the room. He sat on a chair, a few feet away, the Luger held loosely in his hand.

'Do you speak English?' he asked. The man was sweating freely and shaking, as if in a fever. He nodded. 'Then do so, for the benefit of our friend here.' He inclined his head towards Weeks. 'You were very frightened when I appeared in your shop. How did you know I would be coming?'

The man swallowed several times, his Adams apple bobbing visibly.

'I saw the reports in the newspaper.'

Wolfgang tilted his head to one side and smiled. 'What reports?'

'About the bodies. I realised who they were.' He sat hunched, wringing his hands in his lap.

'And who were they? Please tell my friend here.' He waved the gun towards the Englishman.

They were my men,' he said quietly.

'Oh yes? Can you be more specific?'

'They were in my unit.'

'Working for T four.'

Even more quietly: 'Yes.'

Wolfgang pointed the gun. 'Speak up!' he commanded.

'We were working for T four.' More loudly this time.

'Ah yes. *Tiergartenstrasse vier.* The systematic elimination of the mentally and physically disabled. Those poor souls who did not fit the Aryan ideal.' Salz remained silent. Wolfgang went on. 'I remember it well.' He paused and sat quietly, lost in thought.

'I remember your *unit* coming to our house. Unfortunately Ludwig was away, fighting on the eastern front, and only Franz was there to protect me – he didn't stand a chance. But he did delay your men long enough to allow me to escape through a window at the back of the house.' He paused again, remembering - then went on quietly.

'Every day since, I wish I had not.' Weeks could see he was near to tears.

'I only found out later what had happened to Franz… and it was you and your *unit* that did it to him. It should not have happened. He was an Obergefreiter in the Wehrmacht. But you did not care. It was me that you wanted.' He rubbed a sleeve across his eyes. 'But he did not give me up.'

'I'm sorry.' Salz too was near to tears.

'*Sorry*?' Wolfgang hissed. '*Sorry*? It is too late for regrets. You should have thought about that when you took him – instead of me.'

The little German settled himself on the chair and fixed his eyes on the quivering baker. He got out a pack of cigarettes and lit one for himself, taking a deep and satisfying drag. Salk looked at it longingly. 'Huh,' snapped Wolfgang, 'I don't think so!'

'It was a neighbour who informed on Franz,' he began. 'The end of the war was approaching, the Gestapo were getting jumpy – more so than usual – and for some unknown reason the neighbour was concerned they might come after him. So, to put them off the trail, he let it be known that there was a cripple, a young man with a withered leg, in the house next door, hoping that would divert them. And sure enough they came. Our wealthy parents had both died earlier in the war, Ludwig was away in the army and just Franz and I were in the house when the four men in their *feldgrau* uniforms hammered on the door.

'Franz had always been the golden boy – in every way. He was good looking, good natured and a superb athlete. Ironically, a shining example of the Aryan ideal. So much so that it was expected he would have been asked to compete in the Olympic Games - if they had not been cancelled in 1940 and 1944. Sadly he was dead before the resumption in 1948, even if Germany had been allowed to take part. Ludwig had idolised him, acting as his protector, until called up to fight with the Wehrmacht. Franz was the youngest, so he stayed home with me for the first three years of the war. I loved him dearly, vicariously sharing his successes on the track and field in summer and on the ski slopes in winter.

'We sailed together – the one thing I could do – Franz as crew, leaping across the boat as we went about, trimming the sails and keeping the balance - while I perfected my skill as helmsman. After a busy day tacking round the buoys in the lake we would settle down in the evening, discussing boats and sailing and often having knot-tying competitions. I invariably won - my fingers were nimble and my brain quick. Franz was never jealous, delighted that there was something practical 'Wolf' could do with ease. When Franz joined the Wehrmacht, I was heartbroken to see him go but proud of his rapid promotion to Obergefreiter and relished his all too brief spells of leave when we could spend time together.'

Wolfgang shifted his position and drew, in a leisurely fashion, on his cigarette. He was amazingly cool, Weeks reflected for a man about to commit another murder. He continued with his reminiscences.

'When Franz was taken I was distraught. More so when I learnt that he had been viciously tortured for several days before being executed, his wrecked body thrown in a shallow grave. Friends sheltered me but when, a short time later, the war ground to its inevitable end, I was absolutely determined to avenge my brave brother's death. Ludwig came back from fighting the Russians, bowed but not broken, unlike scores of his comrades, and between the two of us we uncovered the chain of events that led to Franz's appalling end.

'The neighbour was the first to be dealt with. One night he disappeared. A few days later he turned up in the lake, drowned but with unpleasant injuries to his body that just *might* have been the result of being in the water - just *might* have.

It took a lot longer to find the whereabouts of the Waffen-SS soldiers who had been responsible for Franz's torture and death. But we were determined to seek revenge and spent the next 10 years, doggedly searching records until we finally tracked them down. Then, together, we captured them, transported them across the continent and gave them a taste of their own medicine. The grisly nautical tortures we inflicted on their bodies seemed fitting, given Franz's love of boats and sailing. Now there is just one monster left to deal with...'

~O~

Wolfgang stared into the distance as he finished his story, seemingly lost in thought for a moment, his face sad. Then, suddenly, he leapt to his feet and ground his cigarette end into the earthen floor with his foot.

'Right,' he snapped. 'Let us finish the job and be gone.' He reached into his satchel, withdrew a coil of rope and held it out to Weeks.

'I want it up there, over that beam.' He looked towards the open framework of the roof.

'What?'

'Do not stand there with your mouth open you fool, just *do it!*' Wolfgang trained the gun on him and Weeks reached for the rope. Taking it he realised, with a shudder, that there was a noose in one end, neatly tied. Wolfgang saw his reaction and smiled.

'That is right, I am going to hang him.'

'B-but you can't!' Salz stammered.

'But I can.' The little German was smiling grimly.

'I have enjoyed repaying *your* men for what they did to my brother. First a keelhauling for Obersturmführer Rudolf Bausewein. I took great pleasure in that. Next it was the turn of Untersturmführer Kaspar Bockelmann. That was a little more complicated, but no less enjoyable.' He chuckled and looked towards Weeks.

'I was rather pleased that we caused so much upset at not one but two of your building sites.'

Weeks spoke. 'But why did you bring those men to England to kill them. Wouldn't it have been easier to do it where they lived?'

'Ah, but then it would not have had the same impact. It did require a lot of organisation and effort but I knew the English press would make a big fuss in reporting it.' He smiled thinly. 'They do like a sensational story - and I gave them several. I wanted to make sure this miserable example of humanity came to hear of our ... exploits with his *men*.' Salz was in pieces.

'But why England when he was in France?'

'I did not know at the time. The rumour was that he had hidden himself in your country. It was our last victim, Untersturmführer Max Krull, who told me where he was. Luckily the French papers had picked up the stories ... so he found out.'

His face darkened. 'It was *your* lot - the British police - who caused the problems we had dealing with Krull. And now my beloved brother is in your British custody.'

He brightened. 'But do not worry, I have a plan for getting him back. But that is for later. Meanwhile, we have to deal with this piece of dirt.'

He pointed the Luger at Salz. The man looked close to death already. 'Now - do as I say!'

A horrified Weeks reluctantly threw the rope towards the beam. With his first attempt it hit the timber but bounced off and fell at his feet. He tried again and this time it curled over the beam and he was able to reach up and grasp the swinging end. He looked towards Wolfgang.

'Right,' the German barked. 'Take the end over to that diagonal wooden brace.' He pointed to the side of the barn. Weeks did as he was asked. 'Now wrap it round then come back and stand by this … *creature.*'

When the policeman had taken his place next to Salz, Wolfgang backed away, aiming the gun at them. He reached the wall, grasped the rope, pulled it taught and tied a bowline, one-handed. He saw Weeks looking at him and smiled.

'Surprised? Now you know who tied all those beautiful knots. Even the disabled have skills.' He let the gun droop in his hand and leant against the wall.

'I expect you're wondering why all those archaic nautical punishments - keelhauling, lashing, walking the plank…' He paused and chuckled. 'I quite enjoyed having an audience for that one. Especially as it was rarely used in actual fact.'

'Like my brother Franz, I have always loved the water and boats. Sailing was the one sport I was good at - with this.' He tapped his withered leg. Yes, it is polio. I understand a specialist in America by the name of Jonas Salk has recently developed a vaccine for it.' His tone changed and he sounded wistful. 'But it is too late for me.' He grew quiet, seemingly lost in thought. Then he brightened.

'However, the thought of this final punishment is cheering me even though, as your Mr Bunyan said: "Hanging is too good for him".'

He pointed the pistol at the other German, whose legs were shaking uncontrollably.

'But it will have to do. Right you - stand up.' Salz got shakily to his feet. 'Now you …,' he motioned to Weeks, 'put the stool underneath the rope.' The young man was appalled.

'But you *can't*…'

'I can and I *will*,' Wolfgang hissed. 'Do it. *Now!*' He clicked off the gun's safety catch. Weeks unwillingly took the stool and placed it beneath the noose then stood back.

'You…' Wolfgang pointed the gun at Salz. 'Get on the stool!'

'B-but…'

Wolfgang fired a shot. The bullet thudded into the brickwork, sending up a little puff of dust. Salz shuffled over and tried to climb on the stool. He was quaking so much he couldn't control his legs and remained standing on the floor.

'Help him!' Wolfgang's light voice became a high-pitched scream. Weeks went over and took the man's arm and half-lifted him on to the stool, where he stood, knees knocking, trousers embarrassingly wet.

'Now, put the noose round his neck.' Weeks hesitated. Wolfgang flicked the gun upwards. The young policeman did as he was bid, the noose hung loosely down the man's back. As he moved to step away Wolfgang threw a length of the chord he had taken from the satchel towards him.

'Wait. Tie his hands.'

Weeks picked up the chord, pulled Salz's hands behind his back and tied them together. While he was doing this Wolfgang had reached round the diagonal brace and deftly untied the end of the rope, pulled it taut, so the noose was tight around the man's neck, and tied it off again.

He pointed the gun at Weeks. 'Now stand back, against the wall; I need you for later.'

Weeks moved to the other side of the barn, his brain whirring. He was desperately trying to work out how he could possibly save the man's life. The German may have been guilty of torturing and killing Wolfgang's brother, but he would rather see him stand trial and be justly punished than suffer this horror now. He thought quickly: If he tried to rescue the man, Wolfgang had the pistol and was obviously not afraid to use it. Likewise, if he tried to rush the little German he'd probably end up with a bullet in him. Talk. That was all he could think of. Get him talking. He tried to keep his voice even… tried not to betray the quaking inside.

'What do you need me for later - Wolfgang?' It was the first time he had used his name to the killer's face. This seemed to catch him unawares.

'What?' The little German looked surprised.

'I said what do you plan for later – with me?'

Wolfgang smiled coldly. 'You are going to help me get my brother, Ludwig, released from police custody.'

'Really? How will we do that?'

'When we have dealt with… with… this…' He pointed the gun at Salz, the man barely able to keep his balance on the stool. 'We will go back to England.'

'But how do you propose to get him out?'

Wolfgang scowled. 'I will work that out on the way over. He may have the brawn, but I have the brains.'

He gave a short laugh. 'Any more questions? Or can we get on with this?'

Weeks thought fast. 'I may know a way…'

'Yes? What is that?'

Making it up as he went along: 'If you can get me back to Collinghurst I can talk to my superior, I know he'll help…'

Wolfgang sneered. 'Detective Inspector Russell?' Weeks nodded. 'But I heard he's off the case.'

'He was, but he's back on it now.' Weeks had his fingers crossed behind his back.

'Hmm. Maybe.' He grew impatient. 'Enough of this idle chatter. I have a final task to complete. Kick the stool away.'

Weeks had run out of ideas. 'No, I can't,' he pleaded. Please don't make me do this.'

'*Gott in Himmel!*' the small German stormed. 'Do I have to do everything myself?' He was just moving across the room to finish the job when there was a hammering on the door.

'*Was ist das? Sei stille!*' he held a finger to his lips. 'Quiet!'

The hammering came again and there was a shout.

'*Monsieur* Salz. Êtes-vous là?'

Wolfgang moved swiftly over to the door. There was a large baulk of timber, pivoted at the centre. He swung it round hard, like a propeller, so it locked into two metal brackets, securing the door. Then he moved back across the room and, reaching down, pulled the stool out from under the baker's feet.

'*Nooo!*' Weeks yelled, and ran towards them.

Wolfgang pulled the trigger. The young policeman froze, squeezing his eyes tight shut as he waited to feel the lethal burn of a bullet… but there was just a hollow click.

'*Scheisse!*' Wolfgang swore. He tried again. Nothing. The gun had jammed. For a moment, the German stared at the weapon in disbelief. Weeks staggered back and held on to a joist for support. His knees shook under him and he thought he was about to pass out.

There was more hammering on the door.

'*Ouvrez la porte immediatement!*'

Wolfgang looked from the door to Weeks, who had run over and was trying to support the weight of the German.

'*Mein Gott*! What now?'

Staring wildly around he suddenly spotted a small door at the back of the barn. Limping, he ran across the room, and pulled it open.

'No! Stop!' Weeks shouted. But Wolfgang, with a quick glance over his shoulder, was gone.

'What's going on?' a voice yelled from outside.

'He's getting away! We're in here!' Weeks yelled. 'Wait!'

Still holding Salz he fumbled with his foot until he felt the stool and was able to hook it round a rung. With superhuman strength, he held up the German and, balancing on one leg, slowly dragged the stool under the kicking feet.

'Stand still!' he commanded.

The kicking stopped, he pushed the support beneath Salz's feet and the weight eased as he found his footing. Weeks ran to where the rope was tied, undid the knot and let it go slack. Rushing back he caught the man as he began to fall off the stool. He laid him on the ground and eased the noose from round his neck. After checking that he was breathing he crossed to the door, and tried to release the beam. It was wedged tight.

'Damn!' he said. Wolfgang had spun it round so hard, it was stuck fast.

The pounding started on the door again.

'What's going on in there?' It was Russell's voice.

Weeks smiled in relief. 'Sir! Oh, thank God! Just a minute. The door's jammed!'

Looking round he saw a length of timber against the wall. He picked it up and swung it with all his might. It hit the beam with a thud and splintered but the beam stayed put.

'*Aah! Shit!*' Weeks swore uncharacteristically.

Searching wildly for a stronger piece of wood he suddenly spotted a sledge-hammer across the room. He ran and grabbed it and was back within a matter of seconds. He swung the tool above his head and brought it down hard. On the third blow the beam spun free.

Almost immediately, the door flew open and Russell rushed in, closely followed by Judd and Bruissement.

'*What the…!*' Russell took in the scene, clapped the trembling Weeks on the back, then quickly knelt by the German, feeling his pulse. 'Alive – thank God. Where's Wolfgang?'

Weeks, stunned by the events, took a moment to react and shook his head in an attempt to clear his brain.

'Wolfgang? He's escaped - *out there!*' he said, pointing to the small door at the back of the barn through which the German had disappeared moments before. Judd and the Frenchman tore out into the yard.

In a few minutes they were back. 'He's gone,' Bruissement said.

'No sign of him,' the American added. 'How's Salz? He pointed to the German on the floor.

Russell looked up. 'He'll live. Although he may not want to…'

'What do we do about Müller?' Judd asked.

Weeks spoke. 'He's probably headed back to the quay. That's where we left the dinghy. He'll try to row out to *Moonshine*. It's hidden in the reeds.'

'Right! We need to get after him.' Bruissement was taking charge. 'Sonny, you stay with Salz. Weeks, you go and get help. Someone nearby must have a telephone. Greg, you come with me.' Then he was gone, again moving at surprising speed, the American struggling to keep up with him.

The two men reached the quay just in time to see the dinghy melting into the mist which was closing in again.

'*Merde*! What do we do now?'

'Look, over there, *Le Bureau du Capitaine de Port* - the harbourmaster's office,' Greg said, pointing. 'Maybe he can help.' They ran the few hundred yards and clattered in through the door.

'*Bonjour messieurs. Que puis-je faire pour vous?*' the harbourmaster asked, looking up from some paperwork. They explained that they needed to get a boat to follow Wolfgang and stop *Moonshine* from leaving. '*Pas de chance!*' he said, and pointed out through the window. In the time it had taken to get to his office the mist had rolled in so thickly that it was now not possible to see the quay outside.

'That's it then,' Judd said in disbelief. 'We've lost him. After all that we've lost him.'

Bruissement sighed deeply. 'For now, *mon ami*, for now...'

Postscript

The local gendarmerie, along with an ambulance, were soon attending the barn next to the big white house. Micha Salz, or Achim Pfeffer, was initially taken off to hospital but in due course would be handed over to the relevant authorities to stand trial for war crimes.

Bruissement persuaded the others that they should have a celebratory lunch, which would allow time for the mist to clear, so it was mid-afternoon before Russell and Weeks were on the ferry, heading back to England. Although it was late when they arrived in Collinghurst, Superintendent Stout was waiting for them at the police station.

'Well Russell. We've got a result – of sorts,' he said.

'Yes, Sir.'

'We now have enough evidence to formally charge Ludwig Müller with the murder of the three Germans. Shame we haven't got his brother, too.'

'Quite, Sir. Don't worry, I'm going to find him. What will you do with Rankin?'

'He'll be charged with aiding and abetting. He won't be going back to the Army any time soon.' Stout turned towards Weeks. 'As for you…' Weeks did his best spaniel impression; all sad eyes and drooping mouth. 'You were lucky to get away with your life.'

'I know, Sir,' he replied quietly.

'However, if it hadn't been for you, we would have had another death on our hands. So don't look so glum.' Weeks brightened. 'Anyway, I expect you're both tired so best get home. We'll go over it in more detail tomorrow. Right, off with you.'

A police constable drove an exhausted Weeks home then dropped Russell outside his railway carriage with a promise to pick him up in the morning. He unlocked the front door, put his bag inside, then set off across the dunes. Before long the sight of a wisp of smoke let him know he was nearing his destination. He whistled and in a moment a little bundle of tan and white fur burst through the marram grass, came tearing towards him and leapt into his arms.

THE END

*Chris O'Donoghue trained in industrial ceramics at
Bournemouth Art College and worked at
Poole Pottery and Cranbrook Pottery in Kent before
setting up on his own in Rye. He later specialised
in model making and sculpture.*

*When much of the kind of work he did began to be made
in the Far East, Chris, having always loved the outdoors,
decided on a change of direction and started gardening.
His design ability led him to create three medal-winning
gardens at the Chelsea Flower Show.*

*A lifetime's passion for the sea, crime novels,
the simple pleasures of the Fifties and railways – he is
well known on the model railway scene – led him to
combine all three in this, his first published book.*

www.chrisodonoghue.co.uk

A second DI Sonny Russell mystery,
'*Blood on the Shrine*', will be published soon.